REVENGE RUNS IN THE FAMILY

A WOMAN SCORNED 2

FAMILY TIES

A SEQUEL BY ERICKA WILLIAMS

المزارطه الله

**Published by Esharan Publishing
P.O. Box 271, Teaneck, NJ 07666**

This novel is a work of fiction. Any references to real people, events, establishments, or locales are intended only to give the fiction a sense of reality and authenticity. Other names, characters, and incidents occurring in the work are either the product of the author's imagination or are used fictitiously, as are those fictionalized events and incidents that involve real persons. Any character that happens to share the name of a person who is an acquaintance of the author, past or present, is purely coincidental and is in no way intended to be an actual account involving that person.

Cover Design: Dashawn Taylor; Ultimate Media.TV

Editor: Joi McClary; <u>All Proofed Up</u>
<u>www.erickaw.com</u>

ACKNOWLEDGMENTS

I would like to thank my Lord and Savior, Jesus Christ, for keeping me.

I would like to thank my family and friends, who have supported me.

I would like to thank my readers and fans, who motivate and inspire me to keep going by showing me that what I do means something to someone other than myself.

I would like to thank my business partner, Lamartz Brown, for being the gas to keep this thing moving. I am the artist and he is the engineer. I would be nowhere without you, and I know I am a handful to deal with, but you are my greatest asset in this challenging and trying game of art and entertainment. Thank you, thank you, thank you for believing in me, pushing me, bigging me up always, and making me the best that I can be.

I would like to thank all of the people who worked on this particular project. You are a part of the ESharan team, and I appreciate your dedication and diligence. Joi McClary of All Proofed Up, thanks, cousin, for holding me down. Dashawn Taylor, thanks for the banging cover and for putting up with Lamartz with his calls and e-mails. Davida Baldwin of Oddball Dsgn, thanks for all your help. Tazzy and Lulubug of Whatsdastory.proboards.com, you guys read *A Women Scorned: Part 2* before anybody did. Thanks for your feedback and everything you did to make this book better. Kita McCrimmon, thanks for all the hard work you do behind the scenes with ideas and just keeping Lamartz motivated to push me and to push our company to the next level.

To the ESharan Street Team, I love you! Keep grinding for me; it will all pay off. The best is yet to come!

Kat and Fontasia, I hope that I have inspired you to be great. Rhonda, we still gonna get there! Megan a.k.a Felicia Verna, you inspire me, thank you!

I would like to thank Life Changing Books for being the first publishing company to give me a shot. I would like to send a shout out to all of my fellow LCB label mates; you know how hard this struggle is, but we can never stop!

I would like to thank the love of my Life, who breathes life and love into me every day, Life. (Yes, that's his name.) I can honestly say, I never knew love like this! You are the man that I always dreamed of. You take very good care of me. I love you 'til the end, Big Daddy-O!

I would like to thank our children, Tori Sharan, Seven Sincere Allah, StarAsia, and Saniya Rain for keeping us together. We love each other more because we see what love can produce. You are our shining stars, and we owe it to you to keep the family together. Tori, you are my firstborn, and I wouldn't trade you for the world. Follow your dreams and live to be you no matter who doesn't like it.

I would like to thank myself for not listening to the naysayers, not giving up, and believing in my own greatness! I love me!

I would like to thank the air that I breathe and let everyone know that you are only a winner if you know it!

DEDICATION

I would like to dedicate this book to people who have been let down by the people who are supposed to love them the most—their family. Many people have had to fend for themselves and nurture themselves. Many have been cursed by the blood that they were born into. Blood is supposed to be thicker than water, but sometimes it is not.

To those of you who have been abused, mistreated, or betrayed by the ones in your life who you never chose—blood relatives—I say, "Love yourself and find family in God's house and in other loved ones and friends."

The only blood that u must be tied by is Jesus' blood; it will get you through.

*B*rielle took off the wedding dress and threw it on the large pile. She stood at the doorway entrance to the garage in her negligee. Brielle had on the two-piece laced outfit that she wore under her wedding dress at her and Dante's wedding. She took the bra off and threw it into the pile and then took the laced panties off and threw them on top of the pile as well.

As Brielle stood there staring at Dante's garbage, she started touching on herself, wanting to have a release. Brielle masturbated sensually and had an orgasm for Dante one last time. She closed her eyes and imagined that it was his hands that were touching all over her body, caressing her vagina, and putting his fingers inside. Brielle started breathing hard and stroking herself faster and harder until she screamed out his name while climaxing. "Oh, Dante! I loved you so much! Ooh, you feel so good. Good-bye Dante." She moaned. "I loved you with all my might. I wish you could have done the same for me."

She stood there for a few seconds, gazing at all of his possessions that were about to be sent to the city dump. She shrugged her shoulders and stepped back. She had all types of emotions that she was feeling, from good to bad.

Brielle closed the garage door and walked upstairs to her bed, still naked. She told herself that she would be strong and make it through the storm. Brielle got under the covers and was asleep within minutes. She had a dream about Dante that felt eerily real.

Brielle was cooking in the kitchen and Dante walked in. He was bleeding from his chest. He walked up behind her and grabbed her. She turned around and was scared by the bloody sight of him. He pulled her and tried to make her sit down.

"Why, Brielle?" he asked.

"Why?" she screamed back. "You want to know why? So do I! Why couldn't you see that it was wrong? Why did you have to be so evil?"

"I felt trapped. I needed my own life. I wanted to do whatever I wanted to do without having to answer to an insecure bitch!"

"Insecure? No, you just didn't love me enough to make me feel comfortable. That was where you lacked. If I didn't feel secure in my relationship with you, it was because you made me feel unloved. So you failed, not me. I loved you. You should have just let me divorce you if you wanted another woman. You should not have begged for forgiveness every time. You should have let me move on! But you wanted me to be your prisoner while you wanted to be free!"

"Why do you hate me?" Dante asked.

"Because you deceived me. You let me live a lie," Brielle screamed. She wanted to kill him again and again.

"I'm sorry, Brielle. I was never good enough for you. I didn't deserve you. I knew that you would be happier without me, but I couldn't let someone else have you." Dante tried to console Brielle but she pulled away.

"So, you should have done the right thing. I hate you!" She continued to scream and pull away from his grip.

Brielle grabbed a knife and started stabbing Dante over and over again. Dante's voice was wailing in a loud, high pitch that made her ears ring. Brielle tried to silence him by stabbing him repeatedly, but he continued to holler at her until tears started falling down his face. All Brielle wanted was for Dante to die. Blood was splattering and gushing all over the floor and onto the walls. Dante was powerless and could not fight back. He yelled, "You will never get over this! You will never get over me!"

Brielle was startled and awakened by a tapping on her cell bars. She woke up in a cold sweat and realized that she was having a nightmare. Brielle also realized that she was still in a jail cell. She had been arrested for the murder of Monique Troy two days earlier and had spent the past two days in torment. When she thought about the fact that Shawn had not come to bail her out, she could not believe it or figure out why.

Brielle sat up on the hard metal slab that was covered by a paper-thin blanket. There was an officer holding a tray of nasty-looking food out for her to take. She stood up, grabbed the tray, dropped it on the floor, and lay back down.

"You better eat that because that's all you will be getting for the rest of the night," the mannish-looking female corrections officer said harshly.

Brielle ignored the advice and remained on her back, staring up at the ceiling, angry and cursing the guard out in her head. All she could think about was her arrest, and she kept replaying the incident over and over again in her mind.

Brielle kept thinking about how the officers knew Shawn's last name and how they had spoken to him as if he had known she would be arrested. They were engaged to be married; it didn't make sense.

How could he turn on me like that? She thought. Shawn had been there for the admission that she had made to her father about being a murderer. *If he was going to leave me, wouldn't he have left after that?* She continued to question herself while feeling abandoned and depressed.

Tears began to roll down Brielle's face and drop into her ears. She sat up abruptly, moved to the bars that held her hostage, and grabbed them.

"Guard!" she yelled furiously. "Guard! I want my phone call."

After a few more minutes and a few more loud beckoning calls, an officer approached, released her, and walked Brielle to the phone. She dialed Shawn's cell phone number, and it went straight to voice mail. She was stunned. There was too much to say, and she couldn't say it to a machine; plus, she was too embarrassed about him not taking her call.

"I thought you loved me for real," Brielle whispered into the receiver, nearly in tears, then returned the phone back to its cradle. She was humiliated. She knew the police were probably gloating and making fun of her for being turned in by her fiancé—a fact that she still couldn't fathom.

There has to be an explanation. Was he messing around with Janay? Was he working with Darren? Did I kill the wrong man? She thought to herself and desperately returned to the cell and tried to go back to sleep but was unable to stop thinking about where things had gone wrong with Shawn. Brielle was crushed.

"If it's over with Shawn, I don't want to live anymore. I can't take another loss of love. I just can't do it," Brielle cried and whispered to herself. She started pinching herself to see if she would wake up.

"I just want to sleep forever. Any dream or nightmare would be better than this reality," she said, rolling on to her stomach and laying her head on her crossed arms, continuing to quietly whimper. After a long while Brielle finally drifted back off to sleep.

Again, she dreamed. She was inside of Darren's apartment the day that he died. They had on the same clothing from that day. They were lying on Darren's bed.

Before she knew what was happening, he rolled over, opened her legs, and began to eat her pussy. She was caught off guard. He kissed the lips of her vagina ever so gently, and although she wanted to bash his head between her knees, she couldn't do it. It felt too good. Her mind started racing as she asked herself what she should do. He feasted on her while she decided what to do. Her legs began to relax, and she started to feel the tension waning.

He looked up into her eyes and said, "Damn, you taste good. But I'm not at all surprised."

She told herself that what was going on at that moment was just a means to an end, Darren's end. It was her excuse to lie back and enjoy being the entrée. She climaxed and came in his mouth, and he sucked and swallowed. She was overwhelmed.

He started rubbing her thighs and touching her breasts. She liked the way it felt.

"Hey, you ain't really sick. You are just pretending," she said and thought, Soon you will not be sick; you will be dead.

She inquired, "Was that your strategy to get me in your bed—to play sick?"

"No, actually, I wish I was well so that I wouldn't be feeling like a lame. I am not trying to rush you. I am not just interested in having sex with you, Brielle. I'm really falling for you."

"Oh boy, should I start playing the violin now or later?"

"No, wait 'til later; we can have violins playing at our wedding."

She burst out laughing. "Wow, you are really laying it on thick, aren't you?" she replied.

He sat up in the bed and took her hand. "Brielle, I'm telling you the truth. I'm sure you have some trust issues—and you have every right to—but I'm here to tell you not to doubt that a man can really care about you. Don't think that you will never be able to find a healthy love. All love doesn't hurt, Brielle." He kissed the back of her hand.

"Well, I can't tell. But if you say so, Darren, I hear you." She pulled her arm away.

"Don't just hear me; listen. I haven't really wanted to get close with anyone for a long time. My wife was a dirty whore. She embarrassed me and made me look bad, and she broke me down as a man. She didn't care that she was letting another man laugh at me because she was sharing a secret with him that made me look like a fool. That's no different than a spy who sells secrets against their own country. It's like they are laughing behind your back with your adversary and then smiling in your face like they have your back. I wanted to forget about love too, until I met you."

She was starting to feel uncomfortable about the way he was expressing his feelings for her. "I agree. It's like your loved one giving your enemy the gun to shoot you with. It's the most painful thing to find out about someone you love. But I'm not ready to hear this right now, Darren." She turned her attention on the TV but wasn't really watching it.

"Well, I'm ready to say it, Brielle." He turned her face to his.

This wasn't supposed to be a part of the plan. He wasn't supposed to be talking like this, *Brielle thought, deciding that he was lying to her in order to get her to trust him.*

"*I'm glad you like taking care of me.*" *Brielle stood up and Darren smacked her ass as she walked away.*

In the kitchen Brielle methodically made Darren's plate and laced it with more antifreeze.

He is sitting here trying to make me feel sorry for him. He wants me to fall for him so he can fuck me over, her mind told her.

Let's go, bitch, handle this business. He's nothing but another twisted man," *Brielle whispered to herself.*

She took the plate in his room, put in another DVD, and watched him devour his destiny.

When Darren was done eating, he put the plate on the TV stand next to his bed and rolled over to face Brielle.

"*Let me have some of you, Brielle. I really want you,*" *he said and then started kissing her and sticking his tongue in her mouth.*

Brielle couldn't resist it. She kissed him back but didn't know why. He started to feel good to her, and she wondered if his little spiel was starting to work on her mind. He kissed her breasts and sucked on them. Her guard was going down and down and down with every kiss on her body.

He kissed her stomach and her thighs and opened her legs and got on his knees. He entered her slowly and gently.

"*I want to make love to you good and slow,*" *he said in her ear while riding her slowly and while she let him all the way in.*

Maybe I'm just giving him some because I feel bad that he's about to die. Maybe I just want him to get some pussy one more time before it's over for him, *she thought, unsure of why she was making love to Darren.*

"*Or maybe you are falling in love with him, you stupid bitch.*" *Her mother's voice stung in her mind.*

Darren made passionate love to Brielle and pulled himself out of her before climaxing. He came on his bedsheet.

"One day I'll be giving you that sperm so we can start a family," Darren said confidently and then rolled back over and sat up.

"Why do you keep talking like that, Darren? Stop it." Brielle sat up.

"No. Listen, I have to tell you something, Brielle. I can't go any further without telling you the truth, because then everything I tell you will seem like a lie when you find out." Darren gently stroked Brielle's face.

"What?" she asked, confused.

"When I met you in Aruba, I was there to find out about you. Monique Troy came into the Fort Lee Police Department and accused you of murdering her lover, your husband. I was given a month to find out if she was telling the truth." Brielle just sat there listening, with no reaction.

"So, I traveled to Aruba and found you. I befriended you. I listened to you talk and tried to see if you would confess. I was there to catch a killer and caught feelings for you before I left Aruba. Brielle, I'm a detective." Brielle still had no reaction because little did he know, she already knew.

"You're not mad?" Darren was confused.

"Mad? No, I'm not surprised. All of you men are liars and cheats." She shook her head.

"Brielle, after I met you, I knew that it couldn't be true. I started falling in love with you the moment I started being in your company. I left Aruba with the intentions of making you mine. Brielle, I love you," Darren declared passionately and then kissed Brielle softly on her lips. She angrily pulled her head away from him.

"Darren, come on, you don't even know me." A tear came to her eye. Brielle really wanted someone to truly love her.

"I never stopped thinking about you from the moment I laid eyes on you." He wiped her tears as they fell.

"That's why you fucked my cousin, you full-of-shit bastard. Shut the fuck up. You're lying." She pulled away from him.

"Your cousin came on to me. Ugghh!" Darren screamed and grabbed his stomach.

"What, Darren? What's the matter?" She sat up and looked at him with wide-open eyes, already knowing what was happening.

"Oh, my stomach feels like a truck is parked on top of it. It's squeezing my insides! Something is wrong, Brielle. You gotta call nine-one-one! Ohhhhhh! It's killing me!" He looked at her and she was looking in his eyes, not moving. "Brielle, call !"

As he was rushing to the bathroom, he grabbed his chest and fell to the ground, convulsing.

"Darren?" she calmly said. His body was shaking and foam started coming out of his mouth. Brielle watched, never moving or trying to assist Darren at all. Darren's eyes rolled up in his head, and he tried to grab for her. She just sat on the bed and watched him shaking and shuddering. His body was going through major trauma. He was squeezing his eyes closed. Suddenly, he reached out and grabbed Brielle's ankle and squeezed it tightly. Still, she just sat there, watching him die. Gradually, the convulsing slowed down, and she heard a gurgling in his throat. He seemed to be choking on his throw-up. He opened his eyes and looked right in hers before his body went limp and his eyes stared blankly. He was looking right at her, but she knew that he was dead.

Brielle was frozen. She sat there, staring at him sprawled out on the floor for thirty minutes before getting the nerve up to check his pulse. She was frightened. She didn't like him looking at her. She put her hands over his eyes and closed them and then knelt down next to him and lifted up his hand. She checked for a pulse and there wasn't one. She put her ear to his mouth and nose to see if she felt the air from his breath. There was no air. She put her hand on his chest, but his heart was not beating.

Brielle was awakened from her dream.

"Brielle Prescott!" an officer yelled. "You're being released."

Brielle jumped up and waited to be let out of that horrible cell. She was taken to a room where she was told to take off the jumper she had been given and put her clothes back on. She felt unclean and her hair was disheveled. It was all over her head. Brielle's body needed a nice, hot bubble bath, and her mind needed rest.

Brielle figured Aunt Janelle had come to bail her out. She couldn't think of anyone else who would love her enough to do it. She walked out into the lobby of the county jail and was stunned to see Shawn, looking handsome as ever. She ran to him and they grabbed each other abruptly and embraced tightly. "Let's get out of here, baby," he said and led her outside, holding on to her hand.

As Brielle got closer and closer to Shawn's car, her blood began to boil more and more. She kept replaying the scene when he had seemed to already know of her upcoming arrest; how he said that she would get the help she needed. He opened the passenger's side door for her, and she checked him out before he closed the door. He looked fresh like he always did, with a nice Polo shirt and jeans and matching Nikes.

Shawn looked well-rested, a far cry from how she looked and felt.

As soon as he closed the driver's side door and started the car, Brielle reached over and started punching him in his head and body.

"How could you?! You set me up!" Brielle hollered.

After receiving about four blows, Shawn was able to grab Brielle's hands and restrain her. He held both of her hands in one of his and grabbed her chin to force her to look in his eyes while he spoke. "I would never do that to you." She unsuccessfully tried to release her chin from his grip. "Listen to me. I did not set you up. Do you hear me?"

"So, what happened, Shawn? How did the officers know your name? Why did they say you knew already? Tell me!" He held her tightly.

"Brielle, I know you must have been in there going half crazy. I know you thought I betrayed you and I will explain. I am going to let your hands go, and I swear if you swing on me again, I'm gonna bust your ass. Do you hear me?" Brielle just stared into Shawn's eyes, fighting back her tears.

"All right, you can act like a badass if you want to. I'm warning you. Don't even think about raising your hand to me again. I'm not Dante." Shawn released her hands and she let them drop into her lap. She decided against trying his word because she desperately wanted to hear his explanation.

Shawn started his car and pulled out of the jailhouse parking lot. Brielle wanted to tell him to hurry up and talk, but she waited patiently and kept her attitude under control. She liked how forceful Shawn was. A strong man was definitely a turn-on. Shawn purposely took his time before beginning to speak.

He drove her home in silence, knowing it was killing her but knowing that he was innocent and making her pay for not having faith in him to know better.

"Oh, so you don't have anything to say?" Shawn looked over at how disheveled and crazy Brielle looked but smiled at the realization that even still, he loved her.

"No, I want you to go get yourself together, and we can talk over dinner? Legal Sea Foods?" Brielle tried to hide her smile but couldn't.

When he pulled into her driveway, Brielle ran inside, washed up frantically, and threw on a Juicy Couture sweat suit and kicks and a matching baseball cap. When she ran back out, she jumped in the car and gave Shawn a big, long kiss. She leaned back in her chair and licked his kiss off of her lips.

"This story better be good, and I am ordering everything on the menu." Shawn leaned over and kissed her and then backed out of the driveway.

Shawn pulled into the parking lot of Legal Sea Foods and parked. Brielle was starving and couldn't wait for Shawn to talk to her. It was four in the afternoon on a Thursday. She hadn't seen the outside since Monday. Food was definitely something that she needed.

Once they were seated, she ordered two appetizers and an entrée, while Shawn ordered two entrées. She passed her menu to the waiter and put her chin in her hands and looked over at the man who she thought loved her, whom she had fallen very quickly in love with, and waited.

"Okay, I received a phone call from a detective at the Fort Lee Police Department. He asked me to come in and talk to him and that it was concerning you." Brielle shook her head in disgust. "The detective stated that Janay had been questioned for the murder of Monique Troy. I asked him why Janay was a suspect, and I was told that her blood was found at the scene of the crime."

"So, she gave them my name, and you told them it must have been true?" Brielle interrupted.

"No, they told me that Janay said that you hired her to kill Monique, and they asked me if I thought it could be possible and whether you had been acting strangely around the time of the murder."

Brielle looked at Shawn with tears in her eyes while awaiting his answer. She needed him to not let her down. She needed him to be the one man she could finally rely on. "I told them that you had been acting very emotional. I said that I had convinced you to get some counseling." He picked up his glass of wine, sipped it, and put it back down.

"Shawn, the officer said, 'But you know that, Mr. Ellison.' What was that supposed to mean?" she asked Shawn accusingly.

"It meant that I knew you would need a lawyer because Janay had pointed the finger at you."

"So, why didn't you tell me? You knew they were coming after me, and you just let me be a sitting duck?" She lowered her voice after realizing she had begun to speak loudly.

"Brielle, what happened at my mother's funeral?" He gently took her left hand in his and touched her engagement ring. Brielle looked down at the enormous rock that she had just received from her bag of belongings at the county jail.

"We got engaged." She stared at the ring without looking up at Shawn. "And then a few days later, you turned me in…" Shawn put his finger over his lips.

"I did *not* turn you in, Brielle. I did *not* tell you they were coming to get you because I knew that you would do something stupid that would make you look even guiltier. I wasn't uncooperative with the police because I wanted them to be cooperative with me. I wanted to find out all I could and appear helpful. I knew that those days would be hell for you thinking that I sold you out, but I had to stay normal. I had to wait for the judge to set bail, and then I had to put in for a bail reduction. They set your bail at a million dollars at first. Paulo—remember Mr. Rabissi?—he got it down to five hundred thousand. I didn't want to have all of that money tied up and then have to put out more to cover your defense. We got a big fight ahead of us, Brielle."

"But you said that Janay told you and she told the police."

"That was a lie. I said it for their ears to hear. I never spoke to Janay. I swear to you. They needed to think that I was on the side of justice."

Brielle let out a long sigh. She was relieved that she still had Shawn. She had contemplated suicide if she ended up going through trial without someone who loved her by her side. Shawn kissed her hand and let it go. She got up and sat next to him on his side of the restaurant booth. He put his arm around her and kissed her forehead. "It's gonna be okay, baby. I will make sure of it."

"But, Shawn, Janay gave me up. She is going to probably get immunity for telling the whole truth. I'm sure they held her pending case over her head and offered her a good deal."

"Yeah, they did. But Rabissi is the best criminal lawyer I know, and I know a few believe me. We have to go and see him in the morning. Is there anything you need to tell me?" He looked at his crazy lover and was consumed with love. He had to help her out of this one, he thought. He had to give her this last chance so that they could put their pasts behind them and be happy.

"Like what?" She eluded the obvious question. She knew that he knew she had Monique killed, so what did she need to say it for? "Shawn, I promise, this is it. If I get out of this, I'm done with the revenge thing. It's just that the bitch wanted to take me for half of my money after fucking my husband and making me lose three children. How could she be so heartless? Hadn't I suffered enough because of her?"

"Brielle, listen and listen good. Your father was a killer." Brielle jumped and turned around to face Shawn.

"What?" she asked as low as she could while wanting to scream it.

"Yes, he told me that day when you went in the living room to talk to Marilyn. He said that you must have inherited his extreme propensity to anger and violence. He said that once he lost his job and your mother died that he started doing hits for a mob guy he knew, but because he was a drunk, they threatened him to leave town or they would kill him because he almost botched a job. That's why he moved to Philadelphia." Brielle's eyes were stuck wide open. "I'm only telling you this so that you will know how serious it is for you to get help."

"Well, at least that explains how I could push my cousin to his death at just ten damn years old. How could I not have known that he would fall off and drown? I know I was just fed up, but I still pushed him off of a boat." Brielle shook her head and put her face in her hands.

"That's the bitch that had my cousin killed!" Brielle looked up to see Shanta standing and pointing at her. The other restaurateurs were staring at Brielle. The man who Shanta was with put his arm around her and pulled her away. "I can't eat here. I'm liable to take a knife to your throat, bitch! I told you where I lived, and you sent your cousin to kill Monique! You knew all along who I was talking to you about, murderer!" Shanta's companion pulled her outside of the restaurant, and Brielle could see them walking past the window, with Shanta still ranting and raving. Shawn looked at his love and shook his head. He knew he must really be in love with her, because Drama was her middle name.

Brielle looked at Shawn, shrugged her shoulders, and put some more of her lobster tail in melted butter and then into her mouth.

Brielle

Brielle and Shawn went home. She was never so happy to see her house. The missing Tahoe was very apparent to her, and she thought back to the day that she and Janay made their plan.

As soon as they walked inside, Brielle went to the phone and picked up the receiver and dialed. Aunt Janelle answered, sounding drained.

"Hello, Brielle," she said dryly.

"Aunt Janelle, what is going on? Where is Janay?"

"I don't know where Janay is. I haven't seen her in a few days. How are you, Brielle? Are you home?" Brielle was concerned about her aunt's complacent and lethargic sound.

"Aunt Janelle, what's wrong? Are you okay?" Brielle probed.

"No, Brielle, I'm not. Do you expect me to be?" Aunt Janelle's voice was harsh. Brielle slid onto the stool and looked at the knife stand that was still on the countertop, still missing the knife that had killed Dante.

"I need to see you and Janay. We need to work this out as a family. I wish that Janay would have waited to get a lawyer instead of turning on me so easily. We are all that we have left." Brielle shook her head and held her fist tightly. She could kill Janay for letting the police interrogation break her.

"Brielle, that's my daughter and you are my niece. How do I choose? You were always more like a daughter to me, and Janay was always like your mother. If I didn't know any better, I would have thought that the two of you were switched at birth. I've done the best I could with Janay, but she has always been evil and vindictive. You have always been kindhearted and mistreated." She sighed heavily.

"Well, we need to sit down and come up with a strategy. She has that case down there, and I'm sure they are agreeing to drop the murder charge up here for her testimony against me, but there's got to be a way around both of us going to jail for murder for the rest of our lives. Me and Shawn will fly down there this weekend," she said, looking in Shawn's eyes for his approval. Shawn quietly nodded his head in agreement.

"Okay, I will try to get in touch with her. I can't lose you girls. I just can't believe this is happening." Aunt Janelle's snuffles told Brielle that she was crying. Tears started falling down Brielle's face as well.

"Well, let's be strong until we can be together, Aunt Janelle. Please don't let this kill your spirit. I'll see you in a few days." Aunt Janelle agreed and they ended the call.

Brielle wiped her face and sat in a daze. *Bitch, ain't no time for tears. You better find a way out of this no matter what! Stop being so fuckin' sensitive all the time.*

"I hate you! Leave me the fuck alone!" Brielle screamed, startling herself and alerting Shawn, who was in the other room, that something was wrong. Shawn entered the doorway and knew that Brielle was responding to her mother's still present torment of Brielle's mind. Shawn lifted her up and hugged her tightly.

"I have got to get over my mother. She cannot continue to try to ruin me from the grave; she did that enough while she was living.

Shawn grabbed Brielle and led her upstairs to the bathroom. He undressed her in between gentle kisses, and they both got in the shower. Brielle stood under the showerhead and let the water run from her head to her toes. Shawn grabbed a washcloth and the shower gel and began to scrub Brielle's body carefully. He lathered her whole body and then his.

He was suddenly overwhelmed by looking directly in her very sad eyes. He dropped the washcloth and grabbed her. He held her tightly in his arms and hid his face in her shoulder. Brielle wrapped her arms around him and rubbed his back after realizing that he had began to cry. Shawn's sobbing began to get louder and louder. She released herself from his grip and looked at him.

"I cannot lose you and I refuse to," Shawn said after grabbing her face and looking directly into Brielle's eyes.

"You won't, Shawn. I'll make sure of it," Brielle assured her man.

"No, *I* will make sure of it," Brielle's man reassured her.

Brielle dropped to her knees and put his manhood into her mouth. The water was gently raining down on her head while she gave him the best head he ever had. The water and her determination to please him like never before forced him to climax in her mouth. She was looking up at him while he released into her. He pulled her up, turned her around, and entered her vagina from behind. He thrust into her forcefully and deeply. He eagerly climaxed again, hoping to give her the child that she desperately longed for. Brielle was bent over, touching the floor when she felt his penis jumping. *Please let me get pregnant*, she prayed.

Brielle stood up and turned around. They had a long kiss and then washed each other with sudsy washcloths. He washed her gently, hoping to wash her pain away.

They left the bathroom and got in bed naked, both of them scared and hopeful at the same time. They slept while embracing each other the whole night long.

Brielle was happy to wake up the next morning fully rested. She had not been awakened by a horrible dream the whole night. Her rescuer was there with her, and his protection allowed her mind to rest and sleep peacefully.

When Brielle rolled over and sat up, she noticed that Shawn was not in the bed or in the room. Suddenly, she got frightened that he had maybe had a change of heart and left during the night. Shawn entered the room just as that thought entered her head; he was carrying a tray with breakfast on it.

"What's the matter, baby cakes?" he asked, noticing the worried look on Brielle's face.

"I thought you had left," Brielle answered, feeling at ease.

"Left as in for good?" He laughed while she nodded yes. "Babe"—he sat down and put the tray in front of her—"you have got to get it in your mind that I am not leaving you. I admit that dealing with you is unlike anything I've ever dealt with before, but I wouldn't trade it for the world. You complete me. You are my other half. Stop worrying so much. Give me some kisses for this big breakfast I made for you. What man would make pancakes, sausage, grits, a fruit salad, and eggs for a woman if he didn't love her?"

Picking up her fork, he began to feed her. "I'm going to get my tray, but I will be back. Okay, baby cakes?" He leaned over and kissed her lips before returning to get his food from the kitchen.

Brielle was about to eat and remembered Darren's statement that she should always thank God for her food. She figured Shawn would know how to say grace. He returned and sat next to her on the bed.

"Why aren't you eating?" Shawn looked into Brielle's eyes with intensity.

"Because I want you to say grace." She blushed.

"What? You mean there is a God?" Shawn asked sarcastically.

"I still don't know for sure, but your mother's funeral sure opened my eyes to faith. And maybe God sent you to me. Maybe he made you love me so I could believe in miracles. No man would want to deal with my baggage, babe I know that." He covered her lips with his finger and then placed her hands in praying position under his closed palms. "Thank you for this food. Thank you for this day. Lord, you are mighty. You know what we don't. I don't know why you placed this woman in my life, but keep her here, Lord. Keep her mine. Let us win this fight. We owe you the glory; we just ask that you fix this situation so that we may be together, giving you all the praise. Amen."

"Amen," Brielle said, smiling. She felt a sobering peace come over her.

"Now let's eat so we can go speak to Paolo."

They finished their breakfast and got dressed. Brielle wanted to look like the powerful woman that she wanted to be and not the scared little girl she felt like. She put on an olive-colored Anne Klein business suit with matching Sam Edelman snakeskin shoes. She pulled her weave back and put it into a tight bun. Shawn put on one of his best suits.

Brielle tried to hide the worry in her eyes, so she avoided looking into Shawn's, but he knew that she was worried; he was somewhat worried himself.

They pulled into the office of Paolo Rabissi at 10 a.m. Brielle was impressed by his plush office. He had it decorated like a living room. The cost of the furniture, paintings, and fixtures alone was in the hundreds of thousands. His office was just as extravagant. She figured he must have won a lot of cases, and she only needed him to win one more.

He greeted Shawn and Brielle and got right down to business. He opened her file and began reading.

"Okay, you have been charged with second-degree murder, conspiracy to commit murder, and murder for hire." Brielle looked blankly ahead without showing any reaction. Shawn shifted in his chair. "Here's what we know so far. Monique Troy was shot and killed on Tuesday, May twenty-third, at 8:30 p.m. She was pronounced dead on arrival to the hospital. There have been no witnesses except a Janay Roberts. Ms. Roberts has issued a statement of guilt for the murder and has named you as the perpetrator of the crime, saying that you paid her to commit the crime." He paused and looked at Brielle and Shawn, who were quiet and attentive, holding each other's hands.

"Janay Roberts has another murder case pending. That is in our favor. She will probably be offered a plea deal if she cooperates and testifies. Now, first and foremost, is there any way to get her to change her statement?" Shawn and Brielle looked at each other.

"I already called my aunt to see if the three of us can sit down and come to some agreement. That's my cousin and even though she pointed the finger at me, I am willing to try to come together with her for the benefit of us both."

"Okay, you must keep in mind that Ms. Roberts may be willing to put a wire on when you meet with her. She may agree to meet with you to get you to incriminate yourself. Do not say anything that may be used against you in court. Do you understand?"

Brielle nodded her head and crossed her legs, moving her leg up and down. In her mind she told herself that she should just kill Janay and get it over with. She looked over at Shawn and pushed the thought out of her mind. "I understand," she said and flashed a fake smile. Her blood was boiling.

"What are the chances that she will renege?" Paolo asked and jotted down some notes.

"I don't know. How do I offer her money without it being a bribe?" she asked, wondering if she should ask that question.

"Brielle, I am your lawyer. Ask me anything. Your life is on the line. We will turn over every stone in an effort to find the trail to an innocent verdict. Although it sounds harsh, it is better that they are trumping up your charges. They would be better off trying to get you on conspiracy than murder. Juries usually don't like to find someone guilty of murder if they haven't pulled the trigger."

Shawn interjected. "Well, not if there is a witness, right?" He shifted in his seat, leaned over, kissed Brielle, then leaned back to await Mr. Rabissi's answer.

"Well, you know, let's not even speculate. What the police have against Janay is that they found her blood on the steps of the back door. The occupants of the house said the killer entered and retreated through the back door. That does not prove guilt, but it helps. She could have just held out until speaking with a lawyer, but she still can recant her statement and refuse to testify."

"But how can she? She is caught red-handed because of the blood."

"There could have been an accomplice. Her being there does not mean that she pulled the trigger. If she had known that, maybe she would not have folded during the interrogation. Nevertheless, her statement is all they have against you. They do not have a murder weapon either. This case is circumstantial. We can beat it. We just have to think of everything. Our defense most certainly can be that she was desperate for money, so maybe she committed the crime with the idea of framing you after the fact. Just because she said you told her to do it doesn't mean that you actually did. Right, Mrs. Prescott?"

Brielle quietly nodded her head up and down. She knew that Mr. Rabissi knew that she was guilty, but she also knew that he was good at his job. "Well, hopefully, we can come to an agreement with Janay so that we don't have to go that route. If she recants her statement and does not plead guilty, what are the chances of them finding her guilty?"

"Well, they have her blood at the scene. She cannot be identified because the perpetrator had on a mask. It can really go either way. Juries are funny and a unanimous decision is not always easy to get. Look, for now I want you to think of anything you can. If you know of someone else who may have had it out for Monique, that will help. Remember, you must be found guilty beyond a reasonable doubt, and Janay having that other murder case is sweet. Just keep your brain working on this, and I will keep you informed of every new development. Okay?" Mr. Rabissi stood up, extended his hand, and shook Brielle's as she stood up. He then gave a firm handshake to Shawn and patted him on the back. "You found your soul mate, I see. A woman after your own heart." They both laughed and all three exited the office.

As soon as Shawn and Brielle were back in his car, she called Aunt Janelle.

"Hello, Brielle, how are you feeling?" she asked, sounding more at ease than the day before.

"I'm okay, Aunt Janelle. I tried to call Janay, but her phone number has been changed. Did you ask her if she is willing to talk to me?"

"She said she would. When are you going to come down?" Brielle mouthed the question to Shawn, and he mouthed back tomorrow. "Tomorrow," she answered. "I'll fly down tomorrow. Can I stay with you, Aunt Janelle?"

"Of course, Brielle. The doctor prescribed me some pills to make my nerves relax. Brielle, what am I gonna do if I lose you and Janay? You two are all I have. I do not want to choose between the two of you, so I am here for you both. I hope we can work this out. I'll see you tomorrow. If you need me to pick you up from the airport, just let me know," Aunt Janelle said, sounding anxious and worried.

"No, Aunt Janelle, I will order a car to bring me. Just please have Janay at your house. This is an emergency. I love you, Aunt Janelle and I'm sorry that we are putting you through this." She hung up and a thought entered her head. "Babe, what if Janay tries to kill me and say it was self-defense? I know that someone can get away with that."

"Baby cakes, she would be dumb as hell to do that. And chance having three different murder charges hanging over her head? No way. What would she get out of it? We just have to find a way to get her to take back her confession. I am trying to figure out if I should go with you or not. In a way, that might make her jealous and vengeful that you have me sticking by your side. On the other hand, though, if I offer to pay for her legal counsel, that's not you bribing her. Think about it. She may be able to get a reduced sentence and cop a plea and then combine her two sentences. Shit, that bitch is in a bad way; she better take all the help she can get."

"Janay is stubborn and ignorant. She will fight a worthless fight to the end. She has this can't–touch-this attitude but you're right. Well, it don't hurt to try. Either she can join us or get beat by us…ole stank-ass bitch. I should have known she was a traitor when she started threatening me about other shit."

Shawn raised his eyebrows. "What do you mean threatening you?"

Brielle thought fast for an answer that would sound convincing. She could not reveal that she had, in fact, killed Darren, especially when his wife and accessories were awaiting trial for his murder.

"Oh, um, she told me that if I told anyone about her being a 'pimp' that she would have someone rape me or some shit, I don't know. Janay is crazy."

"It must run in the family, huh?" Shawn joked as Brielle playfully punched him in the arm. "Shit, I'm cuckoo for Cocoa Puffs, I don't care. You got me all crazy too. Crazy in love with you. If you were Jamaican, I would swear you have put some roots on me."

"Maybe I went to visit the witch doctor in New York and paid to have it done; you never know." Brielle laughed a wicked high witch-type laugh, while Shawn smiled and again shook his head at his nutty fiancée.

They drove to Shawn's brownstone in the city. He packed more of his clothes and changed out of his suit. He put on a pair of Antik jeans and a plain gray short-sleeve T-shirt, which showed his recent tattoo of a dove. He got it in memory of his mother. His braids were freshly done, as always, and Brielle continued to admire her man. They waited for some prospective tenants to come. Shawn had decided to rent out his brownstone since he was practically living with Brielle in Jersey. He had recently put an ad in the paper, and there were three different appointments that day.

The doorbell rang and Brielle opened the door to see a gorgeous hunk of a man standing on the other side of it. They looked at each other for a few seconds before Brielle realized they were both staring at each other.

"Hello. Your name is…?" she said flatly and unenthusiastically after clearing her throat, hoping to change any possible thought that her stare may have given him.

"Rich, Rich Robinson. I am here to see the brownstone for rent." Brielle stepped aside and the visitor stepped into the foyer while Shawn descended the stairs.

"Nice to meet you, Rich," Shawn said and extended his hand to shake Rich's. "This is my fiancée, Brielle." They said a shameful and low hello to each other, as if they had done something wrong. Brielle did not look in Mr. Robinson's eyes nor did he look in hers.

"Okay, well, let's take you on your tour. You coming along, *wifey?*" he asked jokingly, knowing that Brielle did not like to be called that. Her idea was that if a man hadn't given a ring, a promise, and taken a vow, he would not be given the privilege of calling her his wife. She didn't buy into that street dialect of being called *wifey.*

"Just because you called me that, I'm not coming. Go ahead, I'll make lunch." Shawn laughed and squeezed Brielle's ass as she walked past him to go into the kitchen. He explained to Mr. Robinson Brielle's position on the word as they ascended the stairs. They were upstairs for about twenty minutes, and then when Shawn was finished showing the basement, all three of them sat in the living room.

"So, will you be living here by yourself?" Brielle asked.

"Uh, well, I am separated from my wife, so for now it's just going to be me."

"And your mistress?" Shawn joked. Brielle was again offended and spoke up about it.

"Shawn, that's not funny. Hopefully, he will be trying to work things out with his wife before he brings another woman into his mix."

"Oh God. Pardon Brielle, man, she's very touchy about people and their marital issues. She seems to think all problems should be worked out when you're in a marriage. But that's not always possible, baby cakes. Plus, that is Rich's personal business. As long as you pay the rent, man, I don't care if your wife and your mistress stay here with you." Shawn laughed while Brielle gave him a dirty look. "I see that you work on Wall Street as a broker. Isn't that risky work? You don't always get paid."

"Well, I am an officer now. I don't work on the floor doing sales. I verify sales, hire people. I've paid my dues, so my job is pretty secure, along with my salary," Rich replied.

"I see. Yes, looking at this application, you are doing pretty well for yourself. That's a good thing." Rich nodded his head proudly.

"Well, we have some other people who are interested, so I'll get back to you in the next few days." Shawn stood up to shake Rich's hand, and Rich reluctantly stood up and obliged. "Well, please, whatever you do, don't send anything to the address on my application. That is where I lived with my wife, and I don't want her knowing where I may be moving to." He glanced at Brielle cautiously and continued. "You know, marriage is not an easy thing, and I just want to try to end everything amicably. If you need any more information, just call me on my cell phone." Shawn agreed and walked Mr. Rich Robinson to the door.

"He probably does want to have a hideout where his mistress can stay," Brielle said, shaking her head.

"Brielle, listen. You cannot treat every man like his name is Dante. You never know what happened with that man and his wife. Shit, she could have cheated. You have to let go of all of that baggage, girl. You had that man scared to even look in your direction."

He better hope I don't come across his wife, Brielle thought.

A young couple and their baby were the next to come and look at the place. Brielle was very welcoming to them. They were a Spanish couple with a six-month-old daughter. They seemed very interested in the brownstone, and Shawn gave them the same verdict at the end of their conference with him.

The third prospective tenant called to cancel, so Brielle and Shawn decided to turn in early for their trip. Brielle decided to use Shawn as an excuse not to stay with Aunt Janelle, because she didn't trust Janay enough to sleep there. She didn't want to take the chance of waking up dead.

Janay

anay was having lunch alone at Houston's restaurant when her cell phone rang. She checked and saw her mother's number.

"Hello, Ma, what's up? You okay?" Janay picked up a piece of her Hawaiian steak and ate it.

"I've been better. I'm calling to make sure that you come here tomorrow to see Brielle." Janay looked at her fingernails, uninterested in that topic. She did not respond. "Janay, I didn't hear you. Are you going to come so that we can handle this like a family?" Janelle asked her daughter with sternness.

Janay laughed loudly. "Handle this like a family, Ma? Your niece is trying to send me to prison for life. She thinks that she is going to go on living her fairy tale lie of a life while I rot behind bars. This is serious; it's not like we are planning a family reunion."

"Janay, you have to hear what she has to say. We have to see if we can get through this together. Make sure that you come when I call you to let you know that she is here. Brielle has nothing to do with what happened here, so who will you blame for that? What made you go along with her plan? Why didn't you talk her out of it?" Janelle took a deep breath and wiped a lone tear.

"There you go," Janay said, her voice escalating, "taking up for Brielle. That is all you have ever done. Brielle is always the victim, and I am always the culprit. She can do no wrong in your eyes." Janay cut her steak roughly in an agitated manner and put another piece in her mouth.

"Janay, for once, try to be cooperative. You and Brielle both have a lot of issues. You both have nearly sent me to an early grave, but I haven't turned my back on either one of you, and I don't plan to. You cannot blame someone for your own actions. You are grown and you don't let anyone tell you what to do, so I suggest you give yourself a chance to hear what she has to say and what strategy the two of you may be able to take together instead of being hardheaded and stubborn as usual." Janelle hung up the phone, disgusted.

Janay finished her meal, paid her bill, and proceeded to her car. As soon as she got in the car, she made a phone call.

"Hey, Murda Mommy," a male voice answered and then laughed.

"Listen, ain't nothin' funny right now. I need you to do something for me. Meet me in the parking lot of Houston's; it's important. How long? Okay, make sure it's twenty minutes and not an hour." She moved the phone from her ear.

Janay hung up and waited for a local drug dealer named Jarrod to show up. He pulled his Range Rover into the space next to her car and got in on the passenger's side. He leaned over to kiss her and she pulled back.

"I need you to kill my cousin," Janay said bluntly. Jarrod, stunned, slowly moved back, not commenting on her refusal to receive a kiss as his greeting.

"Who, what, when, where, and why?" he asked and Janay laughed.

"You forgot *how*," Janay joked.

"No, the how is up to me, unless you have a suggestion, but let's start with the why." He pulled out a blunt, lit it, inhaled, and passed it to Janay.

"She got me caught up in that murder case in Jersey. I knew I shouldn't have fucked with her, and now I'm lookin' at two murder charges." Janay pulled hard on the weed blunt and passed it back.

"Okay, so don't you think that you'd be the first suspect?" Jarrod smoked and looked intently at Janay, contemplating how much he would ask to complete the task at hand.

"Not if it looks like an accident. Do you have any ideas?" Janay shifted in her seat and looked desperately into Jarrod's eyes.

"Hold up. First of all, how much do you plan on paying for this?" He passed the blunt back to Janay.

"I don't know, man. We'll figure that part out. I need to know how it can be done. I can't stand her and I'm tired of her shit. I let her suck me into this plan, and I want her to pay for involving me."

"Well, is she allergic to anything? Are there any foods or substances that can possibly kill her if she was exposed to them? Does she have asthma or any ailments? Does she use drugs?" Jarrod sounded like a professional.

"Nah, the bitch is on some goody-two-shoes shit, and the bitch is a fuckin' murderer." Jarrod's eyes widened. "Yeah." Janay nodded her head to confirm his confusion and continued. "She had the nerve to get off on killing her husband and has me being charged for killing his pregnant mistress."

"When do you need it done by?" Jarrod paused. "I guess we can make it look like a robbery, or maybe we can run her off the road, but there's no guarantee that she will die if we do it that way. We can always shoot her up with some bad dope, but if she has no history of drug use, that may seem suspicious." Jarrod had a bad feeling about this situation, but he was going to see if they could come up with an air-tight plan.

"She'll be here tomorrow. We have to think fast. I don't know how long she's staying or if she's bringing her wack-ass boyfriend. Bitch think she all of that because she got a man." Jarrod picked up on the jealousy in Janay's voice and comment. "I know she or they will be staying at my mom's, so we are gonna have to do it there. Shit, just come in and shoot her ass and be out. As long as you don't drop no blood and get away, then we are fine. And make sure you don't fold under pressure if you happen to get brought in for questioning."

Janay thought back to the visit the New Jersey detectives paid to her when they arrested her for Monique's murder and wished she had taken her own advice. But when they let her know that her blood had been found at the scene, she panicked and started telling. She shook her head in disbelief that her life had been turned upside down in a matter of days. *It was all Brielle's fault*, she reminded herself.

"Listen, if you just want me to shoot her, that's cool, but I'll need the door to be left open, and I need you to pay me thirty grand."

"Thirty grand? Listen, Jarrod, I'm fighting two court cases. I ain't got it like that right now. And I can't leave the door open. You have to make it look like a robbery." Janay fidgeted in her seat anxiously.

"Well, then you gonna have to put in some work for me then. Do some runs, be my mule, and drop off my product at different locations. Plus, I want fifteen Gs. You'll have to work the rest off. And give me pussy whenever I want it," he said arrogantly.

"Whatever, Jarrod. Give me something now."

"What you want?" he asked, peering at her nonchalantly.

"Give me some pills. My nerves have been shot. I need something to make me feel happy and mellow." Janay gave a fake laugh. She had only used prescription pills a couple of times with Krystal, the girl who was killed by the Russian diplomat. Janay's life was starting to spiral more and more downward, and she ignored that obvious fact.

Jarrod passed her a small plastic bag with two pills in it. "Okay, that's all you're getting on the house. You seem like you are stressing, so that's a gift from me. Call me when you get all the details about your cousin's arrival." Jarrod leaned over and kissed Janay on her cheek and whispered in her ear. "I'm gonna love making you my sex slave." Janay pulled away as Jarrod got out of the car and back into his truck. She pulled off.

Janay went home to find two court documents in the mail. Her court date for the Russian's murder was in two weeks, June 12, and the start of her trial for Monique Troy was in a month, on July 9. She asked herself how that could be. She called her lawyer for the Atlanta trial.

"Mr. Tisch, I received the date for the start of trial, and I have that case pending in New Jersey that I told you about. Is there anything that we can do?"

"Well, for one, you have been charged and arraigned here. You have pled not guilty. I can put in for a postponement. That way you can start your other trial, because that one seems more serious than this one. You are claiming self-defense here. I think the chance of you beating this case is good. You will probably not go to prison for this man's murder. He was there willingly and he knew that he was engaged in illegal activity.

You are a witness to the death of the girl, so I think this case is a sure win. I will try to have a pretrial hearing to postpone the start date. I will get back to you. Do you need a lawyer in New Jersey?"

"Yes." Janay popped one of the pills that Jarrod gave her. She didn't even know what it was that she was taking.

"Well, I have a good lawyer for you. His name is Paolo Rabissi. He is one of the best criminal defense attorneys in New Jersey. I'm not in my office to give you the number; just call information. His office is in Paramus, New Jersey. Give him a call. He's not cheap, though, but it'll be worth it. I'll get back to you about the court date." Janay thanked her lawyer and hung up.

Janay went to the couch and started watching TV when her phone rang. It was a client. She needed the money, so she had to take the call, although she was feeling very woozy from the pill that she had taken.

"Hello, Mr. Jamison. Are you in need of something?" she slurred, as she could barely keep her head up.

"Yes, I would like four girls. I have a business acquaintance who is in town, and he would like two girls, one Spanish and one black. I'd like you and another black girl. We will be at the Marriott downtown in Room 1614 after six this evening. Can you and your girls be there by seven?"

"Sure thing, Mr. Jamison. Any other requests?"

"Yeah, we'd like some speed, like a hundred dollars' worth. Can you arrange that too?"

"I'll work it out for you but it'll be extra. I normally don't supply drugs, but I just started doing business with a supplier. We'll need twenty-five thousand. Okay?"

"You got it, sweetie. Just make sure that the girls know that we want all of our requests met. We are looking to have a wild night. Don't let me down", he said in a low voice. Mr. Jamison, a top executive of a large food chain, hung up.

Janay made some phone calls and put the plan into motion. Jarrod came to bring her the drugs within the hour. She had become rather sloppy with her business. She usually never used her home phone or let anyone know where she lived, but her current unemployment and legal problems had changed those rules. Jarrod showed up with a bottle of liquor. Janay opened the door and let him in.

"What's good with you? You look like you are feeling no pain. You want to have a drink?"

"No, I have some business to attend to. I just need the stuff. The guy wanted a hundred worth." Janay sat down on the couch.

"Give me some head and I'll give it to your for fifty." Jarrod moved toward Janay as she looked up at him. She felt cheap.

"Listen, Jarrod, I'm going through something, so I may need you, but you are gonna treat me with respect. I am not sucking your dick for fifty fucking dollars. You don't know who you are dealing with. I know you casually and you don't know me at all. I get paid well for my services; now zip your fuckin' pants back up and give me the shit. I gotta go."

Janay stood up and Jarrod pushed her back down on the couch. He put his hands on her throat and whispered in her ear. "Bitch, you don't know me neither. Watch how you talk to me."

Jarrod kissed her on the cheek and stood back up, with his hand out. Janay put the money in his hand, and he threw the baggie with white powder onto her coffee table. He walked out without saying another word.

Janay got dressed in a red Tahari dress. It was a wraparound dress that was tapered and fit very well to her shape and matched her crimson hair. She looked very classy but felt worthless. She had told the girls to meet her in the hotel lobby a half hour early so she could make sure they were at the room at the exact time they were supposed to be. The girls were all dressed in red, as Janay had ordered them to be. Their names were Sabrina, Shelley, and Isabella. They had all worked with Janay for more than a year and were very experienced. Janay had lost her spark with the business, but she was doing it out of necessity now and not greed.

They went up to the room and were let in. The two men were already having drinks and were very eager to get the party started. Janay introduced everyone and asked Mr. Jamison and Mr. Burrows what they wanted to do first. They were in a luxurious suite that had two private rooms. They all lounged in the living room area.

"Well, I'd like to see these bodies without the clothes. Can you girls get naked for us? And I'd like you, Isabella, to come and suck on my manhood. My wife never does it, old bag." He laughed and Mr. Jamison chimed in. "Yeah, the wives get the house, cars, and vacations, but they can't be paid enough to act like a whore. It's a disgrace." The men laughed again.

"Where's that stuff you brought us?" Mr. Jamison asked. "I'm celebrating my wedding anniversary with you ladies. You might make me go home and ask my wife for a divorce." He used his credit card to snort the drugs up into his nose. He shook his head. "Man, that's some good stuff. Anyone want some?"

Two of the girls accepted, while Janay and Isabella politely refused. Janay was not going to be under the influence of any drugs for fear of another catastrophe. Since that horrible incident with the Russian, she barely drank while she worked. It just wasn't any fun to her anymore, but she had a thought after hearing what Mr. Burrows had said about his wife.

"Let me taste him, Isabella; move over," Janay said and got on her knees. She wanted to get this one by himself and see if she could bait him. She was tired of doing this work. What she now needed was one good sucker to take care of her money problems. "You don't mind, Mr. Jamison, having the other three? I want to have Mr. Burrows to myself."

"Hey, I only get to have two women when I get lucky and go on business trips and meet up with real studs like Mr. Jamison. I want two." Isabella walked back over and joined Janay in sucking all over Harry, which was his first name.

"Okay, you can share now. But I want some private time with you before the night is out, okay? I don't mind dating a divorcée." Janay stood up and inserted Harry into her while he licked on Isabella, who was straddling his face.

"Whatever you say. Make me a believer," he said. He pushed Isabella to the side momentarily and reached down on the floor, grabbed his drink, and took a sip of his Jack Daniel's whiskey.

The other two girls were tending to Mr. Jamison. The more drugged up and drunk the two men got, the more ideas Janay got.

"Hey, let's play Dare. You either take the dare or pay five hundred bucks. Why don't you guys have a little fun with each other? We'd like to see you put your dick in Mr. Jamison's ass, right, girls? We want to see some entertainment too." The girls laughed and agreed.

"Hey! I'm no homo," Mr. Jamison said, while the other stood there, contemplating if he should go all out.

"Who said you were? We are here to have fun, no holds barred. If your wife isn't sucking it, I know she's not letting you stick it in her butt. See how it feels to do it to a man, Mr. Richard Jamison. We won't tell anyone." The girls started bringing the two men closer together, while Janay reached into her pocketbook and snuck out her camera.

The men were inebriated and very high off of the drugs. They were no longer coherent in their speech or thoughts. The girls immediately caught on that Janay would be blackmailing the two men, and they each wanted to be in on the take.

They very seductively coerced the two men to start fondling each other first. Janay stood outside of the circle that the three other girls formed around the men with their bodies and snapped shots of it all. They were her cover.

Richard's head was slightly and slowly pushed down into Harry's lap, and he began to lick and slob all over Harry's dick. Harry began to make loud noises, and Janay turned to the video function on her camera and began to videotape them. The men were enjoying every minute of their so-called first experience with another man.

Janay gently pulled Shelley and Isabella from behind and whispered in their ear, "Go get your strap-on and meet us in the room." Shelley did as she was told.

"Let's go into the bedroom, guys," Janay said, and Sabrina began to help both men up and watch them stagger into the room. The girls took each man into a separate room and pretended to get ready to engage in sexual encounters with them just as Shelley walked into one room and Isabella the other.

Mr. Jamison was lying facedown when Isabella entered him from behind. He was so out of it, all he could do was moan. Janay snuck up and put the camera back on record. The two girls laughed quietly with each other behind the nonsuspecting fake stud of an executive. Richard Jamison was clueless that his very life and the reputation and stature that he had worked so hard to build was about to be turned completely upside down in a matter of days to come.

Janay snuck over to the other room and witnessed another victim whose life she was about to destroy. She caught the men in positions and acts that they would probably rather die than to have exposed.

Once Janay was satisfied with her bargaining material, they packed their stuff up and left the scene. The men were out cold, naked, and spent. The girls went their separate ways, with Janay promising to call them with the next step of her get-rich plan.

●━━━━━━━━━━━━━━━━━━━━━━━━●

Janay reached her town house at about 4 a.m. and was too anxious to sleep. She viewed the pictures and video and brainstormed about how she was going to put the squeeze on Mr. Jamison and Mr. Burrows and fast. Janay called Jarrod.

"Listen, I don't know what time, but I know she's coming tomorrow, so be on call. Ya dig?"

"Yeah, I will need half up front, so have your shit planned. This ain't no last-minute type of shit, but you makin' it that way. Call me early in the morning with something or it's a no-go. *You* dig?" he asked sarcastically. Janay agreed and they hung up.

Janay finally fell asleep and was awakened at 11 a.m. by her mother, who said that Brielle would be arriving around three.

"Is that pussy-whipped man of hers coming with her?" Janay asked enviously.

"Janay, who are you talking to? You know what? I think you have finally lost your mind. I don't care what you do out there in that street, but you watch what you open your mouth to say to me. What is it with you and Brielle? Never mind, I don't even want to hear the nonsense. Be here by five." Janelle hung up.

Janay got out of the bed and called Jarrod. They met in the parking lot of a local McDonald's.

She used the money that she was paid from the night before to give to Jarrod. "Listen, here's ten thousand; I owe you five. My mom lives on Dunlington Place. You will see my car parked in the driveway. Come around the back and I'll leave the door unlocked; but on your way out, knock over shit, lock the door, and then bust it open. That way you will be on your way leaving, not coming. I need you to come at ten. I'll slip my mom a Mickey. Give me something that will knock her out cold. There's only one problem. I don't know if her man will be with her or not."

"Her man? So what the fuck am I supposed to do if her man is there? You said one; you don't get two for one, bitch," he said viciously.

"Fuck it, shoot his ass too. I'll have the money to pay you. I don't know if he's coming with her, but if he does, so be it. They all dumb and in love and shit, so they don't have to let death separate them; they can die together. Who gives a fuck?"

Janay got out of the car, and Jarrod reached over and squeezed her ass before she closed the door. *This nigga better learn that I'm a high-class ho. I don't fuck with nickel-and-dime boys.* She sighed. *Fuck it, I'll let him think he can mess with this ass until I'm done with him.* Janay laughed.

Janay went to the beauty parlor to be dressed to impress her rival cousin. She ignored the fact that she had just paid someone to kill Brielle. That fact didn't faze her at all. She conducted herself as if it were any other normal day, not like she was a murderer about to kill again.

"Girl, I need the hookup. Today is a special day; give me something different," Janay said excitedly as she sat in her stylist's chair.

"Well, what do you want to do? You want to change the color or stop being scared and get a mohawk? You already have one side shaved off; go for it, girl."

"Why not? I'm a rebel. Do it." Jasmine put a cape over Janay and started cutting her hair.

"So, what's so special today?" Jasmine asked.

"My favorite cousin from New Jersey is coming in, and we are going to have a family dinner." Janay laughed to herself.

"Girl, I don't mean to be nosy, but what happened with you at work? I heard some man tried to kill you and you killed him."

"I was having a business dinner with a sales associate, and he invited me and my girlfriend up to his room. I figured it would be safe since it was me and her. I went to use the bathroom, and he choked my friend to death, so I shot him," Janay said matter-of-factly. She was feeling less stressed about that case since speaking to Mr. Tisch. She figured that she would get off scot-free. It was the New Jersey case that she was agonizing over, thanks to her psychotic cousin. Never did Janay blame herself for making the choice to kill Monique. As far as she was concerned, Brielle was the culprit.

"So, did you have to go to court and stuff?" Jasmine continued to pry in a sly way. Janay contemplated cursing Jasmine out and telling her to mind her business, but she didn't want her hair to get messed up accidentally on purpose.

"Well, I have to go through some court proceedings. It's a technicality. I'll be fine, though. My friend is dead; I was saving my life. If I was white, they would have just let it go, but you know how it goes. They want to drag a nigga through it and see what they can get out of it. Maybe a fine or a lesser charge for me to plead guilty to. Anything to have one less nigga on the street."

"Girl, you ain't lyin'", Jasmine agreed.

Janay got her hair done nicely. Jasmine gave her honey-blond and hot-red streaks on the top of her mohawk and all red in the back. Janay looked like a rock star. She had on a black leather tie-up vest with no bra. She had short shorts on with toeless, knee-high black-leather stiletto boots. The leather short set cost $1500 and was by Akris. Her black-and-white $3000 Versace bag put just the finishing touch on the outfit. She paid Jasmine $175 and went home.

She contemplated changing into something less revealing but decided not to. Because Shawn was probably going to join Brielle on this trip, Janay wanted him to see just was he was missing. She would love to have one night with Shawn, but she knew it would be more than just one night. He seemed like the kind any woman would fall heavily for. Too bad he met Brielle, because she may be the cause of his death. Janay had a thought and called Jarrod.

"Yeah, what up? You gettin' nervous?" He asked, and then laughed. Jarrod was not only a smartass, but he was not fine. He was the type of ugly guy who overcompensated for his own insecurity by trying to mask it with arrogance. Janay saw right through him and saw him for the misguided, ignorant loser of a man that he was. She was in no way impressed with him.

"Are *you* getting nervous?" Janay replied. "Listen, I don't have time for the slick talk. You don't have anything I can slip her to make her just fuckin' die? I am kind of getting nervous," Janay admitted.

"Listen, you are way too late for that. If you would have given me more time, I could have gotten one of my girls who works at a doctor's office get her medical records but you didn't plan. I'm just gonna be in and out. Believe me, I won't get caught. The problem is whether you will break and give the police my name. And because that is always a possibility, I will cover my ass the way I know how. Just don't say my name at any time and after this. Do not call me; I will call you to get the rest of the money." Jarrod planned to send someone else to do the job, someone Janay knew nothing about, so that he could have an air-tight alibi.

"All right, whatever. Bye. Be on time." She hung up and drove to her mother's house.

Janelle had a stressed look that had aged her a bit since this ordeal with Janay and Brielle. She stepped to the side and shook her head when she noticed Janay's outfit. "Janay, you know, I am really worried about you. You seem to be really not in the right place mentally, and I think you need to go and talk to someone."

Janay, not being the least bit interested in what her mother was talking about, decided to play along.

"I know, Ma. I really need to get my thoughts together. Do you know of a good therapist? This is a bad thing that happened, but some bad things bring you to issues that you have to deal with within yourself, to work on and work through," she agreed amiably.

Janelle bought Janay's sincerity and said, "I am so glad you agreed with something I said for once. I'll ask my friend Mildred; she says that she really likes her therapist. I feel a little relieved now. Come and give your mother a hug." Janay walked over to her mother and they embraced. "And please don't wear that getup again. I taught you how to dress classy."

"Okay, Ma, don't start, please." Janay sat back down on the couch. They watched a movie until the doorbell rang at six o'clock. Janay's stomach tightened. Janelle went to the door and returned with Brielle.

Janay's eyes brightened when she saw that Brielle was without Shawn. They stood and looked at each other for a few minutes, and Janelle said, "Please hug each other. We have God and you two are his children. Let's pray and come to a compromise."

Janay and Brielle hugged and looked each other up and down. Brielle had on white linen shorts and a matching white halter top, a $1900 Chanel outfit, with some white $1500 BCBG Max Azria stiletto sandals and a matching white-and-gold chained Chanel bag worth $2500. Together they had on about ten thousand dollars' worth of clothing and accessories.

They sat on opposite ends of the couch, while Janelle sat on the love seat across from them.

"Okay, I am so very glad that the two of you are in the same room. I want to know what it is that we are going to do."

Janay answered. "Well, what is it that Brielle's offering? Why is it that she is here?"

Brielle sensed the sarcastic tone from Janay and ignored it. "Janay, can you please tell me what happened? How is it that the police are telling me that you are going to testify against me?"

"Well, about two days after the girl was shot, the detectives came down here and arrested me. They said my blood was at the scene and that I was facing life in prison, if not the death penalty."

"So, you told them that I told you to kill her? Just like that? Without even calling me or a lawyer? It was that easy for you to confess to killing someone?"

"Shit, they had me in there for hours and hours. I was delirious. I didn't even remember the statement I made until the next morning, when they gave me a copy.

"So, then how do you know you made it? Did you check that it was your handwriting before you bailed out? And who bailed you out anyway?"

"My mother wired the money from my account to Corey, and he came and bailed me out." Janay shifted in her seat. She did want to kick herself for giving up so easily, which is why she lied to Brielle about remembering.

"So, are you sure you confessed?" Brielle repeated after staring into Janay's downcast and eluding eyes.

"Yes." Janay answered without looking at Brielle's.

"Okay, well, do you want to get a lawyer that works in the same firm?"

"My attorney down here referred me to a lawyer; his name is Paolo Rabissi," Janay said, like she had classified information.

Brielle sat up and stated, "That's my lawyer." Janay felt snubbed by Brielle yet again. She checked the clock and it read seven. She had three hours to set the scene and get it ready for Jarrod.

"Okay, so then maybe we should have them put a team together," Janay said enthusiastically.

"I think that's the best way to go," Janelle said.

"Yeah, so will you be handling the bill, Brielle?" Janay asked, and Brielle thought of Rabissi's warning about Janay wearing a wire. Her gut told her that Janay was not wearing anything but a slutty outfit, so she answered.

"Of course. Janay, it is only right, but you could have handled it much differently. Now, instead of us fighting one case, we have to fight two. And then you didn't even call me or anything, like you are mad at me. This should not be happening right now."

"Listen, let's just fight this thing." Janay got a thought to call Jarrod and call off the plans, but she didn't do it.

"Let's eat. I guess that's all we can do for now. I didn't think for a minute that it would go so smooth. You ladies must finally be ready to look at yourselves and your actions and see how they affect others. Both of you are so much alike and so different. But this has shown you both that you can't keep blaming everyone else. And look at the possible cost. The worst-case scenario is that both of you end up in prison for a very, very long time," said Janelle as she scrutinized both girls with her words of wisdom.

Janay and Brielle walked into the dining room while Janelle prepared the plates. She brought them each a plate, went to get hers, and returned to join them.

"So, what's up with Shawn?" Janay asked and raised her eyebrow teasingly.

"He's fine. As a matter of fact, I'm going to join him at the hotel. I'm glad that we came together so easily, Janay. We need to put our animosities with each other to the side right now, because both of our lives are on the line. Seriously, do we really have time for division?"

Janay looked at Brielle and snickered inside and thought, *Shit, you don't have time at all.*

Instead, she said, "You're right, Brielle. We have to come together. So, why are you leaving? Let's continue to talk about this." Janay checked her cell phone and it read 8:30. *Damn, it's too early*, she thought.

"Janay, it's up to us to have a consultation with the lawyers. I will call Mr. Rabissi first thing tomorrow morning."

"So, where are you and Shawn staying?" Janay could not help but sound too interested and Brielle caught on.

"I said we are in a hotel. We are good. We didn't want to stay here, Aunt Janelle, 'cause we can't get down like that in your house." Brielle laughed and Aunt Janelle shook her head and smiled.

"Okay, girl, go enjoy your honey. I'm glad to see you, and I'm glad you took the trip to do this in person."

Brielle got up and took her plate into the kitchen. Janay followed. "Do you and Shawn want to go out?"

Brielle grabbed a knife and cornered Janay at the sink with the knife to Janay's side so that she could hide it if Aunt Janelle walked in.

"Look, bitch, not only did you have me raped, you tried to threaten me that you would blackmail me for killing that motherfucker you had rape me. Then I think that you are feeling my pain with Monique, and you turn me in within days? If you think that we are family anymore, you are wrong. We have to fight these cases and fight them together since *you* fucked up. But anything more than that is dead between us. I'm cutting my *family ties* to you."

Brielle put the knife back in the strainer and calmly walked back into the dining room to say good-bye to Aunt Janelle. She hugged her aunt and told her that she would call her in the morning before her flight back to New Jersey.

Aunt Janelle whispered in Brielle's ear, "Promise me that you will start praying. Promise me that you will pray for yourself and your cousin. I love you. Nobody's perfect but He changes things."

"I promise, Aunt Janelle. I love you too." Brielle walked out of her aunt's house and got into her rental car and drove away from her death and to the love of her life.

Janay was so frustrated that Brielle had threatened her with a knife that she got mad and left to go get some liquor without remembering to call off the hit. She was driving home when her phone rang, and she noticed it was Jarrod.

"Oh shit! I forgot to call it off!" She raced to her mother's house without answering. She frantically drove, hoping not to find Janelle dead when she got there.

Janay walked in the house and it was black. There were no lights on. When she turned on the light switch, her mother was on the floor, tied up. She ran over and snatched the piece of towel that was taped in her mouth. Janelle looked extremely frightened.

"Ma! What happened?"

"Somebody was here but they didn't try to rob me! They were asking who else was here, and they searched the house. Are you in some kind of danger?" Janelle let Janay help her up onto the couch and remove the rest of the tape. She told her mother that she would get to the bottom of it and persuaded her not to call the police.

Brielle

Brielle drove downtown with a lot on her mind. She could not believe that she and Janay were in the predicament they were in. It was simple—Janay fucked up and she should wear that. Brielle was mad that Janay fingered her. She should have waited before giving a statement. That was the last straw as far as Brielle was concerned.

Brielle reached the Embassy Suites Hotel in less than a half hour. She didn't want to burden Shawn with her thoughts. She wanted them to enjoy the rest of their trip. When she reached the room, Shawn was not there. She called him on his cell phone, and he told her that he was swimming in the hotel's indoor pool. She quickly changed into her two-piece Dolce & Gabbana bathing suit that flattered her body all the way around and went to entice her man.

Shawn was relaxing in the hot tub when she entered the pool room. There was no one else in there but him. She put a quick plan into motion.

"Hey, baby cakes. You okay?" He asked, extending his hand to help her step down into the whirlpool.

"No, I'm not. My cousin is a demon. But I don't want to worry you with that. I have something for you." She tiptoed over to him while he still had her hand and turned around, giving him her back. Shawn knew just what to do in that instant. He released his love tool from his trunks and pulled Brielle down onto his lap. He moved her bottoms to the side and entered her from the back. For someone coming, it appeared as if she was just sitting on his lap. Under the water they were joined. Brielle slowly moved her body up and down and took him in. The jets on the whirlpool were masking any splashing that their lovemaking may have made. She felt good with him inside of her. Making love to him took her mind to a better place. All she could think of was how lucky she was to have him. Shawn leaned up and whispered in Brielle's ear.

"So, what is that witch gonna do?" He softly moved his tongue into her ear. Brielle pumped a little faster.

"Oh, baby. Um, she's, oh, she's gonna cooperate with us. I love this dick." She turned her head around and kissed him.

"Oh yeah? Oh, you definitely get dick for that. How did you pull that off? Better yet, do you believe her?" Brielle leaned forward to take more of Shawn into her walls.

"Baby, you feel so good." Brielle pumped hard and fast. Shawn grabbed her waist to slow her down.

"Stop moving so wild, girl. What if some kids walk in here? You don't even care, do you?" Shawn laughed.

"Hell no, I don't. No kids should be coming in here at this time anyway; they asses should be in bed. Shut up and keep filling me up." They both laughed.

"Girl, you are so bad and I love it." Shawn grabbed Brielle's waist and pulled her to him while he thrust into her. She leaned forward and took it all.

"I love it too." They began to go at it as if they were in their own private pool.

All of a sudden another couple came in. Brielle immediately sat straight up and leaned back into Shawn's chest. Under the water he grabbed her waist and pulled her in again. She could feel his penis pulsating to release his deposit into her account.

"Yeah, I just let you have some of my crème. Did you feel it?" Shawn whispered into her ear. Brielle slowly lifted herself up and out of him. She slid over to sit on the ledge next to him.

"Yes, I felt it and it felt damn good."

The other couple entered the hot tub with them.

Shawn, smiling, said, "Hey, how are you guys doing?" The white couple smiled and spoke back. Brielle smiled and said hello.

The couple cuddled on the opposite side of Shawn and Brielle. Shawn tapped Brielle on her leg. "Come on, baby cakes, let's let them enjoy what we just did. It's all yours, guys; have fun." The couple laughed, picking up on Shawn's statement. Brielle blushed and punched him playfully. They got out of the water and went over to the pool. They swam and played in the pool for about an hour. Brielle didn't mind getting her wet-and-wavy weave style wet; that's what it was for—getting wet.

By the time they got upstairs, they were both hungry. "Hey, let's go eat at a nice restaurant. My boy told me I should try this restaurant down in Atlanta called Silk. You ever heard of it?"

"Yeah, it's supposed to be really classy. It's an Asian steak-and-seafood place. Let's go," Brielle answered.

They both got dressed in upscale attire and went to get their car. They drove into midtown and found the restaurant Silk. Brielle loved the ambiance of the restaurant the moment she walked in. Shawn figured he would get her in a nice setting so that she could relax before he started to ask her about her meeting with Janay. They sat down and ordered drinks and appetizers. After small talk and her second drink, he started the interrogation.

"So, what happened at your aunt's, baby cakes?"

"We sat down and agreed that it is in both of our best interests to work together. We have to call Rabissi and get one of his partners to take her case."

"So, it was that simple?" Shawn reached across the table and lovingly wiped her mouth of the crabmeat stuffing that she had on her chin. "So, who has to pay?" he continued.

"I do. But at least she agreed. I thought she was gonna act like a real baby and throw a tantrum to impress Aunt Janelle, but she was rather calm. It was weird, though, because I haven't heard from her since her arrest, but she was acting like she wanted me to stay over. Then she asked where me and you were staying and if we wanted to go hang out. I had to let her know that all we have is this case; all that being close and shit is over. She acts like she didn't fucking rat on me to the police."

Shawn took in what Brielle told him and thought for a few seconds. "For some reason I don't trust her. I think she has something up her sleeve." He sipped his drink deliberately.

"Well, I'm gonna stay a step ahead of her ass. She won't be knowing none of my damn moves. She can play around if she wants to. She was the one who pulled the trigger, so she better try to be on this team. It's her word against ours, but she was there, not me. We will see how she acts when she comes up for the meeting with our lawyers." In Brielle's mind she told herself, *That bitch better watch out before she joins Monique in the afterlife.*

They finished eating and returned to their hotel. The Embassy Suites had a nice jazz lounge downstairs that Shawn and Brielle enjoyed for the rest of the night. By the time they got back up to their room, they were drunk and passed out on top of each other.

The next morning Brielle called Aunt Janelle to say goodbye. Her aunt told her that she was happy to have been able to see her and that everything would be fine.

They boarded their flight and Shawn fell asleep in his window seat no sooner than they put their seat belts on. Seated next to Brielle was a very attractive black woman who appeared to be in her early twenties. She was very nicely dressed and had what appeared to be very expensive jewelry on. She was intriguing to Brielle. She looked very familiar to Brielle for some reason.

"I love that Cartier watch you are wearing. I've never seen anything like it. Where did you get that from, if you don't mind my asking? By the way, my name is Brielle."

"Oh, thank you. I got it from London, at Harrods. It's one of only twenty made. My name is Simone. Simone Alexander." The young lady looked into Brielle's eyes and smiled.

"Nice to meet you. Are you from Atlanta?" Brielle continued to get acquainted since Shawn was not awake for her to talk to.

"No, I'm from a lot of places. Me and my mom moved around a lot when I was growing up, which is probably why I don't mind that I travel a lot for work."

"Oh, what do you do?" Brielle asked interestedly. It appeared that Simone must be well paid, whatever she did.

"Well, I'm a private investigator." Brielle was impressed.

"Wow. How did you get a job like that? That's pretty exciting."

"Well, when I was little, my younger sister got kidnapped and murdered. I vowed to grow up to help people find out things that they want or need to know. I started interning for a firm when I was in high school, and then they hired me when I got out of college."

"Oh, I'm sorry to hear that. Did they ever find out who did it?" Brielle pried.

"Yes, it was our neighbor who lived across the street with his wife and kids. We were friends with his kids too. His daughter was my best friend." Brielle was shocked.

"I'm so sorry to hear that. So, did he get the punishment that he deserved?" Brielle continued since Simone didn't give any indication that she was bothered by their conversation.

"Yes, he was given the death penalty. I came to see him die. That is why I was in Atlanta. I live in New York," Simone said, sipping on her cocktail.

"And I thought *I* had a lot to deal with. How have you held up? It didn't make you angry growing up?"

"Hell yeah. It has affected every part of my life. I was so angry growing up, I wanted to kill somebody." Brielle felt an instant connection to Simone as soon as Simone made that comment.

"Girl, I know the feeling," Brielle responded and they both laughed.

"My life started out crazy, though. My mom left New York when she was pregnant with me without even telling my father that she was pregnant with me. She told me that he was an abusive drunk, and she didn't like how he was raising his daughter that he had from another woman, so she never wanted him to raise me. For a long time I resented her for not giving me the chance to get to know him and make that decision on my own. It still bothers me sometimes, but I've had no other choice but to deal with not knowing my father." Brielle shook her head.

"Isn't it crazy how parents are supposed to be perfect, but a lot of times they are the reason why their kids are so fucked up? Pardon my French. Some people should just never have children. Period." Simone enthusiastically nodded her head in agreement with Brielle.

"Girl, you ain't lying. And my mother had the nerve to say my father was no good. She was a damn lush too. She ended up having me and three more children, all of us with different fathers. And to top it all off, she dies early and leaves us to be raised by another maniac—my grandmother."

"Wow. Yeah, my mom and dad were a piece of work too," Brielle confirmed.

"But for some reason we still hold them up on a pedestal. I still thought my mother was the greatest. I carry her picture with me everywhere I go, and I have one picture of her and my father, the only picture I have of him. I decided that I am going to look for him this year." Simone took a Christian Dior wallet out of her blue-and-gray Christian Dior clutch and opened it. Brielle leaned in. "Here she is right here. The woman who almost groomed me into being a lunatic."

Brielle leaned in and looked at the old photo. It was classic 1970s, with the couple dressed conservatively, the man in a suit and the woman in an unrevealing dress. There was a nice old-model car in the background. Brielle zoomed in to the people in the picture and looked at their faces. She noticed two very familiar faces looking at her, and it took a few minutes for it register in her brain. Staring back at Brielle was a picture of Dorothy, her father's old girlfriend whose house he would always take Brielle to when they were supposed to be having a father-and-daughter outing. She gasped.

"Oh my God!" Brielle whispered, as not to disturb the rest of the air travelers.

"What is it?" Simone asked her, frightened.

"That's my father and Dorothy. That was my father's girlfriend when I was little. No way. I swear to God when you sat down and I looked at you, you looked so familiar, and now I know why. You look just like Dorothy. I spent so much time at your mom's house before you were born. Your dad is my dad?" Brielle paused to come to terms with what she believed had just been revealed while Simone stared at the picture in awe as well.

"So, if that is your father, then you are my sister?" Brielle, covering her mouth in shock, whispered. "I can't believe it." Brielle kept looking back and forth from Simone to the photo of Simone's mother and Brielle's father. Her mouth was open and she was stunned. Brielle continued. "I'm not trying to be offensive to you, but are you sure that is your father?" Simone was not offended.

"That's what my mother told me. She gave me this picture of them when I was very little. She told me that he had died. I always considered him my guardian angel. I didn't care what she said about him; I loved him and missed him. Is he really dead?" Simone asked, hoping the answer would be no. Brielle shed a tear and wiped her eyes.

"Yes, but he just died last month." Brielle said regretfully. She felt sorry for Simone. She also felt good to know that she wasn't the only one scarred by her parents. "But me and him didn't have a great relationship. I hadn't spoken to him for five years before he died. I went to see him one week before he died." Brielle looked at Simone closely and saw Dorothy. She had an instant love for her sister.

"You know, my mother and father abused me, and I always wanted a sibling, especially a sister that I could share the pain with. Someone I could lean on and who I could be there for in return." Simone looked intently at Brielle as she spoke and waited her turn to speak.

They both sat quietly for a few minutes. Brielle just had to be sure. She knew that Dorothy was a shady woman; even when Brielle was ten, she saw the vindictiveness of Dorothy. She hated Dorothy for messing around with her father behind her mother's back.

"Simone, how do you know that your mother didn't just give you a face to identify with? How do you know that she may not have possibly been with someone else and was unsure? I'm just asking."

"I don't. All I know is what she told me and I believe her. Why would she lie after telling me the truth about it from the beginning? She always said he didn't know that I existed. If my father was someone else, I think she would have given me that other man's picture. What would she gain from lying about it? She left, she says, to protect me from him. The least she could do is give me the real face. His name was on my birth certificate, though." When Simone told Brielle her father's name, Brielle thought about it and believed that too.

"So, he was that bad, huh?" Simone asked, hoping to hear another no as the answer.

"Yeah, he was horrible. I was around nine when he started taking me to your mother's house. He would tell my mother that he was taking me to the movies or the park, and he would take me to sit in her living room while they went in the back room. Then I would hear them making noises and stuff. But I could never tell my mother, because not only would he have beaten me, she would have too. They both hated me for being born," Brielle said, reliving the horrors of her past. She could no longer continue without waking Shawn up. He was her sanctum. She nudged him and he instantly woke up, looking dazed.

"Baby, you are not going to believe this," she told Shawn.

He rubbed his eyes and asked, "What is it now?" He looked at Simone, who was also staring weirdly in his face.

"This woman right here, her name is Simone." Shawn interrupted Brielle to say hi to Simone, who returned the greeting. "And she is my sister." Shawn looked at Brielle in disbelief and then shook his head.

"What are you talking about, Brielle?" He readjusted himself in his chair to prepare for the newest Brielle drama.

"Listen. You were sleeping, right?" Shawn nodded his head in agreement. "And this beautiful, young, fly, expensive-looking chick sits down"—they all laughed—"and I'm looking at her asking myself, *Now, what's this chick's story*, you know? Not to mention, she looked so familiar, and now I know why. She looks just like her mother. Tall, slim, and champagne–beige-colored, with those almond-shaped eyes." Brielle looked over at Simone, who was smiling and listening to Brielle's account.

"So, I start a conversation, 'cause, baby, look at her damn watch." Brielle lifted up Simone's arm to reveal her Cartier watch. "This shit looks too rich, so I start probing and asking her questions, and the bitch—pardon me, Simone; I mean that in the most endearing way—tells me that her mother split from her father while she was pregnant and never told him he was having a baby, right?" Shawn says "Right" and Brielle continues. "So, she gets to taking out of her thousand-dollar bag and wallet and shows me a picture of her mother, Dorothy, who was my dad's girlfriend when I was little and then a picture of *her* father. My father. Do you believe that?! I have a sister! I have a sister. I cannot believe this." Brielle puts her arm around Simone and brings her close. "Nice to meet you, my sister," she says and kisses Simone's cheek.

Simone reaches over and hugs Brielle and says, "Nice to meet you too, my sister."

Simone

Once departing their flight, Brielle and Simone continued to talk and walk together to baggage claim, with Shawn shaking his head in awe. Both Brielle and Simone were very excited to have met each other and continued to talk like they were old friends. They exchanged numbers and promised to meet up on the weekend. They went their separate ways, and Simone went out to the cab stand to catch a cab home.

Simone took a cab to her loft in SoHo. She entered the large flat with her bags and threw them down as soon as she closed the door behind her. She picked up the phone and dialed. When the person on the other line answered, she spoke.

"It's done. Yes. I need the balance of my money no later than Thursday." She listens to the receiver. "I told you. I drugged her, took her to the hotel, and then stabbed her. It was clean. She was unconscious by the time we got into the room. I slit her throat and left. I told the hotel clerk that we were sisters. When I left I told him that I was leaving because my sister was expecting male company." Simone paused again. "No, there weren't any cameras in that cheap-ass spot. I know what I'm doing. Please just have my money on time. Okay, talk to you later."

Simone got off of the phone and set a hot bubble bath for herself. She could not believe that she had just met her sister. Although she had two brothers, she missed having a sister after her sister was killed. She was happy to now have a living piece of her father. She knew Brielle without knowing her. She loved her without having spent any time with her. She looked forward to the closeness and the bond that they already shared but that they would nurture. She also knew that she couldn't tell her sister that she was a contract killer.

Simone unpacked her belongings and took out her wallet. She looked at the picture of her father and saw her sister Brielle in him. Brielle looked very much like their father. She looked at the pictures that she and Brielle took before departing from each other. The pictures looked like her mother and father standing next to each other. Simone looked in the mirror. She had her mother's full lips, high cheeks, round face, and pointy nose. "Why, Mommy? Why couldn't you have just stayed with him so that you didn't have to do it on your own and get pregnant by three other men? Why did you have to throw your life away?"

Simone looked away from the mirror and back into her digital camera. "Maybe my sister will be a positive influence in my life to help me get rid of my demons. I hope so."

Simone put the camera and the rest of her things away and called her brothers to tell them the news. Her brothers were teenagers and they were not too concerned with Simone's life. They still lived in Harlem with her maternal grandmother. They were excited and happy for Simone, though. They knew how devastated she was after their sister Mariah had died. Simone was never the same after that tragedy.

Simone got off of the phone and lounged around, watching TV. She decided against going out to the club, which was something that she did often to get work. She would meet various men whose lifestyles and backgrounds were criminal in nature, and most of them, after a short time, would confide in her about their problems.

She started offering her services as a hit girl and had been doing so for the past two years, since she was twenty. She was her own boss, but she got jobs from the same customers at times. She could not offer that kind of service to anyone without being worried about them going to the police, so she chose her clients very carefully and only contracted with strangers through the people she trusted and had worked for before.

Simone began to think about her past and how hard her upbringing was. Dorothy died when Simone was sixteen, two years after her thirteen–year-old sister was killed. Dorothy's drinking got worse after the kidnapping, and she basically drank herself to death. Simone and her two brothers were then sent to New York to live with their grandmother.

Simone was always into trouble, but it got worse after the deaths of her mother and sister. She became pregnant at eighteen years old. She only wanted the baby because she hoped that it was a little girl—to make up for the loss of her sister. She didn't care for the father of her unborn child. He was physically abusive to her, and after a fight they had when she was six months pregnant, Simone lost her baby.

Simone graduated from high school and left home at nineteen. She began staying with various people and started selling drugs and doing whatever she had to do to survive.

Simone recalled how she committed her first unforced murder. There had been other previous murders that she had been forced into doing, but this one was one that she had decided to carry out on her own.

It was the summertime and Simone was staying with a friend named Charlene. Charlene had a cousin who came over to visit. There was an instant attraction between the two. She remembered it like it was yesterday. She was lying on Charlene's couch when he walked through the door, looking cute and rough.

"Who's this cutie, Charlene?" Trey asked after looking Simone up and down.

"My name is Simone. I can speak for myself," Simone answered, sitting up and putting her feet down on the floor.

"Oh, pardon me, Shorty, I'm sorry. My name is Trey and I think I love you, girl. I've seen just about every fly chick from New York to Tennessee, and I must say that I want you for me." He winked at Simone and flashed a smile that revealed a mouth full of gold fronts.

"Well, I've been from Jersey to Tennessee, and I've never met a guy who had words quite like thee. What, did you go to private school, handsome?" Trey chuckled while Simone smiled with pride.

"Can I sit next to you? I need to get closer to that beauty so that maybe some can rub off on me."

Simone patted the couch next to her and continued to return the charm. "Sit down right here, and if you act right, I may never want you to go nowhere."

From that moment on Trey and Simone were an item. Trey's crime of choice was selling drugs and guns. Within a week, they were staying in a room in Charlene's other family member's apartment. They were sharing a two-bedroom apartment with Trey's uncle, who was a veteran and heroin addict. Trey ran his gun-selling business out of the kitchen.

Simone soon found out that Trey had just had a baby with another girl. The girl immediately began causing Trey and Simone problems. She would show up unannounced, drop the baby off, and leave him for days at a time without formula or diapers. The girl did not want to let Trey go and could not accept that he was with Simone, so she was always doing something disrespectful.

Initially, Simone stayed out of it, but her anger began to get the best of her, and when she had the opportunity, she offered Trey a proposition while they were lying on their mattress that was on the floor of their bedroom. It was a day they were at the apartment and his son's mother, Dominique, came by unannounced.

"Yeah, why you got this bitch around my son?" Dominique looked at Simone and then rolled her eyes. "I need you to watch lil' Trey for a little while, and if something happens to him because of her, you can bet you won't see him again."

Simone stared at Dominique with hatred in her eyes. She didn't think to hurt little Trey, but she wouldn't have a problem doing something to his mother. Simone decided not to say anything to Dominique because she had her own plan in mind. When someone made her angry, Simone always imagined killing that person. From the time that her sister was killed, she always felt that if an innocent child could die, then what was wrong with killing people who were more deserving of death? She did not choose to become a murderer; it was something that she was forced into. But it never bothered her because that was how much anger she held within.

"Listen, baby, we have been together for three months, and I really love you. But I don't like how your baby mama acts. She is going to keep you from your son. You should give me money to murk that bitch, and then we can raise him together." Trey sat up and looked Simone in her eyes. He was flattered by her offer and that she would take such a risk for him.

"Are you serious, girl? You love me that much?" he asked and began playing with her breasts.

"Yes. All I want is two thousand and I'll do it."

Simone planned her attack on the mother of Trey's baby, hoping to buy his unconditional love with that act. However, that day turned out to be a disastrous one. Simone methodically became friends with a friend of Dominique's in preparation for the special day and found out that she would be attending a party in St. Nicholas projects that night. Simone disguised herself as a crackhead and lay on a bench in the yard of the project development and building where the party was taking place. She had one of Trey's guns that she knew would end up being sold to someone else.

Simone wore oversize clothes, sunglasses, a hooded jacket, and a cap. For hours she lay there, waiting and watching. Finally, at about midnight she noticed Dominique approaching with her friends. Simone lay in wait while they walked right past her without even looking her way. She quietly got up and began walking behind them. Just as Dominique made it into the lobby of the building, Simone walked up behind her and shot her point blank in the back of the head and fled.

As she was running she heard the screams of Dominique's friends but she felt nothing. She ran all the way from 128th Street to 135th and into St. Nicholas Park. She dipped into the park, where she removed the outer clothes, dumped them in a Dumpster, and ran to 138th Street, where she lived.

She collapsed when she made it into the apartment and was surprised that Trey was not there waiting for her report. She wasn't in the apartment ten minutes before someone was loudly banging on the door. She knew that it could not have been the police looking for her that fast, although whoever was on the other side of the door was knocking like it was a major emergency. She looked through the peephole and saw Trey's sister Tina.

"Damn, girl, why you knocking like that? You had me scared to death." Simone assumed that Tina was coming to tell Trey that Dominique had been shot, as bad news always travels fast.

"Simone, Trey's been shot!" Tina screamed and grabbed Simone's hand to take her to the place where Trey's body was still lying.

Trey had been killed around the exact time that Dominique had by Dominique's new boyfriend. That was the first and last time that Simone let her heart love someone. She had lost her sister, whom she loved dearly, and then her first true love. She vowed to protect her heart from that day forward and never leave it open to being broken again.

Simone shook her head as she recalled how that one day changed the rest of her life. After Trey was killed she started staying with one of his friends, Rocky. Rocky was just as misguided as Simone was, and they set out to destroy anyone who came in their path. Rocky would introduce Simone to men that he would meet who appeared vulnerable, and Simone would go in for the kill. She would pretend to be their confidante, and whenever they began to open up about their problems, she would offer them a solution. She would exterminate their adversaries. She would make sure that the men knew nothing about her identity, but she always completed the job and collected her money.

When Simone met Brielle she was coming from doing a job in Atlanta. She told Brielle she was there to witness the execution of her sister's killer, but she had done that about a year earlier. The feeling she got from seeing him fry only made her more ruthless.

Two weeks before going to Atlanta, she had made the trip to London, where she located and killed a business partner of a store owner in New York who had embezzled his money and fled. That's when she bought that expensive Cartier watch. Most of Simone's clients were rich white men who she had no ties to, except the jobs that they hired her to do. Simone was a lost soul.

Shawn

Shawn and Brielle were driving home from the airport after their trip. He couldn't believe that Brielle had just met her unknown-about sister. He shook his head and thought, *My woman is amazing. Her shit never stops. She is so full of life and energy that she just draws it all to her. Why doesn't she know how powerful she is? I guess she does, having had the power of life and death in her hands.* He reached over and caressed Brielle's cheek. She looked over at her husband-to-be and smiled.

"Baby, I love you so much. I know you are like, 'This chick's life is beyond crazy,' right?" Brielle asked Shawn while they both laughed.

"Yes, ma'am. You need your own reality show. But then again, you might have been to jail by now if everybody knew your story."

Brielle got offended and replied, "Shawn, that's funny to you? My life is entertainment? I'm just your circus clown, huh?" She crossed her arms and waited for his answer.

"Baby, you are my African queen, that's what you are. And a queen can carry a whole country on her back. You are my rock, my rib, and my salvation. You've got so much shit with you, I ain't got time to have no shit. I gotta save you from your drama, and that saves me from mine."

Brielle blushed and said, "You lucky you saved yourself with that answer. That was a good one. It might get you some good head tonight." They both laughed.

"I'm serious, baby. I don't know how you have endured all that you have without faith. I just don't know how you don't know that God has kept you."

"I have always just dealt with whatever happened to me. But I can't lie and say that I haven't felt that there was something holding me, like you said, keeping me sane. Sometimes when I lay down, it feels like some force is rocking me to sleep or has its arms around me. It's weird."

"No, baby cakes, it's not weird; that's God. He will give you peace in the most dangerous of storms. He will give you an enormous strength that surpasses all understanding. You are God's child. I just want you to know it yourself."

"Okay, my teddy bear, I will try and remember that. But it sure seems like you are the one keeping me." Brielle looked out the window and up to the sky. She asked the clouds what her purpose was. *If that is you up there holding me down down here, then please tell me. Let me know that you are real, God.* Brielle looked back at Shawn.

"I am the one that he chose to be your earthly protector and savior. I am who he sent to take care of you. But he takes care of us from up above."

"Well, I thank him for sending you then. And I thank you for agreeing to the deal." Brielle laughed. "You are definitely out of this world with your thinking, Shawn."

They continued to drive and talk about how Brielle felt about Simone. She was so elated to have someone who she was sure would be a better partner than Janay turned out to be. She saw Simone as young and scarred but not evil like Janay.

"You know, babe, I think for some reason me and Simone need each other. I know we met for a reason. I could have never ever known her. We ended up next to each other on a plane because it was time for our paths to cross."

"Of course, baby cakes. That's how life is. Nothing is an accident."

"Even me being abused as a child, Shawn? Why?"

"Because, Brielle, God knows we are not perfect. He knows that we are lost without him. He finds us, chooses us, and takes it all away. You went through that to help someone else. You don't know what Simone has gone through. You are right. She may be here for you to help save her. Jesus saves and he uses others for us to bring to him too. Maybe you and Simone will come to Jesus together."

"There you go with that God stuff again. Okay, maybe you're right. I don't know. I know it's something and we'll just have to wait and see what it is," Brielle said again, looking out of the window. She hoped that Simone didn't turn out to be a nightmare like Janay.

Shawn pulled up to the house and told Brielle that he had something to take care of. She instantly thought back to the night that she killed Dante, when she found out that he was still cheating.

"Baby, please be good. Don't start nothin' and it won't be nothin'," she said with a straight face.

"Oh yeah? I hear that, woman; let me know. No problem, I'll be good. I gotta go with Bryan to Rock's birthday party, but I won't be out too late. Just have that pussy on a platter for me when I get back, okay? And I'm holding you to that good head promise." He then squeezed her nipple through her bra. Brielle laughed, opened the car door, and stepped out. She leaned back into the car, said, "You got it, cowboy; you better be ready to ride," and closed the door.

Shawn went back into the city, and his cousin picked him up from his brownstone. They went to a mob-owned restaurant in Harlem called The Flash Inn. There waiting for him was a connected man named Peter Sicily. They shook hands and both sat at Peter's small table.

Shawn put a small cache case onto the dinner table and opened it. There were about ten pieces of rare and expensive jewelry. Peter started picking up and examining each piece with a diamond scope. Shawn ordered a rum and coke. He watched Peter and surveyed the area. The restaurant was basically empty. There were two other small groups of men at two tables not close to Peter's. Shawn did not feel any bad vibes. He made sure that he had strapped his small pistol to his ankle just in case anything did jump off. His cousin Bryan was in the car, waiting and prepared with firearms as well. This was the part of his life that he was unable and unwilling to share with Brielle. He wanted to make sure she would have no involvement in any way were something bad to happen. He knew that he would only have to conduct this unlawful business for a little while longer, and then everything would be over.

"Well, Mr. Harrison, you have come through for me again. I thank you and, as always, respect your cooperation. I will take all of these pieces, and I will see you next month. Is everything with Zanelli's good?" Mr. Sicily asked, closing the case and putting it under his seat.

Shawn finished his drink and stood up. "Definitely. You know, business is rough no matter what business you are in. You gotta stay on top of everything if you wanna stay on top."

Mr. Sicily laughed a hearty laugh and retorted, "That's why I like you, Shawn. You are straight and to the point. *Salud.*"

"*Salud.*" Shawn walked out of the restaurant and into his cousin's tinted-out and chrome-rimmed white Yukon.

"Everything straight, cousin?" Bryan asked before pulling off. Shawn nodded and drove onto the Harlem River Drive to go downtown. It was their other cousin's birthday, and they were going to his party at Jay-Z's 40/40 Club.

"Everything is straight. I just can't wait 'til it's over. I just wish that this nigga didn't have that information over my head. I don't want to be having y'all stealing from people. We make a good living with the sanitation shit. Nobody needs to go to jail at this point in our lives. But I'll be damn if I give this nigga a million of my hard-earned dollars because he can finger me in a murder. He got the jewelry store in Italy. He says we can pay in jewels, and that's how we gotta do it."

"So, how much left you gotta pay off? We've done mad spots and we've gotten a lot of shit in this last year."

"I got three hundred thousand left to pay him. I hit him with two hundred thousand out of my pocket when he first tried to blackmail me, and then I told him I'd hit him with jewels for the rest. Nigga blew all his money. He's broke as hell, so in order for his stores not to closed, I supply him with the jewels and pay down my bill. It's a good thing there's only two murders that he witnessed. If it was more, I'd probably be paying for life, or I'd have to take *that* nigga's. He happened to be there that night and he ended up with the gun and he disposed of the bodies, so who knows if he has any other evidence."

"Yeah, don't sweat it, nigga. We got it all covered. We'll be all right. It's almost over."

"Yeah. I gotta get out of that shit and make sure my girl gets out of hers. I can't keep her out of prison if I end up there." He looked out of the window at the city streets and people. He knew that everyone had their own sad story whether they had a good life or not.

"Sounds good to me, man. If it wasn't for you giving me this gig, man, you know I'd be twisted. Probably in Rikers somewhere. I'm indebted to you for that. I got you with that Italian nigga shit. And you know Rock got you too. If it wasn't his birthday he would have been right in this truck. We haven't let you down yet, have we? We blood, we gonna go up together; down is not an option. Isn't that what you told us?"

"Hell yeah." Shawn felt reassured that things were going to be okay.

They got to the club, and Shawn was anxious to relax. He had a lot on his mind between having his cousins rob some of the houses on their routes to satisfy Mr. Sicily's blackmailing debt.

Mr. Sicily had worked under his boss and had wanted the company to be left to him. When Mr. Zanelli's will was read and Shawn was left with the business, Mr. Zanelli left Peter a lump sum of money that he used to moved back to Italy with and open a chain of jewelry stores. He has a bad gambling problem, and when he finally went through all of his money, he approached Shawn. He told him that he still had the gun from the night that Shawn and his boys killed two men for Mr. Zanelli and that he would turn Shawn in if he didn't pay him one million dollars.

Shawn agreed to pay, all the while refusing to follow his first thought of just killing the man. Peter had always been a man of his word. Shawn believed that he would keep his end of the deal and leave him alone after being paid the amount he requested. Shawn also knew that if Peter asked for more money after that, he would have to kill him or have him killed, which was something that he really did not want to do.

●━━━━━━━━━━━━━━━━━━━━━━━━━━━●

They went into the 40/40 Club, and it was packed with people from wall to wall. They went straight upstairs to one of the private rooms that was reserved for Rock's party. The room was plush. It had a pool table and all-white leather furniture. There were girls walking around in bikinis, taking drink orders, and others giving lap dances. He definitely could use one of those. He was not going to take advantage of the other private rooms they had for two or three to engage in way more than dancing. He was not going to cheat on Brielle. He just needed a fine-ass chick to take his mind somewhere else for a few minutes.

He called over a girl in a shiny yellow patent leather string bikini. She had a bright-yellow wig and bright-yellow stiletto boots to match. She looked young and fresh. She couldn't have been more than twenty-two. Shawn didn't like young women, but he sure didn't mind getting a lap dance from one. The girl approached and leaned over to talk to Shawn.

"Hey, handsome, you want me for something? My name is Christina. I can give you what you need, Daddy; just tell me what it is, okay?"

"I just need your price, pretty girl. I've had a bad day, and I need you to make it all better. Can you do that for me?" Shawn thought about Brielle and how totally misunderstood he would be if she were to walk in at that very instant. But he also knew that a woman would never understand a man and his simple pleasures. He loved Brielle and—like many a man who's been in love with a woman—knows that what he was doing was totally innocent in his eyes. He wasn't at all interested in this girl, only the moment.

"Price for what?" she whispered in Shawn's ear.

"Just a lap dance, cutie," Shawn replied, pulling the girl down onto his lap.

She sat on him and turned around and whispered in his ear, "Just twenty per ten minutes. You sure, baby? There's a nice room upstairs that we can have all to ourselves. You're cute too. What's your name?" Christina started moving around to the beat of the music. She got a rise out of Shawn real fast.

"My name is Steven. If I wasn't engaged, I might just go upstairs with you. You already got me hard as a rock." Shawn wrapped his arms around Christina's waist and held her tight as she humped up and down on him. He buried his head in her back and closed his eyes. She felt good on top of him. He wished that he could just go upstairs with her, but he knew that he couldn't.

"Steven, you got me all wet. I want to see what it looks like. I don't cost that much, and I'm worth the price. You gonna turn me down?"

Shawn was starting to get weak. "You say this to all the guys. I don't buy pussy, miss. I have a beautiful woman at home who I love. And who will kill me if she found out, literally." Shawn imagined Brielle stabbing him in the heart and lost his erection. He gently lifted Christina up and sat her next to him.

"Listen, I don't offer myself to every man who comes in here. You are hella gorgeous. You so fine, you could make me give this here job up. I know a gem when I see one." One thing he knew was that this girl had game. She was definitely good at what she did.

"How old are you, sweetheart? Talking all grown like you been around the world." He squeezed her thigh and she laughed. Shawn knew that they were both just doing what chicks and men do in clubs, in private thousand-dollar rooms.

"I'm twenty-three. And I have traveled the world. I'm an old soul. My mother was a model, so I have seen it all, been through it all, and know how to hold my own. Is there something so wrong with that? She always taught me to use what I have to get what I want, and I can't honestly say that I know you enough to want you, but I know that I want to get to know you. I'll punch out right now and leave early. We don't have to go use the room upstairs. I'm tired of this scene anyway." Shawn thought for a moment and had to make a move before he sent himself to an early grave.

"Listen, let me think about it, okay? My cousin's party is here tonight. Let me go pop some bottles and enjoy his day, and I'll get back to you. Here." Shawn gave her a hundred-dollar bill for his ten-minute lap dance. He got up and went downstairs to find his cousins, who were no longer in the room.

He was two seconds away from taking Christina up on her offer and it scared him.

Shawn walked downstairs by the bar and dance floor. He noticed Rock at the bar, popping champagne and enjoying his entourage. He had two girls on each side, and he was apparently with both of them. Shawn came up behind Rock, who turned around and let him squeeze in between him and one of the girls.

"Yo! I'm fucked up, nigga! It's my birthday! I made it to see thirty, nigga! I never thought I'd see this day. You see these fine specimens I got with me? They twins, man, and, man, I'm gonna enjoy them later. And I ain't sharing! Tasha, this my cousin Shawn. Tamara, this my cousin Shawn," Rock said. "This man saved my life. He gave me an honest living. Here, man, have some of this good shit!" Shawn took the champagne glass and sipped it.

They moved to a table, where Bryan was sitting with a few more of their boys and some more badass–lookin' females. No matter where Shawn turned, danger, drama, and disaster was there. He thought that he should probably leave, but the party was just starting, and the eye candy was looking too damn good. "Lord, please let me be good," he said to himself.

The partygoers drank, danced, and enticed each other. There was the usual hooking up of the opposite sex in preparation of many after parties that would take place after they would leave the club. Shawn danced and had a good time and continued to avoid the many advances he received from very attractive women. He enjoyed himself and did not feel that talking or dancing with other women was wrong as long as he went home to his woman. He did take two numbers from two ladies who he would surely call just in case. In the event that he and Brielle did break up, those two would be the first two that he would call.

Bryan found someone to leave with, and she got in the truck with him and Shawn. As Shawn was getting into the Tahoe, a familiar face was walking toward him. He couldn't place who she was, but she looked very familiar. He paused as she approached.

"So you were just gonna leave, Steven? Without even getting my number." It was Christina in some regular clothes and without the yellow wig. She was a beautiful, fresh face, and she had the sexiest body. He quickly pulled out his phone.

"I'm sorry, Christina. I never made it back upstairs. You looked damn good in that work outfit, but you look even sexier in your street clothes. What is your number just in case me and my girl run into a separation?" He laughed and waited. By then he was very drunk.

"Oh, come on. I'm sure your girl knows you are out with your cousin for his birthday. Come home with me and, by the way, call me Chrissy."

"Girl, I can't. As much as I want to right now, believe me. But I know I'll regret it in the morning. What's your number?" Christina gave Shawn her number, and he saved it into his phone under Chris. He did not realize that in saving it, he accidentally called her number. "And I apologize but I lied to you. My real name is Shawn."

"Damn, your girl got you shook like that? Think of me tonight while you're fuckin' her, and I'll be thinkin' about you." She grabbed his waist and kissed him and stuck her tongue in his mouth. He slowly moved his head back after giving her a taste of his tongue too.

"Good night, pretty Chrissy." Shawn got into the back of the truck and passed out. Bryan woke him up when they reached the brownstone. He had forgotten that he had to drive to Jersey and wasn't up for the ride.

Shawn went inside and as he was about to call Brielle to tell her that he couldn't make it to Jersey, he heard someone coming down the stairs. He went to get his gun from the coat closet when Brielle said, "Where the fuck you going? You just got here."

"Oh shit. What are you doing here? I was about to shoot your ass, girl." Shawn was startled and became instantly nervous. He thought about what might have happened if he had decided to bring Christina with him. He returned the gun to the top of the closet.

"I called your cell a million times and figured you couldn't hear it in the party. I left you a message that I'd wait for you here since I knew you'd be drunk. I didn't want you to be driving across the George Washington Bridge drunk." He knew that there was more to that story.

"You know you just checkin' up to make sure I didn't tell you I was going to a party and instead was having my own private party. You still on that nontrusting shit, huh?" Shawn was extra relieved that he had followed his mind and not his pants. Brielle laughed.

"Listen, baby, I know what it's like when a man is drinking and partying with hotties in a party. I'm just trying to help you stay alive." Shawn instantly sobered up after hearing such a realistic threat.

"Brielle, don't fuckin' play like that. Are you threatening me with murder? Do I need to start thinking about who I'm really dealing with? That shit ain't funny. Yeah, there was some gorgeous women in there and I came home alone. But I damn sure wasn't driving to Jersey in this condition, and I know you would have started some shit when I called to tell you that I couldn't make it back."

"Like I said, I know what it's like, and I avoided that problem. I thought ahead, okay?" He was too drunk and tired to debate.

"Okay. Well then, give me some bomb-ass head so I can fantasize about them woman but enjoy my lady at the same time."

"You lucky I love suckin' that dick, 'cause that shit you talkin' could really be talking you out of some head right now."

Brielle kneeled down and unzipped Shawn's pants. She took his soft penis out and put it in her mouth. It grew very quickly and released shortly thereafter. They then went upstairs and went to bed. They had to be at the lawyer's office the next morning to have a meeting and set up a conference call with whatever lawyer Rabissi would choose to have working on their team.

Shawn woke up the next morning with a major headache. He was glad and relieved that he was not a bit more drunk the night before, because chances were that he would have ended up taking Christina up on her offer. Brielle walked in the room with her yellow-laced bra and panties and he was stunned. The color of her underwear was the same color that Christina's "uniform" was. He thought, *Whew, you are one lucky dude.*

"What's the matter, babe? You look like you saw a ghost," Brielle said and then placed a tray of breakfast over him. Shawn sat up and saw fried eggs, home fries, and grits. He picked up his fork and started eating.

"Thank you, beautiful. Nothing is wrong; I just have a slight hangover. I kind of overdid it last night."

"Yeah? Well, is there anything you want to tell me? Any confessions you need to make?" He quickly thought of the possibility of one of Brielle's friends having seen him in the club with Christina grinding on his lap or downstairs, where he was dancing up on a few hotties. He knew that he hadn't met any of Brielle's friends, but that that didn't necessarily mean that she hadn't shown anyone pictures of him. He decided to play it safe and not give himself up because, after all, that was just innocent in–the-club stuff.

"Girl, you better stop it. I've been good to you. Don't start that shit that you was doing in the beginning. You still want that canary rock?"

"Hell yeah," Brielle answered and sat on the edge of the bed, admiring her engagement ring.

"All right then. Stop buggin'. I went to the party, had a good time and, of course, there were chicks trying to get at me and yeah, I may have talked to a few, but who did I come home to?"

"Me." She smiled.

"Okay then. Now let me eat so I can get rid of this damn headache. Go get ready. Did you bring clothes for today?"

"Yes, sir." Brielle stood up and saluted Shawn.

"Well then, go wash your funky ass and get dressed. Better yet, give me that head you promised to give me."

"I sucked your dick last night. You don't remember?" Shawn shook his head no, and Brielle said, "Oh well. It ain't my fault," and went into the bathroom to take a shower.

Shawn and Brielle reached Paolo's office around noon and were dressed professionally as usual. Paolo was waiting in his office with another well-dressed gentleman, who stood when they entered.

"Shawn, Brielle, this is one of my most successful partners in this firm. His name is Elliot Cifelli. We went to law school together and have been winning cases ever since. I know he is the best man for this job. We have not been on the same case together in a few years, but the last case we won together we won by a landslide. We tore the prosecution apart, and we are both very excited to have the opportunity to do so again."

Mr. Cifelli shook both of their hands and they all sat.

"Now, I have, of course, briefed and discussed the details of the two cases with Elliot, and we are building a strategy. Should we give Ms. Janay a conference call?" Shawn and Brielle nodded yes. "Well, before we do so, Brielle, can you tell me what transpired during your meeting with her."

"Well, it was pretty simple, which was surprising. She agreed to work with me right away. There was no conflict, no argument." Mr. Rabissi and Mr. Cifelli looked intently at Brielle as she spoke and then at each other.

"Does your gut instinct tell you to believe her words? Do you think that she is up to something, or do you think she will genuinely be on our team?" Mr. Cifelli asked.

"I am not really sure. I had a bad feeling about her when I left, but while we were talking, she seemed genuine. Let's call and see what you think."

Brielle recited Janay's number and Paolo dialed it and put the speakerphone on.

"Hello?" Janay answered, sounding cautious.

"Hello, Miss Roberts, my name is Paolo Rabissi, and I am calling you from my office, with your cousin and your lawyer in the room. How are you today?"

"I'm doing all right."

"Well, I have assigned Mr. Elliot Cifelli to your case, and we are going to put together a plan of action so that you and Brielle can have the best possible outcome from this unfortunate situation."

"Can you get me off?" Janay asked flatly. Brielle felt hatred for her cousin. She had expected Janay to at least say hello to her when she found out that Brielle was sitting in the office. That put up a red flag to her that Janay was still and always going to be someone not to trust.

"Hello, Janay," Brielle interrupted sarcastically.

"Brielle, do you have to interrupt the man to have me say hello to you? Isn't what he has to say more important than me having to acknowledge that you are in the building? Hello, Miss Crazy. Now, sir, can you continue, please?" All three men looked at Brielle and back at the speaker. Brielle felt embarrassed that Janay had pulled her card. She excused herself and went to the bathroom. Mr. Cifelli cut in.

"Janay, this is Elliot Cifelli. Myself and Mr. Rabissi have been reviewing the case, and our first strategy is to find out if there are any other people who may have had a motive to shoot Miss Troy. We are checking into her background. As far as you being at the scene of the crime, that is really not enough to get a conviction without a reasonable doubt. We would like to have you come into the office in about two weeks. By then we should have some more concrete information for you. The first thing we must do is rescind your confession. Are you going to agree to do that? To deny that you killed Miss Troy and that Miss Prescott hired you to do so?"

"If I take back my statement that Brielle asked me to do it, they could still find me guilty and not her, right?" Brielle returned to the room just as Janay was asking the question. She was about to say something, and Shawn put his finger over his lips to advise her not to say anything.

"Well, if you take back your confession, they will have to work around that. Both of you have been charged, so Brielle still has to fight her case as well."

"Okay, because I'm just saying that I'm not going to go down without her. Are we done for now?" They all looked at each other again, and Brielle shook her head.

"Uh, yes, we are done for now," Paolo answered. "I just hope that you will sincerely approach the matter with positive energy. We need everyone to be on the same page. You and Miss Prescott need to not only be on the same legal team, but in concert with each other mentally. It is important to really be on each other's side. Is that possible?"

"Yeah," Janay said flatly. "Miss Prescott?"

"Yes," Brielle said unenthusiastically.

"I am not a lecturer, I am an attorney; however, I must say that family is family, and you two ladies need to try to put your differences to the side right now for the better result. We will contact you two when we need the both of you to come in together. Have a good day, miss, and Mr. Cifelli will be contacting you soon."

"Bye," Janay said and hung up.

Shawn and Brielle shook hands with both lawyers and left the office. They were driving quietly back to the city when Brielle asked Shawn to run in her house and get her debit card that she had accidentally left on the kitchen counter. While he was inside of her house, his cell phone, which was sitting in the cup holder of his car, beeped, signaling a text message had come in. Brielle picked up the phone and opened up the message. The message read, "Hey, handsome, I enjoyed that little bit of time you spent letting me give you that lap dance last night. And I want another kiss like that real soon but a better one. I'm not going to take no for an answer. Call me soon. Chrissy. Mwah."

Janay

anay hung up the phone receiver and threw the phone against the wall. She was furious. She knew that she needed to have her own money instead of relying on Brielle to trick her into thinking that she would help her. She felt that Brielle was only going to save herself and would sink Janay's ship once she jumped it. How could she trust Brielle? She couldn't. Brielle was only interested in getting herself off, not Janay.

Janay picked up her digital camera and started viewing the photos that she had taken of the two married businessmen who had become homosexual lovers. The pictures were graphic and would definitely do the job of getting her the money she needed to find her own lawyer and pay for her own exoneration. She would play along with Brielle until such time. As Brielle had told her in the kitchen, there was no need to keep the family ties. Brielle was no longer her family just because they shared the same blood.

Janay got dressed in some Buffalo jeans and a matching long-sleeve T-shirt and some flat sandals and drove to the nearest drugstore to have the pictures made. She had them printed and saved to a CD. She called Mr. Jamison. He recognized her number and greeted her warmly.

"Well, hello, Janay the Beautiful. How are you? To what do I owe the pleasure of this call?"

Janay felt no remorse for what she was about to do. "I need to meet you. Meet me at Red Lobster in an hour. Your life depends on it." Janay hung up, called Jarrod to have him meet her outside of the restaurant in an hour and a half, and went ahead to the Red Lobster. She sat at the bar and had drinks while she created her strategy. She was rather drunk by the time Mr. Jamison walked in but not too drunk to get her point across. He came in looking disheveled and anxious. He joined Janay, who had since been seated at a table, and ordered a stiff drink.

He looked confused and very concerned when Janay began to share the reason for their meeting.

"Richard, I have something for you to see." She pushed a small envelope containing the incriminating pictures across the table to Mr. Jamison.

He opened the envelope and slowly took the pictures out. She examined his face as he painfully scanned the pictures, with his eyes shockingly wide and his mouth open almost to the floor. He viewed the pictures at least four times and had tears in his eyes by the time he could no longer look at them. He shook his head several times in awe and disbelief.

"I have no fucking recollection of what I am looking at," he whispered. He could not believe what he was seeing with his own eyes. Richard Jamison shook his head and continued to look downward. He did not once look at Janay. He put the pictures into the envelope and sorrowfully looked at Janay and then quickly looked away.

"How much money do you want?" he asked and downed the rest of his drink.

"Fifty thousand to start. And then another fifty. I figure that you and your lover can split the bill fifty-fifty." Janay unflinchingly looked dead into Richard's sad eyes and then put her chin in her hands to await his response.

Richard Jamison looked at Janay in desperation. He quickly realized that she was very committed to the decision to blackmail him and that it would be a waste of his time to try and talk her out of it, but he had no other choice.

"Janay, my wife lost her job six months ago. My house is about to go into foreclosure. I do not have fifty thousand dollars laying around. Is there something else that I may do to help you with whatever you are dealing with?"

"That is the only thing that you can do. I'm sorry, but you will have to come up with the money. You have two weeks to give me the first fifty thousand."

"I don't know if I will be able to do that." He shuddered at the thought of those pictures being exposed.

"Well, you'd better start working on it because if not, they will be e-mailed to the local paper, as well as your corporation head. I really don't want to have to do it to you, but I will." Janay checked the time on her phone and texted Jarrod to see if he was yet outside. He replied that he was. "Okay, I've got to go. I will be calling you in a few days to check on your progress." She got up from the table quickly and disappeared. She went into the parking lot and watched to see which car Mr. Jamison was driving in. As soon as he walked out, Janay texted the information to Jarrod, who began to follow him out of the lot and to his home.

When Mr. Jamison pulled into his driveway, Jarrod pulled up a ways so that his car would not be seen and ran over to meet Richard before he made it to his front door. As he was about to put the key in the door, Jarrod called out to him.

"Hey, Mr. Jamison. We know where you live now. Don't try anything funny by contacting the police. We will be watching you." He quickly exited, ran, jumped in his car, and sped off before anyone else could get suspicious and call the police.

Mr. Jamison slowly put the key in his front door and went inside his home.

Janay was waiting, as planned, in the parking lot of the 7-Eleven when Jarrod pulled in. He got out of his car and into hers.

"Okay, what's the address?" she asked before he could even shut the car door.

"Bitch, where's my two hundred? You think this shit is a game. I keep telling you, I am not one of these lame cornball niggas. I'm tired of you testing me."

"Here, damn. You may not be lame, but you damn sure be beat for some shorts. Now what's the address?" she asked again.

She passed Jarrod the money, and he passed her a piece of paper with Mr. Jamison's address written on it. She put it into the compartment of her car.

"Now, can I get two ecstasy pills, please?" She asked, passing him another twenty dollars.

"Damn, girl, you want some freaky pills, huh? Why don't you take them with me so I can show you what I'm working with?"

"I'll call you if I get horny," she replied and took the pills and put them in her pocket.

"Make sure you do and, trust me, you will. That's what those pills are for. I want some of that pussy, girl. Call me."

Jarrod got out of the car and back into his as Janay pulled off. She drove home alone and popped both pills as soon as she got inside. She did not want to be outside while under the influence of those potent pills. She was feeling very aroused within fifteen minutes and tried to call one of her sex partners, who did not answer the call. She called Jarrod to come over even though he was her very last resort.

Jarrod was ringing Janay's doorbell very shortly after she placed the call. She did not like his attitude, but in many ways she did. He was just as feisty and cocky as Janay was, although he was also violent and disrespectful. But she wanted sex and he would have to be the one to give it to her.

Janay opened the door to her town house in a lace, crotchless bodysuit. Jarrod was instantly aroused. He wasted no time picking her up and carrying her to her living room couch, where he turned her around and, without taking off his pants, removed his penis from his zipper and entered her bare. He grabbed on to the little bit of hair that she had in a Mohawk and yanked her head back. Jarrod forcefully fucked Janay while grabbing her body parts, smacking and biting her. Janay was so high that she did not even realize the torture he was putting her through. She seemed to be enjoying the rough sex. Jarrod grabbed her nipples and squeezed them hard as he released his sperm into her. He pushed her down onto the couch, put his dick in his pants, and walked out, leaving her bruised and sprawled facedown on the couch.

Janay woke up early the next morning with the ripped-up bodysuit still partially attached to her body and wrapped around her ankles. She stumbled to the downstairs bathroom while trying to remember how the previous night had ended. She felt sore on parts of her body, and when she looked in the mirror, she noticed that she had bite marks and bruises all over. Mentally, she recapped the evening and remembered Jarrod coming into her house. She didn't remember anything after that but was sure that he was the person who had left the markings on her body. She instantly started crying and stared at her reflection, *What is happening to me? I have turned into a monster. A drug-addicted whore. My life is ruined.*

Janay pulled what was left of the lace bodysuit off of her and went upstairs to take a bath. She cried uncontrollably while washing her sore body and then suddenly stopped, got out of the bathtub, and went again to the mirror in that bathroom. She looked herself in the eye and said vehemently, "I hate you, bitch. I hope you die. You are through. Your days are numbered."

Janay went to her bedroom and rubbed herself down with baby oil. Her body had purple, red, black, and blue marks all over it. *What kind of person would want to torture someone else during sex?* she asked herself and then realized that she was in the business of giving sexually deviant men any kind of pleasure they paid for, even if it included torture.

She looked in the mirror and realized that she was just like Jarrod, a person who would go to any lengths to hurt others. She was a person with no remorse. She was a person with no accountability, concern, or conscience. She had performed perverted sexual acts for money, and it never appeared wrong to her until then. She began to think of all of the different encounters that she had had with strangers. She had made a lot of money but nothing else. That money had not bought her happiness or contentment. She had only been driven by the possession of money, and now she needed money to buy her freedom and didn't have enough because she had not cared for the money either. She did not take good care of the money; she spent it unwisely because she had no regard or respect for that either.

Janay picked up the phone and called her mother.

"Mommy, I don't feel good," she said when she heard Janelle's voice.

"What's the matter, honey?" Janelle responded.

"I don't know, Ma. I feel lost," she replied and quietly cried so that her mother would not know.

"Janay, you have been moving fast, and you have not listened to any good advice. The life that you are living is a destructive one, and it has caught up to you. What makes you think that you can kill someone, take someone's life, for money? Did God tell you that you had that right? He gives life and you are not ordained to take it away. I have not even been able to fathom that you and Brielle both turned out to be murderers. I have tried to ignore the fact and pretend that it is not so. I just cannot wrap my brain around this. Both of you may very well go to prison for the rest of your lives and for what? Money? What good is money going to do you in prison?"

"Mommy, I just called to tell you that I am sorry. I am sorry that I have been so reckless and unruly. If I get out of these two predicaments, I will change my life."

Janelle had to take the phone from her ear and look at it to make sure she was actually on the phone and her daughter actually said what she just said. "Janay, I hope you are telling the truth. Many people make promises that they don't keep, and when it's too late, it's too late."

"I just have to do what I have to do to get out of this, and then I can try to change my life."

"Janay, I pray that you will come out of this. But whatever you *must* do to get out of *it,* as you say, may be just the thing that will be your downfall. God does not have to cover you when you are doing wrong. He is not obligated to protect and cover you in your sin. I just want you to know. You may want to change now, before it's too late."

"Ma, I don't want to hear that shit. I have one more thing I have to do to get this money up." Janay was yelling at her mother like she was a stranger in the street.

"For what?! Brielle is paying for your lawyer."

"I don't trust that bitch one bit. She wants to pay for my lawyer to guarantee her freedom and my death! If you are so concerned, why don't you give me fifty thousand dollars so I can save my own life?" Janay screamed into the phone.

"Janay, I thought you and Brielle came to an agreement?" Janelle said, trying to remain calm. She paused and then continued before Janay could answer. "Janay, I can't deal with this right now. My blood pressure is sky high over you and this nonsense. I pray that you stick to your agreement. Let Brielle handle it and get yourself together. Stop selling your soul to the devil!"

Janelle hung up and immediately got on her knees to pray for her daughter and niece. "Lord, please cover Janay and Brielle, and make it so that they may have another chance at life. Please do not send them to prison. Make everything right, Lord, if it be your will. Amen."

Janelle got up, picked up her Bible off of the end table, shut the TV off, and started to read her Bible.

Janay hung up the phone feeling just as overwhelmed as she did before she called her mother. She was tired of her mother always talking about God. She wanted her mother to help her. She wanted someone to make everything right. She dialed Corey's number. They had still been dealing with each other, although she hadn't spoken to him in a few days.

"Hey, is this my bad bitch from the ATL?" Corey answered and laughed.

"Yeah," Janay answered unenthusiastically. "I need to see you."

"So, you gonna come to Brooklyn? We can stay up in a hotel. I got this chick staying with me right now."

"Yeah, whatever. I just need to get away for a couple of days. Plus, I might as well stay up there until the trial. It's starting in a few weeks. You gonna send me some money to come?"

"Yeah, you know I got you. Go to Western Union. I'll send you a G. You sound like you sad and could use a little shopping spree. Hold your head. I gotta go. The money will be there in, like, an hour, okay?"

"Okay. Thank you. I can't wait to see you," Janay replied, but Corey had already hung up. She knew that he wasn't the least bit concerned with her like that. They were basically sex partners, and she knew that he just liked the fact that he had an older woman in Atlanta whom he could brag to his Brooklyn boys about. She knew that the relationship between the two of them would never go anywhere, but she was equally glad to have a getaway up North. She would not have been interested in a young drug dealer from where she lived, but an occasional few days with Corey was always fun. His crew was well-known and they always hit the exclusive clubs when she was in New York with him.

Janay got dressed and waited an hour to go get the thousand dollars that Corey would be sending her. She called Richard Jamison's phone, and it went straight to voice mail. "I hope you are putting in preparation what you have to do. I hope that you have contacted your friend about it too. I will call you in a couple of days."

Janay hung up and called her lawyer, Mr. Tisch. When his assistant put the call through, she received some good news.

"Janay, I have some great news. I got the case postponed for two months. I hope that this gives you enough time to handle your other case. As I said, this seems like a shoo-in, so don't worry, honey, okay? It's in the bag." It was so funny to her how different cultures used different sayings and slang.

"That's great, Mr. Tisch," Janay sang, trying to sound happy and stress-free. "I will let you know how the other case is going. Did you get me the okay to leave town?" she asked even though she would be leaving whether or not she had permission from the judge to leave the state.

"Oh, certainly. You have another trial. You just need to keep in touch with me to check on new developments. Did you get in touch with Mr. Rabissi like I suggested?"

"Yes, he is actually representing my cousin, so another lawyer from his firm is going to represent me. I can't think of his name right now."

"Oh, don't worry, all the lawyers in that firm are bulls. You're in good hands. Take it easy."

"Thank you, Mr. Tisch, I will. Talk to you soon."

Janay hung up, packed her rolling Louis Vuitton suitcase, and went to get her money. She went directly to the airport after receiving the thousand dollars. She wanted to shop in New York. She took the first flight out and took a taxi straight to

Fifth Avenue. She was also equipped with her debit card because the way she shopped, a thousand dollars may get a pair of shoes and a half of an outfit. As Janay walked down Fifth Avenue, she looked at all of the affluence. The street was crowded with the hustle and bustle of the city. She felt like a loser among royalty. She didn't feel the usual thrill of shopping. She just didn't feel good about anything at the moment.

Her attitude quickly changed when she walked into the shoe department of Saks Fifth Avenue and saw a pair of Christian Louboutin sandals. They were brown, snakeskin, and $795. She knew that months ago, it would have been no problem for her to buy those shoes. She had a great-paying job at a successful marketing firm and her escort business. Now she was unemployed and burdened with two murder cases. On the one hand, she figured she'd better enjoy spending all the money she could, because in prison there would be no shopping. On the other hand, she should be stacking her money to use for her defense just in case Brielle tried to pull a fast one. She put the shoes down and was drawn to another beautiful pair. She was struck by love for a pair of black gold-studded Giuseppe Zanotti sandals that were less expensive. They were $695. She could not pass them up. As she was walking to the clothing department, she passed a mirror and notice how puffy her eyes were. She looked mentally drained and stressed. She stopped at the sunglass counter and picked up a pair of Chanel sandals that were $325. She proceeded past the bags and also picked up a small Fendi purse that was $1960. *Fuck it*, she thought and got on line to pay. Clothes would be out of the question.

As she was waiting to be checked out, she felt an enormous pressure. When she got to the register, she threw the bag to the side of the counter and told the cashier that she was only interested in the shoes and shades. She was humiliated, frustrated, and infuriated. She snatched her bag from the clerk and walked out of the store without looking at another item.

Janay called Corey and he said that she would have to go get them a room and wait for him. He would be busy for a few more hours, he said. Janay hailed a cab and took it downtown to the W Hotel. She reserved a room and then went to the spa to have a Shiatsu massage. When Janay's massage was done, she walked around to a trendy restaurant on Madison Avenue called Asia de Cuba.

As Janay was having dinner, a man approached her and asked if he could join her. She noticed his expensive-looking tailored suit and said that he could join her. They talked and got acquainted. His name was Rich Robinson.

Simone

Simone woke up to prepare for her day. She had a date with a man she was going to kill by the time the date was over. Peter Sicily's nephew, Joey, had hired her two weeks before to act as a girl interested in a blind date with her intended victim. He had been working as an informant and dropping dimes on Joey's illegal number-running business and gambling spot, and he knew some information about a murder that Joey was tied to, so he didn't want to take chances and let the guy give up that information to the police. Joey wanted to let the guy have it before the cops called Joey in for questioning so that he wouldn't appear at that point to have a motive to want to kill him.

Joey contacted Simone and told her that he needed her to have a blind date. She always knew that those jobs involved her to be around the victim in an intimate setting, up close and personal. Those jobs held more risk and paid more money.

Simone went into her closet of Frederick's of Hollywood, Victoria's Secret, and other lingerie labels to find the perfect trap.

She would meet her date, Melvin, at Ruth's Chris Steak House in Times Square, and they would have dinner, go to a show, and then to the Hilton for sex. Not only was he going to pay her a thousand dollars for her service, she was going to get thirty thousand once the job was done and there was no police involvement. She would get half up front and half six months later if they had not been suspected of the murder. If she were to get called in for questioning, she would receive fifty thousand not to implicate anyone and have her legal fees paid for.

Simone went to get a manicure, pedicure, body wax, facial, and massage. She had to pump herself up mentally to be able to pretend that she was interested in the loser before she would take his life.

Simone spent a week talking to Melvin over the phone and acting like a desperate tramp looking for a relationship. She portrayed herself as a vulnerable, heartbroken woman so that the guy would presume that he would be able to take full advantage of Simone, whose name for this purpose was Candy.

She made it fully clear that she needed some love and affection, which most men would take as an open invitation for sex.

Simone got home and began to replay in her mind how she would carry out the demise of Melvin Cullen. She already knew from watching a *Snapped* episode that using potassium chloride to kill someone left no trace. The only difficulty about it was that the person would have to be injected with the chemical directly into the heart for sudden, untraceable death.

Simone knew that she would have to render him powerless to be able to get the needle into his chest and to release the injection into his heart. She knew that her power would come from her sexiness and his weakness from his lust and desire for her.

Simone was restless. She could not relax, so she decided to write Mariah a letter. Simone had been writing letters to Mariah since she died. She put them all in a box marked "Heaven," which she intended to have put into her casket when she herself died. She decided at Mariah's funeral that she would not lose contact with her. She would record every part of her life with Mariah, so as not to ever completely lose her.

Dear Mariah,

Here I go again. My life continues to be built on destruction and death. You are not going to believe this, but I met a sister that I didn't know that I had. She is beautiful. We have the same father but he died. I happened to meet her on the plane coming back from Atlanta. I wish I could tell her the truth about me, but I will lose her for sure. She has had enough drama in her life too. If I tell her, she might not want to have anything to do with me. Oh, her name is Brielle. She is twelve years older than me. We both miscarried before but she did three times, and then she killed her husband in self-defense. I don't know if it's better to be you or to be out here in this horribly crazy world. Well, please watch over me. I hope to make it back home safe, sound, and free tonight.

Love, Simone

Simone lay around until it was time to get dressed. She looked at the clock, which read 8 p.m., and she jumped up and got dressed. She wore a slutty outfit, which was too cheesy for her real taste. She had on tight black spandex with pumps and a shirt that looked like Peg from *Married...with Children* would wear. She felt like a black Peg. She put on a long, straight jet-black wig and went to hail a cab to meet Melvin at the restaurant.

Simone hadn't been in a serious relationship in a while. She didn't want one. She knew that love did nothing but hurt, so love she chose to do without. She hadn't been seeing anyone in the past month, and her body was yearning for a man to be inside of her.

Simone was sitting in the lounge area, waiting for Melvin and sipping on a drink. When Simone saw Melvin she was stunned. The moment she saw him she wanted him.

When he walked in she knew it was him from the description he gave over the phone. They had e-mailed each other but agreed not to use photos; they wanted to see if they were compatible before relying on physical attraction, which was Simone's concocted story. She knew that she could not have him with pictures of her on his computer because she would be the one who was going to kill him.

Melvin approached and his body was calling for her from the moment she saw it. Simone was caught off guard and scared. She didn't want him to have enough charm to make her change her mind. She didn't want his conversation to be soothing to her mind enough for her to want to engage in him past the night.

I have to carry out this job, or my life will be in danger.

Melvin was well-built and groomed, with curly hair and hazel-brown eyes. He was not light-skinned, but more of a butternut tone. He was not tall or short, heavy or thin. He was just right. He had the build of a naturally toned, muscular man. His eyebrows were thick and his eyes twinkled with his smile. His teeth were straight and white. Simone loved a man with nice teeth. Melvin looked like an R&B singer with the swagger to match. Not only that, he had some Mauries on his feet and a watch that looked like it cost tens of thousands. Simone was in trouble. She stood up as he approached and quickly sat back down, realizing that she looked like a prostitute. She extended her hand as he sat.

"Damn, you makin' me look bad with that outfit. I thought we agreed to dress casually." Melvin shook Simone's hand and reached down and kissed her cheek.

"Well, hello to you too, Candy." Melvin sat across from her and gave her a wink. "You lookin' good, don't worry. It's just the wig I don't like. Maybe I will get you to take it off later and see what you got up under there." Simone was offended when she normally wouldn't give a fuck.

"I'm sorry, Marvin, I should be mad at myself. This is really not my style, but I figure I might be trying to turn you off before I get my feelings hurt. You know how you handsome men do, nothing but wrong." She shook her head at him as if he had already done something wrong to her.

"You will get a second chance to make a first impression. Does that make you feel better?" Simone sensed some arrogance in Melvin, but what else should she expect from a good-looking black man?

"Well, let's see if I even want one by the end of the night." The host came to lead Simone and Melvin to their table.

Simone felt so uncomfortable that she could not think straight. She wanted Melvin to like her and not to think of her as a slut, although she looked like one. She didn't know why she even cared. Melvin was charming her with every word he said. They had small talk while they ordered and waited for their food to come. She knew that he was a sales manager–slash-criminal who had gotten arrested for stolen property and had decided to give information up on Peter's nephew.

To Marvin she made herself appear needy and gullible on the phone to appear vulnerable, so Melvin would have his guard down and his dick way up.

"So, Candy, what would you like to do after we finish dinner?" Melvin cut straight to the chase. Simone felt that Melvin must have read her mind or maybe her eyes as he caught her in the middle of daydreaming about sex on a platter with him. She had just unbuttoned his pants in her mind when he interrupted her with the rhetorical question. She knew that his question was actually whether she was going to fuck or not. He wanted to know that early.

"Well, I can honestly say that I haven't had dick in about a month and great dick in about three, so, as R. Kelly says"—Simone continued and sang the melody—"Your body's callin' for me, if you want to know the truth." She shot him a smile and licked her lips while looking him in the eye. Melvin shifted in his seat and gave a big, fat grin.

"Well, if you want to know the truth, great dick I do have." Simone sipped her cognac and put the glass down.

"Just how great is it? Will it make me scream? Can it make me cry?" She leaned back with her elbow on the chair arm, awaiting his response. Melvin leaned in and answered.

"Candy, it will make you melt." Simone picked up the glass that was almost empty and downed the rest of it. She had only had two drinks, and she knew that she should not have any more if she was going to do the job right. She knew that she could handle herself when it was time to, because at that point the adrenaline would take over, but if she got drunk, she was bound to slip up, and she knew that was not an option.

"Okay, so are we going straight to the Hilton then? We may as well not waste any precious time getting to the bottom line."

"I can tell you one thing. In person you seem way more confident than you do over the phone," Melvin told her.

"Well, this is the real me, baby and, believe me, I bite."

"Ooh, well, I don't like to be bitten, though, sexy Candy." Melvin took the cherry out of his drink and twirled it in his mouth by the stem.

"Oh," Simone laughed, "I didn't mean it that way. All I was saying is that you don't cross me and get away with it."

"Well, you ain't even gotta think that far ahead. I ain't thinkin' about crossin' you, just twistin' and rippin' you and maybe twirlin' and whirlin' you. Is that okay, Miss Candy baby?"

Simone felt her pussy twitch to his comments, and the wetness told her that she was definitely in trouble. She just knew that this would be a fuck to remember. She just didn't know if she would be able to follow through and kill him afterward. She had never been in this type of situation before.

They finished their food and walked a few blocks downtown to the Hilton hotel. Simone had already told Melvin to get the room, as she could not have her identification on a room where a dead body would turn up.

She was also very careful about her DNA, as careful as she could naturally be. Hence, the reason for the wig—so that her own hair follicles would not be found on the mattress, because her hair was under a wig cap. The black wig was also a disguise for Simone's very identifiable blonde hair. The camera shot of her leaving the hotel would show a black-haired woman, not a blonde one.

They got on the elevator, and Melvin grabbed Simone around her waist and brought her close to him.

He whispered in her ear, "Is it gonna make me howl like a wolf? You sexy bitch." He kissed her lips after she nodded yes, and then he stuck his tongue slowly in Simone's mouth and sucked gently on her tongue. Simone liked the feeling.

Bitch, you better not get caught up in this moment, you hear me? Ain't no man worth dyin' for, Simone told herself. She began to slowly kiss Melvin back until the elevator rang and stopped at their floor.

Melvin squeezed Simone's ass and held it as they walked down the hotel corridor. Simone wet as a faucet, and Melvin was hard as a rock.

He opened the door, let her walk in, and then he locked the door. He wasted no time taking off all of his clothes, dropping them right on the floor, and stepping out of them to reveal an eleven-inch piece of meat waving at Simone.

Simone took her hooker outfit off to reveal a peach-colored all-in-one teddy with short shorts. She stepped out of her clothes and lay on the bed with her teddy on.

Melvin pulled out a bottle of Hennessy and opened it. He poured them two glasses, and Simone quickly went from tipsy to drunk and very horny. Simone was not thinking about what she was supposed to do. She was thinking about that tool that Melvin had and how well he was going to use it. This was the first time that she let anything come in between her job and her money.

Simone slowly took her teddy off to reveal her young and tight body. She was a nice shape with nice measurements. Instantly, Melvin fell in love with Simone's plump breasts, her big areolae, and long nipples. He grabbed her and started sucking on them. She was so aroused, she could no longer hold out.

Simone pushed Melvin back on the bed. He landed on his back, and she ripped a condom open with her teeth and put it on him with one hand while caressing his already ready penis with the other hand.

She straddled Melvin and sat up so she could see his every expression while she rode him like a wild bull. She kept in stride and in control. She thrust herself in and out and slid herself up and down on Melvin's soldier, which stayed at attention for a long time.

Simone loved every minute of the sexcapade with Melvin. She climaxed three times while on top of him. By the third time she was leaning down and tongue kissing him passionately to every stroke that she rode. Melvin kept his hands or mouth on her breasts the whole time, which turned Simone on to the point of ridiculous bliss. She was on a cloud, if not in Heaven. They fell asleep in each other's arms.

Simone frantically jumped up at about ten the next morning. She looked over and saw Melvin right next to her. They slept in each other's arms. She jumped out of bed and checked her phone. She had received about twenty calls from Joey. She knew that he was awaiting the report that the mission had been accomplished.

Brielle

Brielle was furious. She could not believe that Shawn had been kissing on another woman the night before. She intently watched the door of her home and hurried up and wrote the number down before Shawn came back to the car. She saw her front door open and her so-called man step out and approach the car. She didn't know how she should react. She wanted to play it cool, but her coolness went right out of the door when Shawn opened the car door. With lack of self-control, Brielle threw the phone at Shawn's head. "You are just like the muthafuckin' rest of them!"

Shawn was lucky enough to duck, and the cell phone hit the car window, putting a small crack in it, and fell to the floor. Brielle grabbed the card that Shawn went to retrieve and flung her car door open.

"Call that bitch back! She wants another kiss!"

Brielle grabbed her pocketbook and got out of the car, slamming the door behind her. Shawn was stunned. He watched Brielle storm into her house. He reached on the ground, retrieved his phone, and opened it up. He read the message that Brielle discovered and sat in the car, thinking of what he should do. He was in no mood to fight with Brielle and figured she wouldn't believe anything he had to say at that moment.

Brielle watched from an upstairs window as Shawn pulled off and drove down the street. She became hysterical over the fact that he hadn't tried to diffuse the problem. She snatched the cordless house phone off of its cradle and dialed Shawn's number.

"That's it! You just drive away? What you gonna do, go get that kiss?"

"Look, Brielle, it was innocent. It was nothing," Shawn answered calmly. These were the times that most men wished they were unattached and free to *do them*. A nagging, accusatory woman is always annoying to a man whether the man is wrong or right.

"Oh, it was? Okay, so I guess I'll find myself a new *friend* to kiss on too. Is that okay with you?"

"Brielle, I'm not cheating on you. If I wanted to cheat, I could have left with that girl."

"So what are you doing with her number, or what the hell is she doing with your number?" Brielle started tearing her nail tips off of her fingers, with some fingers ending up bleeding from the tear.

"Listen, the girl asked me to take her number. I wasn't going to use it. I must have dialed it by accident when I put the number in my phone, because I never gave her my number. She a young waitress-slash-stripper chick. Not my style."

"So then what would have been wrong with telling her, 'No, I have a fiancée?' That would have been too corny, right? You didn't want to seem like a man who turns pussy down to your cousins, huh?" she challenged aggressively.

"Brielle, they know I love you, like everybody else does. I was just a little drunk, and maybe I was just enjoying her attention." He thought about it after he said it and knew that it wasn't the right thing to say.

"What? Oh, so you were spending time with the little slut? Okay, no problem. Have a great day." Brielle hung up and threw the phone against the wall. It dropped and the back of the phone opened up, expelling the battery. She walked over to the phone and put the battery back in and it rang.

"What?" Brielle answered, thinking it was Shawn.

"Is that how you speak to your little sister?" Simone asked from the other end.

"Oh, Simone, I'm sorry, sis. How are you? I've been meaning to call you. What are you doing?" Brielle sucked on some of her bruised and sore fingers.

"I was thinking we should hook up and do lunch or something. Are you busy?" Simone was stretched out on her sofa, flipping through the channels. She had left Melvin at noon checkout and went home. They planned to see each other again, and she knew that she would have to handle her business at their second meeting. She told Joey that Melvin stood her up. She said that Melvin didn't answer her calls but that she would persuade him to set up another date with her. Joey was adamant in letting her know that she only had a few days to handle it.

"Not at all. Actually, I need to get into something. Do you want me to come to the city?"

"Sure. I live in SoHo. Do you know how to get here?"

"I know it's way the fuck downtown." They both laughed. "When I get on the West Side Highway, I will call you so you can tell me where to go from there." Simone sat up, excited and smiling.

"Okay. I can't wait to see you. I'm feeling a little lonely and down. Maybe my big sis can cheer me up," Simone said genuinely.

"I'm feeling all fucked up myself. But I'll tell you about it when I see you. I'm so excited and I'm glad you called! Let me get dressed. Talk to you in a few." Brielle got ready to hang up when Simone cut in.

"Brielle, do you have any pictures of Daddy? Or pictures from your childhood that we can look at together?" Simone asked timidly.

"I'll see what I can find. My childhood wasn't that happy. We didn't do many family outings or take a lot of pictures like other families, but I should have some stuff to share. See you shortly."

Brielle hung up and looked at her jacked-up nails. She was mad that she let some girl cause her to mangle her fingers. She didn't want Simone to see that. She went upstairs and changed out of the suit that she wore to the lawyers' office. She wanted to look sophisticated for her little sister, so she put on a colorful paisley-print cherry and aqua wraparound dress by Etro. She put on some aqua Jimmy Choo leather sandals to match and wore her Prada shades. Brielle filled up her matching blue Prada bag and strutted to her Bentley. She was going to make a night of it.

Brielle was in New York City within fifteen minutes and downtown even sooner. She was excited. She was eager to see how Baby Sis was living. She had found about ten or fifteen pictures that she liked and wanted to share with Simone. She called Simone, who told her how to get to her loft, and parked in a parking garage when she was in the vicinity. She walked up three flights of stairs and knocked on Simone's door.

Simone came to the door in jean short shorts and a wife beater T-shirt with no bra. She had a very shapely figure, and Brielle assumed that she used her figure to get what she wanted. She was a pecan color and had honey-blonde hair that was cut in a bob style. Simone was a little hottie.

"Hey, you lookin' like you 'bout to get a booty call. You sure I'm not coming at a bad time?" Brielle joked and walked in and started looking around. "I meant to tell you that I like that blonde hair. I went blonde a couple of months ago. Is that your real color?" Simone smirked at Brielle and shook her head as if to say, "Come on, you know this is not my real hair color."

"Girl, I been in the house since we got back. I have been feeling kind of down. Usually, I'd have no one to call, but when I remembered I had a big sister, I knew I should reach out. How's that man of yours?"

"Girl, please," Brielle said, sitting on the couch and taking her shoes off to put her feet up. She felt comfortable and at home. Simone was sitting on her chaise lounge across from Brielle.

"Do you want something to drink? Girl, what the hell happened to your nails?" Simone asked while looking freaked out by the sight of Brielle's hands.

"I ripped my tips off after that *man* pushed me to the limit. I was mad after I did it. Is there somewhere around here that's clean where we could go to get our nails done?" Simone laughed at Brielle.

"What you mean that's clean? Don't tell me you are one of those prissy girls from Jersey who thinks that everything in New York is dirty. There's a nice spot two blocks away. We can go in a little while if you want to, but first, I want to catch up, look at pictures, and learn about my family."

Brielle smiled, reached in her purse, and pulled out the pictures. She passed them to Simone as she explained who the people in the pictures were. She showed her pictures of her paternal grandparents, who had both died before Brielle was ten. There were pictures of Brielle with her cousins and by herself.

She showed Simone and told her about the people in the pictures who were related to Simone. Then she showed Simone a picture of her parents.

"Damn, Daddy must have taken this picture the same day that he took the one I have with my mother. Look." Simone reached in her purse and took out her lone picture. They laughed when they saw him in the two pictures with their mothers and the same suit on. They started laughing loudly.

"Yup, look at him. Girl, he was a mean man. I don't know whether you should really feel like you missed out. He never took the time out to be a good dad. I may be worse off than you because I saw him for who he was. At least you got to fantasize that he was a great king all of your life. I only got to love him for a day—on his death bed." Brielle stared at both pictures and thought back to the day she first met Dorothy. She had a blank look on her face.

"Damn, girl, what's the matter? It was that bad?" Brielle snapped out of her daydream and shook her head.

"You damn right it was, girl. Not only was I abused by my mother and my father, but I was molested by my cousin from, like, eight to ten." Simone shook her head in disgust.

"What? So what happened when you were ten? Did he get in trouble, or did he just stop on his own?" Brielle was not expecting Simone to ask such a question. She did not know whether she should tell Simone the truth, although she wanted to share everything with her sister.

"Can you get me something to drink? Do you have any wine?"

"Girl, I only drink the hard stuff. I've got some Cîroc vodka." Brielle laughed. "What's so funny? That's Diddy's brand of vodka," Simone said defensively.

"No, I'm laughing because vodka is my drink too. Just some more proof that we are blood. Let's get ripped so we can talk no holds barred. We have so much to talk about." Brielle took her time thinking about just how much she would actually share, but two drinks in and they were both spilling all the beans. Simone noticed that Brielle was nice and tipsy when she repeated her original question.

"So, what happened to the cousin that molested you? I would have killed his ass if I were you. It would have been self-defense, and you were a young girl too. You wouldn't have gotten in trouble." Simone took a sip of her drink. Brielle looked intently at her baby sister and let her guard down.

"I did kill him," she said flippantly and took a sip of her drink as well.

"What?! You gotta be kidding me! You killed him for real? Did they send you to a crazy home?" Simone sat up in her chair, eagerly awaiting the information she had requested.

"No, I told everyone that he was playing around and that he fell." Simone looked confused, so Brielle clarified her statement.

"We were visiting family in North Carolina, and we took some rowboats out. Of course, he wanted to go in the boat with me. So, when we got out in the middle of the lake, no one else was around, and he tried to get me to suck on his dirty-ass little dick."

Brielle downed the rest of her drink and put the glass on the floor in front of the couch and continued her story.

"When he stood up, unzipped his pants, and came toward me, all I could think of was to push him away. He ended up falling backwards off the boat, and I stuck to the story that he was playing around, rocking the boat, and fell out. Then I kind of forgot about what really happened until years later."

Simone jumped up and put her hand up for Brielle to give her a high five, which Brielle did. "Girl, that's what I'm talking about! What goes around comes around! I feel you on that. And they believed you too? That's wassup!" Simone jumping around was a little confusing for Brielle.

"Damn, girl, you act like you got molested too."

"No, but I know about an eye for an eye. I have no problem settling scores." Immediately, Brielle thought of Janay and how Simone could probably give her a run for her money in the grimy department. Simone seemed like she was 'bout it. "So, did that shit fuck you up in the head?" Simone finally sat back down to hear the rest of Brielle's life story.

"I don't know. I didn't have much time to dwell on that, because after that my dad and mom were messing my head up. They were constantly taking their frustrations with each other out on me. I think that affected me more than anything else. But I was strong. I decided not to live like them and be a screwed-up person. I went to college and graduated and met my husband Dante." Brielle stopped, thinking of where she was going to go with the story next.

"Oh, that was your husband? I thought his name was Shawn? Or maybe I'm buggin'. His name was Dante?" Brielle cut Simone's confusion off.

"No, you are so fast. Slow down. Shawn is my fiancé."

"Oh, okay. So, you are divorced?" Simone took a sip of her third drink and awaited the rest of the story. Brielle stared at Simone strangely. "What? Why are you looking like that?" Brielle was good and tipsy. She was ready to drop the next bomb on Simone.

"I killed him too," she said matter-of-factly. Simone's eyes widened and a big smile came across her face.

"What? You killed your husband? Girl, I'm scared of you. Nah, I'm feelin' you. What did he do to you?"

"He cheated and made me lose three babies. He belittled me, degraded me, and mistreated me. I lost three babies because of him," Brielle repeated, thinking about the children that she had so desperately wanted. She stared off and imagined herself walking through the park with her children.

Without warning, Brielle started crying hysterically. Simone slowly walked over, sat down, and put her arms around Brielle. She rubbed her sister's shoulders, remaining quiet but supportive.

"I know that it must be hard for you to think about the children that you lost. But at least you gave that nigga what he deserved." Brielle was shocked that Simone agreed yet again with her confession of committing murder.

"When did this happen? You didn't do any time for that?"

"It was self-defense."

"Oh, and he was putting his hands on you too? That motherfucker." Simone was taking personally what had been done to her sister. "Well, it's good that you got him before he got you. And that man you have now seems like a good dude. He seems like a keeper." Brielle thought about the argument she had with Shawn. She thought about the fact that he said she was overreacting. She didn't know what to believe.

"So, sis, enough about me; tell me about you. What have you been up to for twenty-two years?" Brielle did not want to reveal that she and Shawn were having a problem at the moment.

"Well, I have been a nomad, moving from place to place and surviving. I am a survivor and I take care of myself by any means necessary. I would have killed that bastard that killed my sister if I had gotten to him first. I know about death way more than I know about life. I haven't had the opportunity to be stable, go to college, and meet a good man. I have been around murderers, shady characters, and criminals all of my life. I left home early and the streets raised me."

"I thought you were a private investigator? Don't you have to go to school for that? You said you have traveled the world. You seem to be doing very well for a young lady of twenty-two. This loft must be at least a thousand dollars a month." Brielle was starting to suspect that Simone may not have been so honest in the beginning. Simone laughed a devious laugh.

"Sister, if you only knew what I've been through. Let me just say that you are not the only one who ended it for someone else. I have had to take a few people out myself. I always wanted to be a private investigator after what happened to Mariah, my baby sister, but the streets got in the way of my education. I do what I have to do to survive."

"Simone, you need to start thinking of something concrete, because men will only take care of you until they want to take care of someone else." Brielle pictured Dante and Monique walking hand in hand, with their baby in a stroller. She smiled after realizing that it was a picture that would never be. "You know, my husband nearly destroyed my life. I could have gone to prison for killing him. I can still go to prison," she said without thinking.

"What do you mean you can still go to prison?" Simone asked, sobering up.

"Well, I'm kind of going through a murder trial right now." Simone could not believe her ears.

"You killed someone else too? Girl, who else did you kill?"

"Listen, we have covered a lot in a short amount of time. I was in a bad place. I lost children, my husband was in love with another woman who he got pregnant at the same time as me and...I just snapped. I didn't kill the girl, but my cousin is charged with her murder and she implicated me. Let's go out for a while. I need to gather my thoughts. I just don't want another woman to be misled, mistreated, and misused the way I have been. We all have a right to choose our lives, and if someone does not choose to have an open relationship, no one should impose that on the other person. There are plenty of women with HIV or AIDS because they believed that their men were being faithful. I have come out of it, but I know plenty of women who have not. You said that you killed someone?"

"It was a few years ago, and it was self-defense too," Simone lied. "My boyfriend's ex-girlfriend shot him, and I shot her before she could shoot me. I was never charged for it because there were witnesses who corroborated my story."

"I cannot believe how similar our lives have been. I guess it's true when they say families have curses. We have been cursed with the killer gene because our dad was a killer." Brielle shook her head.

"What?!" Simone yelled.

"My aunt told me that his drinking got so bad that he was fired from his job, and he started doing hits for the mob. I don't know how true it is, but he sure was an evil enough man for me to believe it."

"Wow!" Simone said and they both shook their heads.

"Now can we go get something to eat? I'll get my nails done tomorrow."

"Have you ever heard of Asia de Cuba?" Brielle shook her head no. Well, it's a posh, trendy spot on Madison Avenue, and I know you will love it. It's my treat," Simone bragged.

"I hear that. Well, go get dressed so we can go," Brielle instructed her baby sister.

Simone went behind the partition to her bedroom to change. She wanted to look as wealthy as her sister, so she put on a Giorgio Armani two-piece set that was a silk top and skirt worth $2000. She returned to the living room and succeeded at impressing Brielle.

"Wow, little sis. I guess you have been cursed with a fine fashion sense like your big sister."

"Yes, ma'am, I have. Let's go."

The ladies walked to Brielle's car, and Simone ranted and raved over Brielle's Bentley coupe.

They drove to Madison Avenue and found a parking space around the corner from the restaurant. As they were entering the restaurant, they bumped into Janay and Rich, who were leaving. Brielle was shocked to see Janay in New York and couldn't place who the familiar-looking gentleman with her was.

"Janay, what are you doing here? I thought you would be up in two more weeks?" Brielle asked without even greeting Janay in a cordial manner. She moved back out onto the sidewalk to interrogate Janay.

"Hello to you too, cousin. I came up early. Is that okay with you?" Janay looked Simone up and down.

"Well, you could have called to let me know." Brielle looked intently at Rich and remembered exactly where she knew him from.

"I don't have to call you to tell you my whereabouts, Brielle. And this is Rich, since you can't keep your eyes off of him," Janay replied sarcastically.

"Hello, Rich, nice to see you again." Janay felt snubbed as usual.

"Oh, you two know each other?" Janay pried.

"Well, we've met. How are you, Brielle?" Rich answered.

"I'm fine. Did you speak to Shawn yet?" Brielle asked Rich who replied, "He actually called me about an hour ago to tell me that I got the place. I'm so glad because my wife was about to give my belongings to the Salvation Army." Brielle thought of the day she gave Dante's belongings away and met Shawn.

"Good for her," she answered and didn't mind the confused look that she received from Rich for that comment.

"Oh, so you're buying Shawn's brownstone?" Janay smiled, thinking of a possible plot to get back at Shawn and Brielle by way of Rich.

"Well, I'm just renting it for now," Rich answered and then continued to converse with Brielle. "What did you mean 'good for her'? I'm just asking." Rich gave a fake smile. He did not like Brielle and felt that she was a bitch from their first meeting.

"Don't worry about her; she's just a hater. So, hi, young lady, my name is Janay. I didn't know my cousin had friends," Janay said sarcastically and extended her hand for Simone to shake.

"Well, my sister doesn't need friends now that she's got me. I'm all the friend she needs." Simone reciprocated the sarcasm, already gathering that Janay was the evil cousin who was trying to send her sister to prison. She did not shake Janay's hand.

"Sister? Wow, Brielle, you are full of surprises. You have a sister now?"

"Yes. We actually met on the flight back from Atlanta. She is my dad's daughter, and guess who her mother is? My dad's old girlfriend Dorothy. Isn't that crazy? She left town because she was pregnant by my dad and didn't want him to raise her."

"Lucky girl. Your father was a piece of shit. So, I should stay and get acquainted with my cousin. I just ate but I could surely drink and talk."

"She's not your cousin. She's my sister from my father, and you are on my mother's side, so there's really no need," Brielle stated.

"Oh, come on, Brielle, you know that families include both sides. Rich, I think I'm going to stay with the girls. Can we get up later or tomorrow? I'm sorry."

Brielle began walking into the restaurant without waiting for Janay. Brielle gave Simone a look that told her that she didn't want Janay there. Simone welcomed the guest. She wanted to see how grimy Janay really was.

The three ladies were seated at a small table on the top level of the restaurant that overlooked the ground floor. Janay wanted to get to the bottom of the questionable story of Brielle's sister. She didn't buy the information.

"So, Simone, how did you find out that you and Brielle had the same father?" Janay asked after they had finished ordering their food and drinks.

"Well, as fate would have it, we were seated right next to each other. I felt an instant liking for Brielle and her look. She felt the same way and asked about my seven-thousand-dollar Cartier watch. We started talking and I showed her a picture— the only picture I have—of my parents, and she said that my dad was her dad."

"So, how do you know that your mother told you the truth?" Janay asked harshly.

"Because I know," Simone answered, with no explanation or remorse.

"Oh, so I guess you're happy to have a little sister, huh? Someone you can manipulate and maybe have commit murders for you." Janay looked Brielle in the eyes and continued.

"You know your sister had me kill her husband's pregnant mistress," Janay whispered while looking into Simone's eyes and hoping to turn her against Brielle.

"Do you tell everyone that?" Simone asked, and Brielle spoke before Janay could answer.

"Janay, I thought you were recanting your confession. I thought we are about to go to trial and fight for our lives. What the fuck is wrong with you? Maybe you want to go to prison but I don't, so let me know if you keep planning to tell this story, and I'll save my money instead of paying what could end up being hundreds of thousands of dollars for your defense," Brielle hissed angrily.

"Actually, I would do anything for my sister and I wouldn't tell," Simone cut in and looked sincerely at Brielle, who smiled at Janay.

Janay realized that Simone was just as crazy as Brielle after that statement. She was jealous that Brielle had someone to be close with. She always wanted a sister too. She could not take sitting with the two comrades any longer. They were acting as if Janay wasn't even there, talking around her and not including her in their conversations. After finishing her first drink, she decided to leave.

"Well, ladies, it's clear that I am not welcome here, so I'll be leaving. I'll see you at the lawyers' office next week."

"I thought you'd never get the hint. Bye-bye, sweetie," Simone said and gave her a phony smile and a wave, catching Janay off guard. Janay knew that Simone was going to be a problem, but she would make sure that she would be ready to handle it. She had a good in. She would have to get very close to Rich to make sure to put the odds in her favor. She decided not to respond to Simone and grabbed her bag and left.

Janay

anay stormed out of the restaurant and walked back around the corner to her hotel. She immediately called Rich.

"Well, that was fast. I thought I wouldn't hear from you until at least tomorrow," he said, happy to hear from her so soon.

"I'm sorry about that. I wanted to get acquainted with my cousin, but they were acting like they didn't want me there. My cousin Brielle is a demented chick. I don't even know why I try to get along with her," Janay said innocently.

"Yeah, she seems kind of bitter." Rich chose his words carefully, knowing that blood is usually thicker than water.

"She's a bitch. There's no other way to put it. She's mad because she lost three babies and her husband got another woman pregnant," Janay said, not intending to tell the full story just yet.

"Who, Shawn?" Rich asked, confused.

"No, she was married before Shawn. Her husband died. But enough about them. Do you want to see me again tonight?" Janay said, looking into her compact mirror and redoing her makeup.

"Sure. I was just about to see if I could crash at my boy's house. I've kind of been rotating between all of my friends until I could find a place. I'm so glad I'll be moving into Shawn's brownstone in two weeks. I was sure not wanting to be homeless through the winter." Janay was not paying attention to Rich's conversation. She had a plan to create.

"Well, meet me at my hotel. I'll be waiting patiently." Janay hung up after telling Rich where she was staying. She would call Corey the next day; this meeting was way more important.

Janay got to her hotel and went to a liquor store and bought a bottle of Moët Rose. She was going to have to find a way to get in with Rich without seeming like a loose woman. She knew that the next best way to a man's heart, after cooking good for him, was by way of his pants. But she also knew that a man will treat you like a whore if you act like one. She was going to make him fall hard for her and become her slave.

Rich got to Janay's hotel room and knocked on the door. Janay opened the door in a Victoria's Secret lounge set. It was classy and conservative. She had her nails and toes freshly done with a French manicure and pedicure. Rich's eyebrows rose when he saw her.

"Wow, you're looking rather dreamy," he said, entering the room.

"Well, I was hoping to look steamy," she teased.

"Well, I'm sure you can get steamier than that, but I like to take things slow. I don't want to see it all at once. That's a good choice for a first, quote-unquote, home visit." Rich laughed.

"Well, I'm looking forward to my first home visit to your home. Do you need me to help you move?" Janay asked, trying to seem like a helpful lady.

"I don't think you can help me move, but you can sure help me put stuff away when the movers are done. That will be nice to have a new friend and a new place." Rich sat on the bed and picked up the remote. "So, we've already ate. You up for some spirits? I can walk to the liquor store." He patted the bed for Janay to sit next to him, which she did.

"I'm way ahead of you." Janay walked to the small refrigerator in the room and took out the bottle of champagne.

"Oh, excuse me. Give it here, let me pop it." Janay passed Rich the bottle, which he popped and poured into the plastic champagne glasses that she got from the liquor store and made a toast. "To honesty, understanding, and fun!" He tapped Janay's glass with his and downed his first glass and refilled his glass and drank the second one right down as well. She wanted him to be drunker than she was so that she could try to pump him for information.

"So, how did you meet Shawn?" Janay asked after sipping lightly.

"I didn't know him before. I just answered the ad for the brownstone. I instantly hit it off with him, but Brielle was kind of ticked off when I said that I was married but separated."

"I told you that she's touchy because of what happened with her husband. She actually killed him." Janay downed her first drink.

"Cut the shit. Get the hell outta town," Rich said and poured a third drink while Janay began to rub his back and neck. Inside she laughed at his proper speech.

"You sound white the way you talk," she joked.

"Oh, please do not tell me you are one of those black people who think educated blacks should be ashamed of their intelligence and talk ignorantly."

She was instantly turned off by his statement and hoped that he wasn't going to put on airs and make her tell his ass off. She was pretending to be mild-mannered and calm, not the aggressive chick that she really was.

"Oh, and please do not tell me that you think you are better than other blacks because you were lucky enough to get a good job."

"Lucky enough? Luck has nothing to do with it. I have worked very hard to get where I am today and I am very proud of myself and no one is going to make me feel bad about being successful. I earned the right to speak right. I put myself through school. I'll be damned if I play dumb to make lazy-ass people that don't want to make something of themselves feel good. I have no tolerance for people who cop out and blame society or, quote-unquote, the white man for our problems. The slaves had more motivation than these sorry-ass motherfuckin' niggers who want a handout and who are mad at a black man for taking charge of my destiny." Janay didn't want to hear the bullshit he was talking.

"My God, you are way too serious. Do you need to loosen up a little bit?" Janay asked, still rubbing on Rich's body.

"I sure do. Do you mind if I get comfortable like you are?"

"No, not at all. Get comfortable." Janay said, getting aroused.

Rich took his pants and shirt off and exposed his muscular body. He was a tall brother who had nice, curly jet-black hair that he had tapered off on the sides. His complexion was milk chocolate, and his muscles were tight and cut. His body proved that the gym was his friend. He had almond-shaped brown eyes, a nice, thin nose, and full, juicy lips that looked like they could suck a good clit. He was handsome and Janay was ready.

Rich took his pants off, and his legs were cut up as well. He had the perfect six-foot-three build. Janay went to her makeup tote bag and took out the Victoria's Secret body lotion that was scented cinnamon and apple and began to rub it on Rich's back. She straddled him from the back, while he remained on the edge of the bed, watching TV. She planned on distracting him from a show that he was very intensely watching.

"So, I wonder if I take you home, will you still be in love, baby, because I need it tonight," Janay sang, mocking the old Lisa Lisa and the Cult Jam song. They both laughed. "But on the serious side, what would you think of me if I fucked your brains out right now? Would you love it and then hate me or love it and understand that we are grown, and a part of getting to know someone is getting to know them on the inside too?"

Rich looked over at Janay. He scanned her body up and down and wanted to see it without the silk covering. He was ready to tear the nice two-piece suit off of her.   "Well, I can't tell you whether I will love it or not until I get it. Am I about to get it or something?" He squeezed her thigh.

"I'm thinking about it. I mean, we talked and got acquainted at the restaurant. I think we are both interested in getting to know each other better, which, of course, takes time and being in each other's company. I know that a woman is supposed to be a lady, and in society's eyes I am not supposed to sleep with you yet. However, I always thought that it was a waste of time to like someone, love their company, and then find out months later that their sex is repulsive. Sex is a part of the prerequisite to a successful partnership venture. How can I know if I want to continue to see you unless I know that we are compatible in the bedroom?" Janay said while undressing. Rich watched her drop her pants and step out of them. He intently waited for the shirt to come over her head.

"I totally agree," he said.

"Of course you agree. You agree now but what about later? I don't want to be calling and you never answer. I am gonna want to see you again," Janay said, exposing her breasts and bare body by pulling her blouse over her head and throwing it to the side. She stood in front of him completely naked and allowed him to be enticed by her firm breasts and nearly bald pussy. She had her pubic hair shaved in the shape of a heart. It was dyed crimson red like her asymmetrical haircut.

"Wow! That looks tasty. Well, from the looks of you, I'll be calling before you even get the chance to dial my number. Now, prove to me that looks are not deceiving. If you feel as good as you look, you have nothing at all to worry about. Come here, hot-red-pussy girl. Damn, I guess I been married too long. That's what women do now with their stuff?"

Rich reached forward and fondled Janay. He rubbed her pussy and stuck his finger inside of her. He pulled it out, smelled it, and sucked her juice off of his finger. "Okay, well, it smells nice and tastes even nicer. Come here, girl." He pulled her close and she pulled away.

"Let me see what you are working with now. Take your stuff off."

Rich leaned back on the bed and pulled his boxers down. He was lying flat on his back, but his tool was reaching for the ceiling. Janay was impressed by his soldier and how well he was standing at attention. Rich kept his feet on the ground because he imagined the rough ride he was about to take. He held his penis and put the condom on it.

"Get on it," Rich said, holding it steady for Janay to straddle.

"I'm ready to ride that buffalo like a real cowgirl." Janay lifted one leg over and straddled Rich. She gently grabbed his dick and guided herself onto it. She slowly began to move up and down, while Rich closed his eyes and held her legs. His hands stayed on her, while she gradually began to pick up momentum. Janay was sliding her body up and down on his pole faster and faster. She began to moan and express her delight. Janay was in control but she began to lose it with every thrust. She was filled up with him, and every pump felt better and better. She knew that she was about to climax and gave him the heads up.

"Rich, baby, I'm about to cum. I don't know how you got me there this fast, but you want me to wait, or will you join me?" She pumped harder and faster.

Rich grabbed her thighs tightly and took over. He brought her up and down at the pace that would bring him to the point of climax as well. "Come on, baby, let's do it. I'm ready. I'm ready, girl! It's about to come! Come on! Yeah! Yeah! Let it go! Let it out! I'm cumming!" He pumped his groin up in the air, deeper and deeper inside of her.

"I'm there too! I'm letting it out! I'm cumming all over that dick! I'm cumming! I'm cumming, Rich! It feels so good!" Janay moaned in between her deep breaths.

They climaxed together and she collapsed on top of him. For a few minutes she lay on his chest, with his manhood still inside of her. When she regained her composure, she sat up. She grabbed her breasts and held them.

"That was good. I know I'm gonna be calling you." Janay lifted her body off of him and crawled up to the top of the bed and lay on the pillow. Rich pulled himself from the bottom of the bed to the head of the bed and lay on the other pillow beside her. He moved onto his side and put his arm around her waist. Rich looked into Janay's face to try to see what he could tell from her eyes. She looked directly back into his.

"You don't have to worry. I'll answer every time," he said and leaned over and kissed her mouth. "That was just what I needed." Rich put his hand between Janay's legs and rested it on her pussy. "That was short but sweet. Not bad for a test run. So, we both agree, there will be more where that came from; that's good. I gotta go, though." He got up to go in the bathroom, and Janay sat up in the bed. She didn't want to make a big thing of it, but she had assumed that he was staying the night.

"Where are you going?" she yelled to him. He came out of the bathroom with a washcloth and cleaned himself.

"I have to go to work tomorrow, and I didn't bring any clothes. When you called me I hadn't made it to my boy's crib yet. I just came straight here. All of my furniture and stuff is in storage, but my clothes are all over the place. I'm sorry, I have an important meeting tomorrow, or I'd just leave in the morning and go get dressed and go to work late but I can't."

"Oh okay," Janay said, feeling insecure.

"Seriously, don't think anything bad," Rich assured her. "I'm not going home to my wife, if that's what you think. It's really over with me and her. I'm not one of those guys who pretends he's having trouble with his wife to get in a woman's pants. Okay?" he said and awaited her response.

Janay looked at his naked body and said okay. Rich got dressed and promised that he would call her the next day. He kissed Janay and left. As soon as he walked out, she called Corey.

"Damn, what took you so long to call me?" Corey asked from the other end of the phone.

"I ran into Brielle and her sister. The bitch found her long-lost sister, and I was having dinner with them. What's up with you?" she asked seductively.

"Nothing. Where you at again?" he asked.

"At the W Hotel on Thirty-eighth and Madison. You coming or you gonna front?" Janay whined.

"I'm coming. And you better be butt naked in the bed, waiting for me. I miss that good loving. I'm on my way."

Janay got up and took a shower. She popped one of the OxyContin pills that she still had from Jarrod. She was beginning to rely on the prescription pills more and more to get her through her disastrous life. She wished that she still had her job and the life that she was used to. The fact that she didn't was too much for her to handle without some assistance. While she was in the shower, she heard banging on the door. She jumped out of the shower and viewed Corey through the peephole. She opened the door with no clothes on and stepped aside for Corey to walk in.

As soon as Janay closed the door, Corey pushed her up against it. He pulled his dick out and thrust it into her ass before she could move. She leaned forward and received his entrance into her. He pumped into her savagely and aggressively. Janay was high. She was out of it. She just stood there and took it until he came and pushed her, taking himself out of her. He walked over to the bed and sat on it, his penis still out of his pants.

"So, what's up with you? You ain't lookin' too hot. That shit is really getting to you. And you look like you on something. You better get yourself together." He looked her up and down in disgust.

"I know. I am. Can I have the money you supposed to give me?" she asked with slurred speech.

"I ain't got it on me. So, when your trial is gonna start?" he asked nonchalantly while flipping through the channels.

"In two weeks. I came up early to get ready and to get with my lawyer. I'm scared, man," Janay confessed.

Corey leaned down to untie his sneakers to take them off and noticed an empty condom wrapper on the floor. He immediately stood up.

"Bitch, you tryin' to play me? You got me coming here after another nigga done already peeled you?" He stood up and grabbed Janay by the neck.

"No, I don't know what you talking about." Janay did not try to fight him or release his grip from around her neck. Corey let go and reached down and picked up the wrapper.

"I'm talking about this, bitch! Now what you got to say?" He threw the condom wrapper in her face.

"Nigga, maybe the bitch that cleaned up the room overlooked that. I just got here. That shit was up under the blanket; maybe she didn't see it." She looked at Corey with a straight face.

"You're lying. You think I'm a little dumb nigga, huh? Okay, let's check the bathroom." Janay hoped that Rich had flushed the condom instead of disposing of it in the garbage, but her wish was not fulfilled. Corey came back into the room holding the garbage can.

"I guess the bitch that cleaned the room left this used condom in the garbage too so she could get fired, right?" He grabbed the condom out of the garbage with his bare hands and threw it at her.

"You played yourself. How you gonna fuck a nigga in a room I'm supposed to pay for and sleep in with you? You should have made that nigga get a room. Shit, you could have had another room in this here hotel and then came back in here. I'd have never known. You fucked up now. I ain't payin' for shit. I'm out." Corey turned around and walked toward the door. Janay had to drop her pride because she needed the money that he was supposed to be bringing her.

"Oh, it's okay that you got some other chick staying at your apartment, but you gonna black out on me for seeing someone?" She tried to grab his shoulder but he pulled away.

"Listen, I know you think I'm young and dumb, so I'll give it to you like a grown-up. I don't care what you do on your time with your money. I don't care who you let fuck you. But you ain't gonna do it on my watch or with my wallet. You got that?" He turned around, opened the door, and walked through it. Janay called out to him as he walked toward the elevator.

"Corey! Corey, I need you. Don't do this to me!" Janay was not concerned about who was on the floor and could hear the commotion. She needed that money.

"You did it to yourself. Lose my number," Corey said calmly and disappeared around the corner of the corridor.

Janay closed the door of her hotel room and went and sat on the bed. She was numb. She didn't really care about Corey like that. He was her boy toy, but the extra little bit of money that he would give her when they saw each other always came in handy. She was not going to call him again. She had a new project to work on: Rich Robinson. She did remember that she needed to follow up with her extortion plot, though. She called the other Rich, Richard Jamison.

"Hello, Mr. Jamison. Are you making any progress with our business arrangement?" she asked when he answered the phone.

"Janay, I'm trying to get you some money. I have five thousand so far. Mr. Burrows is refusing to give you a dime. He said that you better watch who you are threatening. Janay, are you sure you want to go through with this?"

"Are you and your gay lover threatening me? Of course I'm going through with it. Tell Mr. Burrows that I will take out an ad in the paper with the two of you if he doesn't come to his senses."

"Janay, he has a lot of family, and they are connected, if you know what I mean. I think you should reconsider—"

Janay cut him off before he could try to appeal to her again. "Look, Richard, we've done business together, and you've never given me a hard time, but everyone has to pay for their actions sooner or later. My life is on the line, so it's your turn to pay."

"Okay. I hope you know what you are doing. I'll keep trying."

"Well, in the meantime, send me the five thousand dollars through Western Union. I am out of town right now."

They discussed the secret question that she would need to answer to get the money, and he agreed to send the money first thing the next morning. Janay felt like she had gotten some of her power back. She was used to being in control, and she had lost control of her life since the murder of Monique Troy.

Janay drank the rest of the champagne that she had bought for her and Rich to enjoy. She fell asleep drunk and woke up with a hangover. She got in the shower and got herself together. She was happy to know that she would have five thousand dollars in her hand in a matter of minutes.

Janay went to a grocery store that she was directed to go to by the hotel concierge, because they have Western Union. She was nervous when she walked in. She thought, *What if that motherfucker called the police to report that I was blackmailing him?* That was all she needed, another criminal charge against her. She boldly walked to the counter and gave her name, while the clerk looked to see if she had money coming to her. The woman looked at Janay and back at her computer screen. She asked the question that she and Mr. Jamison had agreed on and prayed that no one would be approaching her to put her under arrest.

"I'm sorry, miss, but I must have my manager handle this transaction."

Janay remained calm. "For what reason? That is my boss. I'm here on a business trip, and he is sending me money for business expenses." She knew that it was uncommon for a legitimate company to do business with cash. Normally, a bank transfer would be the appropriate method of exchanging that kind of money. She thought about running out of the store while the clerk left to go get the manager, but something told her to stay.

The manager appeared from the back of the store and asked Janay to follow him to the management office. As she walked behind him, she thought of all types of excuses and lies that she could give the police if they were to question her about the money. The store manager did not speak to her until they were in the office, with the door closed.

"I'm sorry, Miss Clark, but for your safety and ours, we did not want to exchange that amount of money out in the open. How would you like the bills?"

Janay exhaled after having held her breath for way too long and smiled. "I understand and I really appreciate that. I'd like all large, please." Janay watched as the gentleman counted out fifty hundred-dollar bills and gave it to her without any suspicion in his eyes.

"Thank you so very much, sir. Have a great day." Janay breezed out of the Food Emporium like she was floating on air.

Shawn

Shawn flipped through the *Daily News* as he ate his dinner at the local diner. He did not want to be at the house when Brielle got back. She was furious when she left, and he was not in the mood for her theatrics. He knew that he loved Brielle, but she was just never drama-free; she always had some shit going on, and he was not always wit it. He had enough problems to deal with, trying to get Mr. Sicily off of his back. He must have thought Mr. Sicily up because at that moment Mr. Sicily was calling him.

"Hello." Shawn was agitated and it came across in his voice.

"Shawn, I'm gonna need to see you tomorrow. I need seventy grand." Shawn was instantly infuriated.

"I just saw you. What are you talking about, man? I only see you once a month or every other month. I don't have it. You know our agreement." He didn't care and he wasn't scared.

"Shawn, I owe somebody and there will be hell to pay if I don't pay. I can only give you two days at the most."

"Give me? And then what happens if I don't have it? Are you threatening me?" Shawn held his knife tightly in his other hand.

"Shawn, we've been over this. Don't make me do anything drastic." He looked at the phone to make sure that he had heard correctly.

"Look, Peter, I am a man. I am not your little puppet. Don't make threats to me. I don't give a fuck what you owe somebody else!" Shawn slammed the phone down forcefully.

Shawn was tired of having to have his family commit crimes to pay for something that was already said and done. He did not want to resort to violence, but three hundred thousand was a lot of money to hand over to someone else because he has a gambling problem. Shawn's phone rang again and interrupted his thoughts. He answered the call without first looking at who was calling.

"Hello?" Shawn said in a disturbed tone.

"Hey, handsome, it's Chrissy. I thought you'd return my text or call me or something." He looked at the phone and saw the name Chris. He was not in the mood for another chick either.

"Listen, you are a real cute, sexy girl, and if I didn't have my fiancée, I probably would spend some time with you, but I'm sitting here at a diner eating because my lady read your text. I can't—"

Christina cut Shawn off before he could finish. "Whatever happened to friendship? I know you have a girl. I just thought that we could be friends," she said innocently.

"Friends? You asked me to go home with you. And the bad part is that I was tempted to do it. I cannot fool myself into thinking that I would be around you and nothing will happen. Why me, though? There are plenty of men that can give you the attention that you are looking for. I'm sure you meet twenty new men a day."

"I meet lames, perverts, and men full of games. Every day. Not only are you gorgeous, but you are obviously a good man if you don't want to cheat on your woman. I need me a good man in my life."

"Yes, but I'm a good man to my woman. How can I be a good man to her and you at the same time? That will make me a cheater."

"Listen, Shawn, I don't know why I can't stop thinking about you. I don't know why knowing that you have a girl is not enough to make me leave you alone. I just know that since I've met you, I've wanted to see you again. I want to see you," she said in a whiny, sexy voice.

Shawn was tempted to have an innocent meeting, but he knew it would only lead to trouble. "Listen, I have to go. I hope you meet a good man, because you seem like a sweet girl. Take care of yourself."

"Before you hang up, listen. Don't lose my number; just keep it just in case, okay?" Chrissy pleaded.

"Yeah," Shawn agreed and hung up. He imagined Chrissy in that yellow outfit and pictured himself taking it off of her. He pushed the thought out of his mind and finished his food. He wished that he could control his male hormones, but women always make it hard for a man to be true. It seems that women like you better when you have someone.

Shawn paid his bill and left the diner. He wondered if Brielle was home yet and drove by the house. Brielle's car was not in the driveway. He wondered where she was and if maybe she was cheating on him because she thought that he was cheating on her. He pulled over in front of the house and sat outside, looking at the front door. He knew that he should just go inside and wait for Brielle to come home, but he didn't feel like it. He wanted to be caressed and held, not yelled at and accused. He looked at his phone and his last incoming call. He toyed with the idea and then called.

"Wow, that was fast," Chrissy said, smiling as she answered. "Did you two break up already?"

"Listen, I'm a little stressed. I just need someone to talk to. Would you like to go and have a few drinks?"

"Yes, I know just the spot that we can go to. Are you in the city?"

"No, I'm on my way now. Where should I pick you up?"

"I live Midtown on the East Side. I'm right across the street from Central Park, on Ninetieth and Fifth. How long, handsome?" Chrissy was excited. She knew that it didn't take much to get a man to change his mind, because she knew from her line of work that men are weak and led by their flesh.

Shawn had no intention of going into her place, and he really just wanted to get a female's insight. He just wanted to be in the presence of a woman, with no strings attached and no turmoil. He just wanted to rest in the comfort of a pretty little thing for the moment. *I'm not going to cheat. I'm not going to do anything inappropriate. I just want to talk*, he told himself.

Shawn was nervous the whole ride to Christina's place. He didn't know why, though; he was doing nothing wrong. He was not going to go home with Chrissy or have sex with her. He contemplated whether going out with someone of the opposite sex was wrong in itself. He pulled up and called Christina to come downstairs. She offered her place as their place to relax, and he refused the invitation. She said that she would be right down.

Christina walked out of her swanky apartment building looking like a star. Had he not already known differently, he would have thought she was famous by the looks of her. She had on a flowing yellow and aqua paisley print that was loose-fitting and classy. She had her hair pulled back into a bun, which revealed her very pretty face and young, fresh look. He again assured himself that he would be good.

Chrissy opened his passenger's side door when he waved to signal that it was him in the CLS 550 Benz parked directly across the street. She got in, smiled, and leaned over and kissed Shawn on his lips.

"It's good to see you. I'm glad you came." Christina sat back in comfort and began devising her plan to get him in her bed later on. She would be subtle, not pushy, and very helpful in removing the stress that he said was on him.

"Before we go any further, I just want to be clear. I know that I probably should not be here right now. My girl is mad at me because of you and here I am. I am not sure why I decided to come, but I do know that right now, I just need a friend. I have no real girlfriends. Most of the women I am so-called friends with I have slept with, so I do not want to go open up a can of worms by corresponding with them. My sister is pretty much a square, so I can't really get any good advice from her when it comes to my woman. So, I met you and I cannot say that there is no attraction, but I just need someone to talk to." Christina listened intently and thought hard about the best response to give to get some points in her favor.

"Listen, Shawn, there are no mistakes. Maybe we just met so that we could be friends and be there for each other. You never know, but just because you have a woman doesn't mean that you are dead. You can only be friends with me because you are in a relationship with someone? I never understood women who are so insecure that their man can't even say hi to a female without her thinking something is going on. I may be young but I come across too many men who feel trapped because they can't move a step without their woman right there on their heels. A man needs to feel like he is in control, not like a woman is his dictator." Shawn realized that what Christina had just said may be the reason why he was sitting there with her. Brielle had accused him and he had done nothing wrong. "So, now can we go and have some drinks and talk? Don't feel guilty; you haven't done anything wrong," she said and said, ...*yet,* in her mind. "Let's go to The Whiskey Bar in Times Square." Shawn had a thought and hoped that Brielle wasn't at The Whiskey Bar. He realized that he should have called her to see where she actually was.

"Do a lot of black people go there?" Shawn asked, concerned.

"No, silly, I know you don't want to run into anyone who might know your fiancée. The Whiskey Bar is a mixed crowd but primarily white. I want you to be able to relax and have some clean fun." Again, in her mind her motive was clear. *Clean until we get to my house and get dirty,* Chrissy thought.

"Yeah, I don't need any more drama. You don't know, messing with you, I could end up dead, literally. My girl don't play."

"Don't worry, you are in good hands. Let's go."

Shawn drove to Times Square and parked in a garage. He and Chrissy started walking to the lounge. He did not notice Brielle and Simone coming out of a movie theater, but they spotted him. Simone spotted Shawn first but convinced Brielle not to say anything, but to follow the two. Brielle was furious, hurt, and shocked. She could not believe that Shawn was out with another woman and hadn't even called to try to plead his case about the text message. She had a feeling that the girl he was with was the girl who had sent him the message.

They stayed a good distance away, and as they followed, Simone tried to console Brielle. She told her that it could be innocent, although she did not believe it herself. She was just as angry as Brielle was but kept her composure and hid her emotions. She did not want her embarrassment to show.

Shawn and Christina walked and talked the three blocks from the parking garage to The Whiskey Bar. He instantly liked the atmosphere in the lounge. They walked downstairs to the bar, which had a lit-up dance floor and private lounge areas for small parties to enjoy the ambiance of the place while being able to be in a secluded area. The private areas had small tables and love seats. There were curtains that could be closed for the patrons to enjoy the music without the rest of the crowd's company. The two got drinks and sat down on one of the open couches that adorned the club as well. Shawn began to relax more once they were inside and sitting down. He took a sip of his Captain Morgan rum runner and almost dropped it on the floor when he turned around to see Brielle and Simone approaching him and Christina. He could not believe his eyes, and when Chrissy saw his expression and turned around, she gathered that it was his fiancée coming toward them because of the look on Brielle's face as well. Brielle stood in front of Shawn and Christina.

"So, Shawn, is this Chris?" Brielle asked calmly, although she had tears in her eyes. She felt more hurt than angry. She was stunned into a numbness that made her feel like it was all just a dream. She could not believe that she was looking at her fiancé, who was on a date with someone else.

"Yes," Shawn answered and said, "but we are just friends, Brielle."

"You're friends with a woman who knows you have a woman, who wants you to be physical with her? Is that what you are telling me? The woman that texted you about kissing her?" Brielle looked at Christina to see if she could figure out the reason he would be there.

"Why, Shawn?" Brielle spoke calmly, which somewhat frightened Shawn. He would have preferred her to be mad as opposed to calculating.

"Brielle, we are just having drinks and talking. There's nothing more to it," Chrissy replied and sipped her drink as if she had said something that was okay.

Brielle contemplated knocking Christina's drink out of her hand, but she did not want to make a scene. She leaned in closer to Chrissy and said, "I don't believe I asked you anything. I am talking to my man."

"See, that's what's wrong with you older women. You have to own your man, like he's an object. He is not owned by you. And if he's feeling like that, he's probably just looking for some free space." Shawn stood up, preparing to block Brielle's reach in case she decided to smack or punch Chrissy in return for her brazen comment.

"Miss, I would advise you to leave this area," Simone suggested to Christina.

"Who are you? I don't understand what the problem is," Christina said, not budging. Simone clenched her fists and replied, "I can show you better than I can tell you. Now, would you really like to know, bitch?"

"Simone, it's okay. I guess Shawn felt that he needed a friend. I guess his fiancée is not friend enough. Not only did we argue earlier over this woman, but he ended up with her instead of trying to make up with me. That's big, Shawn."

Christina looked Simone up and down and spoke directly to Brielle. "Brielle, don't you think that maybe he didn't want to argue? Maybe he wanted to be able to come out, have fun, and leave the grief at home. You women with men just don't know how to keep them. And you get mad at women like me, that are carefree and can let a man be who he is. Why must you women put your men on a leash when you know that they want to roam free?" she challenged Brielle arrogantly.

"Shawn, is she your spokesperson?" Simone asked. "Why is she speaking for you?"

"Well, you must be hers, because you are speaking for her," Christina retorted, rolling her eyes with an attitude.

Shawn sat there, not knowing what to do. He knew that this would be a major problem. He had to try to resolve it before it got out of hand. "Listen, ladies, this is my fault. Christina, I had no business calling you back after I told you that I was not interested. Brielle, I just didn't want to fight with you. I didn't want to go out with the boys 'cause all they do is fuck with women anyway. I just wanted to get some insight from a female on why women are so irrational and emotional. I really just wanted to enjoy myself without any conflict."

Brielle was still stunned. She had no fight left in her. She answered meekly, "Shawn, you couldn't have at least called me to see if we could talk? Us, not an outside party who wants you to fuck her. Do you really think this woman wasn't going to try to get you to come home with her? Come on, Shawn, she's playing the friend role now. Look at what she texted you. That's what makes this wrong. You know she is interested in you and—"

"But that would be up to him, not you, and yes, I am attracted to him—" Christina cut in again.

Simone punched Christina in the face before she could finish her sentence. Shawn grabbed Simone and Brielle grabbed him.

"You're gonna defend this bitch, motherfucker? You know what you can do? You can go home with her and make sure she's okay. Forget about me! Let's go, Simone." Brielle started walking to the exit.

Simone ran up to her and grabbed her arm. "Listen, go home. Take Shawn with you. Don't worry about me. I'll take a cab. At least you caught it before it went further. You okay?" Shawn walked up behind Simone and faced Brielle.

"I'm sorry, Brielle. Can we please go home?" He tried to put his arm around her and she pulled away.

"I'm going home! Do what you want to do!" Brielle turned to Simone. "Come on, Simone." Brielle looked at Simone and went to grab her hand.

"Listen, sis, I think you should go home. I'm gonna stay here for a little while. Don't worry about me; go fix your relationship." Simone gave Brielle a hug. Brielle left and Shawn humbly followed.

Simone walked back into the lounge area. She noticed Christina sitting alone. She went over to talk to her to deceive her.

"I'm really sorry about hitting you. That's my sister and I do not want to see her hurt." Simone put an apologetic look on her face to convince Christina. Christina was drunk, not realizing the danger that she was in.

"I didn't do anything wrong. I was just trying to be there for him."

Simone felt her blood boiling. "That's not your job." She looked at Christina and sized her up. She knew she could take her.

"Listen, I don't owe another woman anything. If her man wanted to take me out, then that's his choice." Christina grabbed her pocketbook and walked away. Simone stayed in the club until an hour later, when she saw Christina leave. When she left Simone left the bar as well.

Simone

Simone did not follow too closely behind, but close enough to stay on Christina's trail. Christina hailed a taxi, which pulled over and let her in. Simone hailed one right behind that one. She told the driver to follow Christina's taxi. Christina got out and went into her building. As she was putting the key in the front door, she felt a knife in her back. Simone knew that there were cameras, so she hid her face in Christina's back and forced her into the lobby and onto the elevator. When they got in the elevator, Christina panicked.

"What are you doing?" she asked Simone.

"Oh, don't worry. I'm just gonna rob you and go. It's your punishment for trying to mess with another woman's man. It's just Karma, baby. But if you scream, this knife will slit your throat, so be calm."

Christina followed Simone's directions. She put the key into her door but tried to close the door on Simone before she could walk in. Simone pushed the door open and closed it. She quickly pounced on Christina and started choking her. Christina grabbed Simone's hands but could not release Simone's grip.

Simone whispered in Christina's ear as she strangled her to death, "How does it feel, pretty girl?"

Christina desperately tried to fight Simone off, but Simone was stronger than she was. Simone noticed that they were on the floor, next to the computer. With one hand, she snatched the mouse out of its socket and began to wrap it around Christina's neck. Christina's eyes widened. She stared at Simone with extreme fright, knowing that she was about to die.

"Little missy, you think your shit is so sweet, huh? This is what you do with yourself? You mess with other people's lives? I can tell you are a whore. Well, I'm sorry to let you know that you messed with the wrong bitch's man this time. My sister has gone through enough, and here you come trying to take her man? Bye-bye, sweetie, lights out," Simone hissed vindictively as she pulled the cord as tightly as she could.

Christina's body went limp. Simone took both hands and pulled on the wire from both sides, making it even tighter around Christina's neck. She checked her pulse to make sure that she was dead. She undressed Christina to make it seem like someone raped her and killed her. "This bitch is a slut. I know she gotta have somebody's fresh cum in her. I feel sorry for that dude when the police find him."

Simone looked through Christina's closet. She took a baseball cap and shades from her room and put them on. She then left Christina's building and walked about ten blocks, discarded the hat and shades, and hailed a cab home.

While in the cab Simone thought about her sister Mariah. They had been so close growing up because they were only a year apart. Tears began to stream down her face and she silently wept. She thought back to the day when she was thirteen and Mariah was twelve, about a week before Mariah's abduction, when they both went over to their neighbor's house to play with one of their friends. The girl's father told the girls to come inside and wait for his daughter to come out of the bathroom. As they were waiting, Mr. Jones sat down next to Mariah and put his arm around the girl. Simone instantly felt uncomfortable but she didn't know what to do. She became nervous.

"Mr. Jones, my mom doesn't want men touching on us," Simone said meekly. Mr. Jones laughed a laugh that seemed evil to Simone, a laugh that she still hears in her mind from time to time.

"Oh, be quiet, Simone. I'm just making Miss Pretty Mariah feel comfortable. You mad because I didn't come and sit next to you?" Mr. Jones started to rub on Mariah's leg, and Simone jumped up and went over to Mariah and grabbed her hand.

"Let's go, Mariah. We have to go home."

Mariah jumped up and followed Simone to the door. As Mr. Jones was unlocking the door, he reached and brushed his hand over Simone's breast. She knew that he had done it on purpose, but she didn't say anything to him. He laughed again as they two girls ran back across the street.

When Simone told her mother what happened, Dorothy told Simone that she was fresh and that she was making something out of nothing. Simone knew that Mr. Jones would sneak over and mess with her mother sometimes when his wife was at work. A week later when Mariah went missing, Simone suspected it was Mr. Jones who had taken her. It wasn't until a year later that he was found out to be Mariah's abductor, rapist, and killer. Simone always felt responsible for not saving her sister from being hurt. She was going to make sure that nothing ever happened to her *new* sister, Brielle. Simone didn't care who came to hurt Brielle; she was not going to lose another sister again.

When Simone reached her block, she got out of the cab and walked down the street and into her building. She was mentally exhausted. She went right to bed but could not rest without having a horrible dream about something that happened seven years earlier.

●━━━━━━━━━━━━━━━━━━━━━━━━━━━━━━━●

Simone walked into her grandmother's room to ask her for some money to go to the store. Her grandmother's third husband was sleeping, and Gammy motioned for her to go out of the room. Her grandmother followed her into the living room.

"Now, listen, Simone. I don't have the money to take care of you and your brothers and give you money for stuff you don't need. You are fifteen years old. You need to start thinking of a way to earn your keep."

She looked at Simone and continued. "Now, Rufus in there is my third husband. Do you know how I survived my first two husbands?" Simone was confused. She didn't know what her grandmother was leading to. She shook her head no.

"Well, your mother's father died in the Vietnam War and left me his veteran's pension and social security. Then my second husband died on the job, so I got his benefits too. Now, that sorry-ass motherfucker in there don't seem like he is ready to go nowhere. He ain't good for nothing but his benefits too. None of them are. But I don't see him croakin' no time soon. So you know what you can do to make it better for us?" Simone's Gammy looked her dead in her eye. Simone shook her head no again.

"You can take me out of my misery and get rid of the bastard." Simone was unsure what her grandmother was asking her to do. "Yes, when it's time for his medicine, I want you to mix some poison in there and give it to him. Here, take this twenty dollars, and go get some rat poison from the hardware store. Tell the man we got bad rodents. Buy some traps so he won't get suspicious. And then later on tonight, when I call you in to bring the medicine, make sure you have doctored his syrup up with some good die serum so we can say good-bye to his ass. I'm about tired of him, and Mr. Johnson down on the third floor want to take his spot. I'm sixty-two years old, and I still got a lot of life in me. I got about two more husbands to get through before I die." Her grandmother started laughing shrilly. It was a laugh that reminded Simone of the evil shriek her sister's killer, Mr. Jones, had made.

Simone could not believe her ears, but she knew her grandmother was serious. Simone had no other choice but to do what her grandmother said, or she would get beat with a broom handle or an iron cord. Simone's grandmother was not your normal average grandmother. She was a young-minded one who hung out in the local bar and was the neighborhood gossip queen.

Simone went to the hardware store and bought the poison, as she was told. She went back upstairs and got her stepgrandfather's liquid phenobarbital that he took for seizures. It was a thick, red syrup. She took a teaspoon of rat poison and poured some of the liquid in a bowl and stirred it together. She could not see the granules in the thick serum. She then took another teaspoon full and mixed it with some more of his medicine and left it in the bowl until her grandmother called her.

Simone went in her room to write Mariah a letter.

Dear Mariah,
I miss you so much. I am so sorry for what Mr. Jones did to you. I hate myself for not protecting you. I hope he didn't hurt you too much before he took you

away from us. I have nightmares about you being hurt like that. I will never be the same again. I'm fifteen years old and you and Mommy are dead. You were supposed to grow up to be a teacher and me, a lawyer.

I will never be a lawyer, because Gammy wants me to poison her husband. She is so mean. Me, Billy, and Brandon hate living here. Gammy is a drunk and so is her nasty husband. He's dirty and he stinks. She just made me go to the store to buy poison to put in his medicine. I wish I could give it to her too. But then me, Billy, and Brandon would have to go to a shelter or a foster home, and we might be separated.

I have to protect them too. And I can't even protect myself from having to do this for Gammy. I'm scared that if they find out Mr. Rufus was poisoned that she might tell on me, that's why she won't do it herself. If I get caught, I'll kill myself so that I can be with you and not go to jail. She's calling me to bring him the poison now. I'm so scared, Mariah. Ask God to help me.

Love always, Simone

Simone was startled by Gammy's voice.

"Simone, Goddamn it! Bring your fresh ass in here, and bring Rufus his medicine. Now!" Simone jumped up and hid Mariah's letter under her pillow. She slowly went into the kitchen. As she walked, she prayed. *Lord, I don't know why all this is happening to me. I believe there is a God. My teacher, Ms. Lawrence, used to take me to church, and I felt something there. I know that you are real, but I don't know why my life is like this.*

Simone went into the kitchen and chose to fill another dropper without the poison. She refused to follow through with it but would tell her grandmother that she did. She took the dropper and filled it up with the phenobarbital and also made Rufus a glass of Kool-Aid, like she always did. Her hands shook as she walked to her grandmother's closed bedroom door.

She pushed the door open to see her grandmother and her husband lying in the bed. Rufus had nothing on but a pair of boxers, and Gammy had on her bra and panties. Simone shuddered at the thought of the two of them naked and being nasty with each other. It was disgusting to think of. Rufus sat up in the bed and smiled at Simone with a smile that she didn't like. Ever since Mariah's rape, Simone trusted no man. She actually hated them. She felt that they were the reason the world itself was so fucked up.

"Hey, baby, thank you for coming to doctor me up." His rotten teeth turned Simone's stomach. She looked over at her Gammy, who had a scowling look on her face that said, *Bitch, you better do what I said and do it right.* Simone looked back at Rufus and went over to his side of the bed.

She passed him the dropper, and he sucked the liquid in and handed the dropper back to Simone. He made a horrible face and took a big swallow and coughed. Simone jumped.

"What the hell you jumping for? Something wrong with you?" Gammy asked. Simone shook her head no.

"That medicine is nasty as shit. I hate that damn medicine. Oh, you brought me my Kool-Aid too, Simone? Thank you, darlin'." Rufus took the glass from Simone and drank it down in nearly one gulp. He made a loud burp and handed Simone the glass back. Simone walked out of the room, put the cup and medicine dropper in the kitchen sink, and rinsed out the concocted dropper and put it in the strainer. She went back to her room.

Simone went right to bed. She put a movie on, got under the covers, and put a pillow over her head. Her mind kept racing as to how the day could have ended had she brought the poison into Rufus. She pictured the ambulance workers and then the CSI team coming in and then herself going out of her grandmother's apartment in handcuffs, with everyone outside looking at her and whispering. She imagined the news reporters and the lights glaring in her face and the microphone in her mouth. "Why did you do it, Simone Alexander?" the reporter would ask.

Simone dozed off to sleep and was awakened by her brother Billy, who was very excited. "Simone, Simone, get up. Rufus is in the bathroom throwing up blood! He said to call nine-one-one. Gammy left to go downstairs to the third floor for something!"

Simone jumped up and went to the bathroom. Rufus was laid out on the floor. He was moaning, grabbing his stomach, and rolling around on the floor, screaming, "Call the ambulance!"

Simone told thirteen-year-old Billy to call 911, and she went in her room and closed the door. She sat on her bed and covered her ears from Rufus' agonizing screams.

Ten minutes later she heard the EMS come through her door. Their walkie-talkies were blasting and they were talkin to Billy and Rufus. Simone heard Rufus screaming as they quickly took him out. Gammy never came back before Rufus was rushed to the hospital.

Simone tossed and turned all night. It was August and it was muggy and the air was suffocating. She kept trying to figure out how he got sick if she didn't give him the poison. She wondered if her grandmother had given it to him without her knowing.

At about 6 a.m. Gammy came through the door to the apartment. She had stayed out all night. She pushed through the door of Simone's room and sat on her bed. "So, what happened?" Gammy whispered, allowing Simone to smell the strong alcohol odor that escaped out of Gammy's mouth.

"The ambulance came," Simone answered matter-of-factly.

Her grandmother looked surprised. "Oh, somebody called the ambulance? Did the police come with them?" Gammy asked Simone, straightening herself up as if the police were in her home.

"There was an officer waiting outside," Billy said. "The EMTs asked Rufus, like, three questions and took him. They ain't ask me nothing."

"Well, where the hell were you? You couldn't act like you were calling and not call? They probably going to just pump his damn stomach or some shit. I figured you would know to let the bastard just die here before anybody was called."

"Gammy, he was screaming and calling me and Billy to help. He could have laid there for hours, and then if he didn't, you know, then he could tell on us that we didn't never call. Me and Billy could get in trouble for that."

At that moment Simone hated her grandmother. Her grandmother was cold and heartless, something that Simone always thought, but it was then confirmed. Her grandmother was an evil woman, and Simone planned to leave that place as soon as possible.

Gammy went to the kitchen to call the hospital to inquire about Rufus. She came back and told Simone that he was in intensive care, that Rufus had to be given an emergency bypass surgery because they found that a valve to his heart was clogged. The doctor told her that had they not been called, he could have suffered a heart attack on any given day.

"They also had to pump his stomach because they found him to have suffered a gastrointestinal attack, which means he had a badass stomachache. They believe the artery blockage led to the buildup of toxins in his intestinal tract, which led to the excruciating pain he was in. So, in other words, we gotta do the poison in smaller doses. We gotta poison his body over time."

Simone looked at her grandmother in horror. "I don't want to, Gammy." Simone had to speak up.

"Oh really? You see they didn't even check for poison, because they don't even expect it. They are not going to think that he is being poisoned. There would be no reason for them to suspect that, Simone." Her grandmother tried to make light of the extremely horrible charge that she had given her granddaughter.

"Gammy, I'm fifteen years old."

"Listen to me, Simone. It will be okay. We will figure it out. I don't want you to think too much about it; don't worry about it. We will do what we have to do, and it will be okay.

Trust me, I'm your grandmother. His body has gone through a major trauma, heart surgery; his body will already be very susceptible to succumb to something."

Simone looked right past her grandmother's eyes that were looking at her. *How could a grandmother suggest such a thing to their grandchild?* Simone asked herself.

Two weeks passed and Rufus was sent back home from the hospital. He was very weak because of the heart surgery. He seemed to have aged five or ten years. He had more medicine to take and a wound that had to be cleaned properly so as not to cause a life-threatening infection.

Simone would not even look Rufus in the eye or go around him. She was scared that he would feel that something was going on and figure it out. He called her into the room one day when Gammy was out.

"Simone, what's wrong? Do you feel like this was your fault?"

Simone got defensive. "Hell no! Why would I?"

"Because I got sick after you brought me my medicine, and I just wanted to tell you that my body was not releasing, or should I say, the blood wasn't freely carrying the toxins through my body. My artery was blocked. In turn, it affected my stomach. I just basically had a gas attack, but it was good that I did, because they would have never known about the blockage in my heart. So, don't worry, I'm not mad with you."

"Okay," Simone said, feeling relieved. She walked out of his room and was glad that she went against Gammy's plan. She listened to herself and spared herself the guilt of killing an innocent person. She felt relieved that Rufus didn't blame her for getting sick or feel that she had done something to him.

When Gammy came home she called Simone into the kitchen. "Simone, go downstairs and go by the garden and bring me some dirt upstairs."

"What you need dirt for, Gammy?"

"To plant a fuckin' flower, Goddamn it. Just go downstairs and collect some dirt in this pot right here! Is that all right with you?"

Simone jumped up and took the small cooking pot downstairs to the front of her project building and scooped up some dirt with a big stirring spoon and brought it back upstairs.

Gammy took the pot inside of her bedroom and closed the door. Simone wondered what she wanted the dirt for.

The next day Gammy called Simone in the kitchen and told her to put dirt on Rufus' dressing before taking it in and putting it on his open wound.

"I don't want to hear no shit. If you'd have done it right the first time, we wouldn't have to keep trying."

Every day for about five days, Simone brought fresh dirt upstairs and rubbed it on Rufus' dressing for her grandmother, who would take it in her room and put it on his open flesh.

The following week Rufus was rushed back to the hospital, where he died two days later.

Gammy never discussed with her what led to Rufus' death, but Simone knew the dirt had something to do with it.

Brielle

Brielle did not talk to Shawn as he followed behind her, trying to talk to her outside. They had to go in separate directions to get their cars, and she refused his offer to walk with her to her parking garage. Shawn walked off to get his car, while Brielle went to the garage and got hers. She drove home in tears, barely being able to see the road.

"Is this what my hand calls for? Does every man on this Earth have to look elsewhere when he has it all right in his hands? What makes a man need so much that is superficial? Why is not one good woman enough?"

Brielle swerved to avoid a car that she had gotten too close behind. She pulled off onto the side of the highway and put her car in park. The voice came back. *What you gonna do now? You see he ain't no better than Dante. What the fuck you gonna do?* She tried to ignore it, but it kept getting louder, asking her what her next move was going to be. She screamed in response, "I'm not going to kill him! I cannot kill anymore! I can't! I don't want to!" She knew there would be more.

You are weak! He is going to do it again and again! Stop him! the voice commanded.

A police officer pulled up behind Brielle's car, and the officer got out of the car and approached her side. Brielle rolled down the window.

"Are you okay, ma'am?" the officer asked, looking into the backseat and around her car with his flashlight.

"Yes, I'm sorry. I just had a fight with my fiancé, and I was unable to see the road. I'm okay now." Brielle wiped her eyes and gave a fake smile.

"Well, Miss, it is very dangerous for you to be on the side of the road alone at this time of night. Do you need a police escort home? I'll be happy to follow you. How far do you live from here?"

"Oh no, I'm okay. I live right here in Fort Lee. I am only a few blocks from here. Thank you for offering, Officer." She smiled again.

"Well, just be careful. Are you fearful of your fiancé? Is this a domestic violence issue, Miss?" He looked at her intently.

"Um, I don't think so. I don't think he is going to do anything to me physically. I'd just like to go home." She looked straight ahead of her, with her hands on the steering wheel, awaiting her release.

"Okay, I'll just need to see your driver's license." He reached in and held his hand out for her to put her license into it. Brielle became agitated.

"Have I broken a law? What are you detaining me for, asking for my ID?" Brielle was frustrated and just wanted to get home. She rummaged through her bag to look for her wallet.

"Ma'am, I need to know who you are in case something happens to you. It's for your safety. We can send a car to ride by your home tonight to make sure you are okay." Brielle's mother's voice egged her on. *Go ahead, give it to him. That way you can kill Shawn, say he came to harm you, and this cop will corroborate that you were upset over a fight with your boyfriend! Do it! Give him the license!*

"On second thought, I am feeling a little frightened." Brielle felt manipulated by her thoughts as she passed the license to the officer and tried to ignore her mother's evil spirit.

The officer took down her name and address and passed the license back to her. "Please be safe, Miss Prescott." He turned and walked back to his vehicle.

Brielle, with shaking arms, drove home. Shawn's car was already in the driveway. He had already been there a half hour, waiting for her. Brielle sat in the car, contemplating whether she should leave and stay somewhere else for the night.

"I don't want to hurt him," she told herself but reneged with another idea. "But he was about to go fuck that girl. I know he was." Brielle wiped her tears and anger replaced her sorrow. She put the key in the door and walked into the kitchen, where Shawn was having a glass of wine. He had guilt written all over his face. Brielle's hands shook as she walked in the kitchen. She kept seeing flashes of Dante's face replace

Shawn's. He summoned her to come to him, his arms open, just the way Dante had before she plunged the knife in his chest.

"Let's go in the living room, Shawn." Brielle did not want to be near any knives. He followed her with two glasses of wine for them to relax and talk. They sat down on the couch. Shawn looked deep into Brielle's eyes and saw the hurt and pain that he had caused her and he felt bad.

"Brielle, I'm sorry." Her eyes widened. She felt the rage rising inside of her yet again.

"Sorry? Sorry for what?! I thought you weren't doing anything wrong! So, you apologizing means that you were doing something wrong." Shawn shook his head in disagreement.

"Listen, calm down. No it does not. It means that what I thought was innocent you didn't. I hurt you and I didn't mean to."

"No, you didn't mean for me to find out. If I hadn't happened to be in the city, in Times Square, I would be none the wiser. You would have gone home with that girl and began an affair. I would have never known, and then you would do it again and again and aga—"

Shawn grabbed her arms and interrupted her rant. "Brielle, I just wanted to see…" Shawn paused in an effort to choose the right words.

Brielle finished his sentence for him. "You wanted to see?! See what? If you felt like fucking her at the end of the night? After all the liquor, you sure would have! You wanted to see if you still want to be out there, free to do whoever you want? You are not sure anymore because you meet some little chickenhead bitch? Get out! Go see now!" Brielle stood up and motioned for him to leave. Shawn tried to calm her down but she was hysterical. "Get out! Now see that! And take your fucking ring!" Brielle threw her enormous canary-yellow diamond ring across the room. Shawn took a moment to think. He was angered that she would react that way.

"It's all that, Brielle? I did something wrong enough to have you throw our engagement ring out like that? You don't want it? Fine!" He walked over to the corner of the room, picked up the ring, and stormed out.

Brielle screamed, "No! Not again!" She ran to the door to call Shawn back, but he was pulling off. She tried calling him but his phone went straight to voice mail.

Shawn was in his car, calling Christina. Her answering machine picked up, and he left her a message. "Please do not call me again. I am fighting with my girl over you, and we didn't even sleep together. I should not have led you on. I'm sorry."

He drove to his brownstone, realizing that it was about to be occupied by someone else. Shawn had every intention of trying to patch things up with Brielle, but he would give her some time to cool off. He went inside and had another drink and was again amazed by Brielle.

He laughed. "Only Brielle could show up at the wrong place at the wrong damn time." He thought about his statement and changed it. "I guess she saved me from really getting into some shit. I really probably would have been dumb enough to go home with that girl and risked losing my relationship for real. How can she break up with me when she knows that I didn't do anything physical with the girl?" He downed his drink and went to bed.

Shawn was awakened by a knock on his door early the next morning. When he looked through the peephole, he noticed two detectives at his door. He was scared that Brielle may have done something to herself. He slowly opened the door.

The officers displayed their badges, introduced themselves, and Shawn agreed to let them in. He led them to his living room, where he sat to hear some bad news.

"Mr. Ellison, do you know a Christina Melvin?" Shawn thought for a second and couldn't place the name, and then it hit him. They were asking him about his date the night before. He shuddered at the thought of what they were about to tell him.

"I went out with a girl named Christina last night, but I don't know her last name."

"Well, does she look like this?" the officer asked sarcastically and showed a mug shot of Christina. Shawn slowly nodded his head that he knew her.

"Well, Mr. Ellison, her body was found by a relative this morning. She was murdered last night."

Shawn was shocked but he kept his composure. "Wow, that's crazy," he said quietly. "I wonder what happened to her."

"Well, we cannot divulge how she was murdered, but we do see that you were the last person to be in contact with her by phone. You said that you saw her? Can you tell us approximately what time that was and where and the condition that she was in, when you left her?"

Shawn began to answer and thought against it. "Am I a suspect or something?" he asked seriously, knowing that he had nothing to do with Christina's murder and hoping that Brielle did not either.

"At this moment we are just doing our preliminary investigation. Can you tell us the time that you were with Miss Melvin?"

"I can tell you that I am sorry to hear about what happened to her; however, my lawyer has advised me never to speak to authorities regarding a situation as serious as this without him being present. I'm sorry. Here is his card and if you need to speak with me again, you may call him and have him set up an appointment for us to talk. I can tell you that she was fine when I left her." Shawn walked the officers to the door and let them out.

Shawn paced the floor of his living room, trying to piece last night's events together. He knew that he left the club with Brielle, but he also knew that he reached her house before she did, about a half hour before. He wondered if that would have given Brielle enough time to kill Christina. He could not figure out how Brielle would have been able to kill her and be home that quickly and how she would have seen her, unless she saw Christina walking out of the club after she got her car.

"Did she see her and offer her a ride? Did she pretend that she just wanted to talk to her and then end up killing her?" he asked himself out loud.

He sat down and thought long and hard about the possibility of Brielle killing the girl. He also thought about the fact that she was a stripper-barmaid and that she probably had many suitors and stalkers. "Maybe I'm wrong for thinking that Brielle is responsible, but what if she did do it?"

Shawn decided to call his woman and see the reaction he was going to get from the awful news. He knew that it wouldn't be that awful for Brielle; she probably couldn't care less.

Before Shawn called he got on his knees and prayed. "Dear Lord, please do not let Brielle be guilty of this murder. I cannot be with her if she is still killing, Lord. I love her. I honestly do. Save her, Lord. Deliver her. Heal her mind and her spirit. Show her that you are the way. Choose her so she can choose you. Let her live a spirit-filled Life. Amen."

He stood up and happened to glance at a picture of his mother. He took it off the stand and looked at it. He spoke to his mother's spirit. "Ma, I hope that you are enjoying Dad again. I hope that you are smiling. Please be resting peacefully. I wish that Brielle was more like you. She has so much that she must put behind her. Watch over me and her, Mom. I want us to make it."

Shawn stopped procrastinating and made the call. Brielle picked up, sounding distraught. "What's the matter, Brielle? Are you okay?"

"Am I okay? Hell no, I'm not okay! The man that I love had to go fucking around with some young whore to make himself feel good!" Brielle was still in bed. She had slept in her clothes, and her hair was disheveled. She sat up and reached for the liquor bottle that had put her to sleep. She took a long swig.

"Brielle, that girl is dead," Shawn said calmly.

"She should have been deaded before it went that far. Now you wanna dead her because I found out? Why, Shawn? What am I doing so wrong?" She looked in the mirror and tried to fix her hair.

"No, Brielle, dead as in murdered. Someone killed her last night." Brielle stopped patting down her hair and froze.

"What? Somebody killed her?" Brielle smiled at herself in the mirror and thought, *That's what the bitch gets for trying to fuck my man.* She continued trying to sound concerned. "What happened to her?"

"I don't know. The detectives came to ask me about her because my number was the last number in her phone."

Brielle was instantly infuriated. "So you called the bitch after you left me? What were you trying to do, go back over to see her?" She paced the floor and started to pull at her hair.

"I called to tell her not to call me again."

"Yeah right! Who gives a fuck if that bitch is dead? That's what she gets! What are you telling me about it for anyway?" Brielle sat on her bed, trying to figure out what was really happening to her and Shawn.

"Brielle, did you kill Christina?" The question slipped out of Shawn's mouth before he could think about it, and once it did he knew Brielle would get even angrier.

"Is that all you care about? That fucking little-ass girl. So, if I did, what would you do, leave me over some trick you said you don't even know like that? Is that what you want to do?" Brielle took Shawn's picture off of her dresser and stared at it.

"What if you did? Bitch, one fucking murder trial is not enough for you? You think you can continue to go around taking people's lives? What is wrong with you? Have you really lost your fucking mind?" he roared.

"I didn't do it, Shawn, I'm just saying." She calmed down after realizing that he wasn't going to back down and appease her just because she was mad at him.

"Are you telling me the truth? I don't even know what to believe anymore with you. Did you kill that girl?" Shawn asked sternly.

"I said I didn't. And now you don't even believe what I say? Look what one night is doing to us; we both lost trust. You know what I've been through, and you go and do the same thing to me for some little girl that probably just wanted to get in your pockets?"

"Brielle, I know what you've gone through, but it's not all about you all the time. Yes, I was wrong. No, I shouldn't have wasted my time, got you upset, or been out with that girl knowing that she wanted to have something going on with me. I guess I was just tempting myself, which was dumb. I did something that could have turned into something more. Yes, I admit it. But, Brielle, you have got to realize how you are. You read a text and accused me. You have not let go of the past, and how are we going to move forward if you are still putting Dante's face on mine?" Shawn was starting to become stressed. He had a deadline to meet, and he did not feel like worrying about Brielle and her issues at that moment. He was losing his patience with her.

"How am I gonna trust you, and you are going on dates? Doesn't an engagement mean that you are done with the dating thing, or at least aren't you supposed to be?" she reiterated.

"Listen, we need to go to counseling. You haven't been back to the therapist since your arrest. We need to put these issues on the table and decide if we can get past them."

"Oh yeah? So, now you don't know if you want to be with me? Well, you don't have to be. You don't have to be with a crazy woman, and I don't have to be with a man that is still searching for a woman when he already has one that loves him. I guess my love wasn't sufficient enough for you, like most men. It's over, Shawn. I will bring you whatever you have here and leave it at your brownstone, and I will leave my copy of the key with your belongings! I'm gonna make it easy for you. I will give you the freedom that you wanted to have *on* the low. Now you won't have to sneak."

Brielle hung up the phone and refused to cry. She had cried enough tears behind men. As a child, she cried because of her father and her cousin Tony. As a young woman, her failed relationships had given her pain. Dante had given her a cruise ship full of tears, not just a boatload, in the years that they had spent together. She was not going to let Shawn make her another victim. She had gotten her revenge on Peyton and the scumbag that Janay set up to rape her. She was not going to let anyone ever make her feel so bad about herself that she would want to take his or her life and jeopardize her freedom. She was not that crazy. She was looking forward to nurturing her relationship with Simone and enjoying her life. She agreed with Shawn that she needed to put the past behind her, and he was now a part of that past.

Brielle looked at the clock and decided to go to church. She got dressed in a simple pantsuit and went to a church close to her house. She had always been intrigued by a local church that always had a packed house on Sunday mornings.

Brielle walked up to the line that was formed for the service and stood by herself, waiting to go in. She felt nervous but determined to go and see what she would get out of it. As she walked up the steps and into the foyer, she was greeted by two elegantly dressed women with a cheerful, "Good morning and God bless you."

Brielle said, "Um, Good morning," and she was ushered to a seat in between a heavyset lady, who appeared to be in her early seventies, and a little girl, about seven.

The congregation welcomed each other as a small group stood up and sang. They sang a song that Brielle had heard on the radio, which said, "I pray for you, you pray for me. I love you, I need you to survive… I won't harm you with words from my mouth. I love you, I need you to survive…"

The lady next to Brielle was singing the song right in Brielle's ear. Brielle looked over and the woman smiled at her and turned her head back to face the podium and continued singing. As the song was almost over, the lady, along with other people, were getting up to stand and sing the ending. Brielle saw them raising their hands and waving their arms. She held her hands clasped together and couldn't help but begin to gently tap her feet to the song.

Brielle wanted to stand up because the song was reminding her of what Shawn had said, how God was going to make sure she made it and that he only had protection and love for her.

The service seemed pretty customary, with the announcements and offering being taken. The choir sang during the offering, and Brielle, again, was moved. This time they sang, "He saw the best in me when everyone else around could only see the worst in me…"

The woman next to Brielle stood up and gently rubbed her shoulder and extended her hand for Brielle to stand up next to her. The woman squeezed Brielle's hand. Brielle was apprehensive at first, but she relaxed and began to clap. The song touched Brielle because not only did she think of how everyone in her family had always mistreated her, but she thought of her mother. The woman next to her was about the age that Brielle's mother would have been. Brielle also noticed how affectionate the little girl's mother, who was sitting next to the little girl on Brielle's left side, was toward her daughter.

Oh, so you wish you'd had another mother, huh, bitch? Well, too bad. I wished I had had a different daughter."

Brielle looked over at the lady, and her eyes welled up with tears. The woman wrapped her big arm around Brielle's shoulder and pulled her close. Brielle's quiet teardrops turned into her releasing a shower full of tears. She sobbed into the woman's shoulder as the woman embraced her and held her close.

Brielle felt something tugging on her leg, and she looked and saw the little girl reaching her hand out. Brielle took the little girl's hand, and the woman continued to hold Brielle.

The lady whispered in Brielle's ear, "It doesn't matter now what happened. What matters is that you open up your heart and let *Him* in. *He* will take it all away. *He* will forgive it all if you never look back. *He* will give you a new life." The lady gave Brielle one more hug and let her go.

The song was almost over, and Brielle raised her hand and waved it. She felt an unusual calm come over her. She felt a wonderful peace.

It was time for the sermon, and the pastor looked like he had once been in the streets and could bring the message in a street-friendly way.

The pastor stood and walked to the podium and got right to the point. "Okay, we got a lot to cover. Good morning and turn with me to Second Timothy 2:22. It reads: 'Flee the evil desires of youth, and pursue righteousness, faith, love, and peace, along with those who call on the Lord out of a pure heart. Don't have anything to do with foolish and stupid arguments, because you know they produce quarrels. And the Lord's servant must not quarrel; instead, he must be kind to everyone, able to teach, not resentful.'"

Brielle thought for a moment. *Shit, oops, I'm not supposed to be cursing in my head while I'm in church. Shoot, I been fighting my whole doggone life. I am tired of fighting. I am ready to surrender.*

The pastor continued. "Now down to chapter three, verse one. 'But mark this: There will be terrible times in the last days. People will be lovers of themselves, lovers of money, boastful, proud, abusive, disobedient to their parents, ungrateful, unholy, without love, unforgiving, slanderous, without self-control, brutal, not lovers of the good, treacherous, rash, conceited, lovers of pleasure rather than lovers of God—having a form of godliness but denying its power. Have nothing to do with them.' I hate to be the bearer of bad news, but we are living in those days. I don't know how much time we got, but I know that what has just been described as the way of this world right here and now. So, if you ain't got your armor of God on or if you ain't asking the Lord to cover you, then please get your mind right and do it now!"

As the pastor—who was fashionably dressed in a three-piece thousand-dollar suit—received a roar of agreement and acceptance of his declaration, he delicately took a sip of his orange juice, cleared his throat, and continued.

The older lady looked over at Brielle and smiled as Brielle returned the gesture. Brielle looked over to the little girl, who was looking at Brielle with concern, as if she knew Brielle's troubles. Brielle put her hand out to let the girl know that she was okay, and the little girl gave Brielle a high five and smiled. Her mom then smiled at Brielle with a look of permission, as if to okay Brielle's exchange with her young daughter.

Why is everyone so nice? Brielle thought to herself, and the big lady leaned over and whispered, "In this house there is love. When the joy of the Lord is present, there will be nothing but peace."

The pastor continued. "I am here today to tell you people that you need to serve and praise your way through your hell. All that trouble that you were able to get into, and now some of you are wimps and sissies when it comes to dealing with God. 'Oh, it's too hard, Pastor, I can't get it right,' is all I hear. Where's your will to do His will? Where's your will to survive? Y'all must like this here Hell on Earth, because you sure keep running back to it. As soon as you leave the church house, y'all need some drama to pray about." Everyone laughed. The handsome, young pastor sipped on more of his juice.

"I am just the messenger. Don't kill me. Don't act like I'm trying to tell you something for my own benefit. I can only tell you what is in this here book. This here book is the Book of Life. If you apply this doctrine, you will really live. We all suffer and have trials and tribulations, but it is not for the bad if God has his hand in your life. Who said that because you were abused as a child that you cannot have a fulfilling adult life? Who said that because you are not a perfect being that God cannot love you to improvement? *He* can. I said *He* will. I said your life will never be the same if you praise *His* holy name. And walk with *Him*. Talk with *Him*. If you are here today and you know nothing about a relationship with God, then the one thing I want you to do is try. Start. Just pray once a day and keep coming back, or make sure you fellowship somewhere else, but, please, get to know Jesus. He will make everything all right!"

The congregation stood on its feet and clapped while the pastor led an a cappella version of "To My Father's House." Brielle was on her feet again. She felt great. She felt like she could take it one day at a time. She didn't have to be perfect to go to church; she could work on herself and keep giving it a try. She knew it would take time, but she wanted to have the happy glow on her face that the older woman next to her had.

It was time for the pastor to offer the doors of the church open so that people could join. Brielle stayed seated. The woman patted her leg and said, "Do it when you're ready, but make sure you get ready."

Brielle nodded in agreement and said, "Thank you so much for today, Miss; you made me feel very comfortable."

Brielle picked up her cell phone and called Simone to tell her the good news about that whore who ruined her relationship. *I know I just came out of church, but I'm not saved yet.* She laughed.

"What's up, Brielle?" Simone answered tiredly.

"Damn, sis, you still sleep? Wake up. Guess what? That bitch from last night got killed," Brielle informed Simone excitedly.

"What?! Get the fuck outta here! How do you know that?" Simone sat up in bed, surprised that Brielle knew about the murder already.

"The detectives went to talk to Shawn. He said a relative or something found her. That's crazy, right? See, God don't like ugly."

Simone started cracking up laughing after Brielle made that comment. "Brielle, you not supposed to use God when it comes to somebody getting murdered. Murder is a sin."

Brielle started laughing with Simone.   "Shit,   God knows that bitch wasn't right by trying to fuck my husband, so he turned his head and let that bitch's lights get put out. I don't give a damn. Shit, she probably did that shit to one last bitch too many. I know I ain't do it, but another bitch may have. Or a nigga that she probably tried to play. She seemed like she thought her shit ain't stink. You live dirty, you eat dirt. That's how it goes."

Simone smiled at the thought that Brielle and her thought alike. "You ain't never lie, sister. And what's going on with Shawn? Did y'all make up?" Simone opened her refrigerator and took a swig from the orange juice container and put it back in the refrigerator. She had on a pair of male boxers and a wife beater, her favorite at-home attire.

"I broke up with him. I can't trust him now, and I'm not going to spend my time searching through phones, trying to figure out passwords, and checking receipts and shit. He messed up." Brielle turned the water on in the shower to prepare for her day.

"Are you sure that's what you want to do? I mean, he probably learned his lesson, and you caught it before it did get physical. He looked shook as hell when he saw us." They both cracked up laughing again.

"He really did, didn't he?" Brielle chuckled again. "I just don't know, Simone. I need time. But don't worry, I'm fine. My trial starts this Thursday. I'll probably be in the courtroom all day every day for, like, months. So, tomorrow I'm gonna pick you up, and we will have a girls' day. "

They got off the phone and looked forward to the next day, when they would see each other again.

Simone

imone hung up the phone with Brielle and thought about Melvin. She liked him. He did not seem like the type of guy to be a snitch. He seemed like a slick-talking nigga who was about his business—just her type. She began to replay in her mind the entire previous evening. She imagined him dropping his boxers and replayed that part over and over again. Her cell phone rang.

"Hello." Simone turned her television down.

"Did you speak to that fuckin' prick yet?" It was Joey.

"Oh, no, but I left him, like, three messages telling him that I have to go out of town and that I want to see him before I leave," she lied easily.

"Yeah, because I gotta get that son of a bitch. This guy I got on the inside let me hear the interrogation tape. He is pointing them in my direction. He mentioned my name."

"Yeah, did he give details about you?" Simone tried not to sound too overly interested in the answer, but she wanted to know.

"No, not yet. But they asked if he knew me, and he said he did."

"So, that doesn't mean he's gonna tell on you, Joey."

"Hey, listen. I paid you half; now you better do it. You sure you didn't meet this guy? He's a real ladies man. He could talk the panties off the most stuck-up cunt in the world. You better be careful."

"Joey, shut up. You know I don't mind no fuckin' dick. I get it and leave it alone. All the time. It's nothing to me. But that's too much information."

"Yeah, you are a fuckin' heartbreaker. Okay, keep callin' this dude until you get him. You hear me?"

"Yeah, yeah, Joey. I'm on it. I'll call you when I speak to him." Simone hung up and her phone rang again.

"Yeah," she answered, frustrated.

"Yeah? Do I need to come and dick you down some more to help you with that attitude?"

She smiled after recognizing Melvin's voice. "Oh, I didn't hear you. I thought you said were you wack in bed." Simone started laughing. She caught a glimpse of herself in the mirror and noticed a look that she hadn't seen in a while—the look of love.

"Oh really? So then my next question is: Can I get a do-over? Now?" Melvin asked playfully.

Simone could not believe that he was calling so soon and wanting to see her again right away.

"You for real?" Simone got serious and sat on her canopy bed.

"Why wouldn't I be? You gave yourself a bad rap over the phone. You made yourself seem pitiful, but, girl, you ain't no joke. You ain't no weakling and you ain't who you seemed to be."

"Oh, I ain't? Whatever, nigga; if I ain't. You'll never know what I am." She tried to resist the urge that was building to see him right then and there.

"Why not? You mad because you didn't fool me into thinking that you are a worthless woman? I saw how uncomfortable you were in those clothes and that horrible wig you had on."

"Well, damn, rip me, why don't you?" Simone joked.

"I want to. Meet me at the same room. I kept it. I went to work from here, and I'm back, baby, waiting for you. You comin'?"

Simone was speechless for three seconds, and then she couldn't help but blurt out a breathless Yes."

She went back to her sexy closet and picked out a treat nicer than the first. It was time to impress Melvin and then kill him.

She picked a white breast–out, feathered bra with a crotchless bottom that had feathers around the seams. It tied on the top and sides with white ribbons. Simone looked like a dove. She hesitated before putting her black wig back on. She knew Melvin didn't like it, but she still could not be seen leaving the scene of the crime that would occur with her blonde hair. She made sure that she dressed more classy and upscale.

Simone put on a linen dress with some Anne Klein wedge heel tweed sandals. She looked like a sexy businesswoman. She took the syringe that was already filled with the potassium chloride that Joey had supplied her with and put it in her over-size matching Gucci tote bag.

Simone reached the hotel and went straight to Melvin's room. He opened the door and had a towel on. He grabbed Simone and started kissing her like he loved her and hadn't seen her in months. She kissed him back like he was the love of her life.

He held her tightly and pulled her in the room while continuing to caress her tongue with his. He walked her over to the bed. Simone dropped her bag next to the bed so that she would be able to reach in and get the syringe when the opportunity came.

Melvin released his grip on her and began to undress her and reveal her negligee. He was turned on even more by her perky breasts sticking straight out of her cupless bra. He began to do an instant replay of the night before. Melvin began sucking on Simone's breasts. He lay back and had her lie on him. He lay there hugging her for a few minutes. She sensed that something was wrong.

"What's the matter, Melvin? You are hugging me like you just lost your mom or something. Are you okay? You can't possibly be that into me." Melvin sat up on his elbows, and Simone rolled off of him and onto her stomach. She sat up on her elbows as well to hear his response.

"Candy, listen. I'm going through something right now. I think I just need the comfort of a loving woman right now. I know we are strangers, but sometimes it's easier to take refuge with one that knows nothing about you who just feels right. You feel right to me. I don't know how and I don't know why. I just know that you do." Simone was drawn in by Melvin's eyes and what seemed to be sincerity.

"What are you going through?" Simone wanted to see if she could get any information out of Melvin.

He thought for a few moments and looked Simone in her eyes. "I got into some trouble with the police, and now they want me to tell on some dangerous people to save my freedom and my career. If I get charged, then I will be facing ten years in prison, but if I tell on someone, I won't even be charged."

"Yeah, but you don't want to put your life in jeopardy for no fuckin' stinkin'-ass cops either." Simone was asking herself whether she should try to help Melvin by talking to Joey or setting up some kind of meeting with the two; however, she didn't know if that would be detrimental to her health. She couldn't believe that she was even considering such a thing.

"I didn't say I was. It's just that they have put the offer on the table, and I gotta plot my next point with the other side. I don't know how to approach the situation. They may not believe that I'm not cooperating and want to kill me anyway."

Simone was confused. She didn't know what to do. "So, what if they don't? What are you about? What are you into?" She lay on her side with her head in her palm and looked in his eyes for his answer.

His eyes said, "Be with you." The thought made her look away. He took her chin in his hands and turned her face back toward his. "I will cut that criminal shit out. I will find me a woman and settle down. This is the turning point for me. I have had a lot of opportunities. This is my last one to get my shit together, for real. I have a good-ass job. I was just being greedy, takin' shit when I had the world at my fingertips. I am in line for a promotion at my company. If this all goes away, I can make a positive change."

"Well, good for you." Simone forced herself not to give a damn about his sob story. She got up and put her ass in his face and bent over in front of him, putting her hands on the ground. She turned her head around and said, "Now, can you suck some pussy from the back and maybe eat some ass out too if you get the urge?" Simone suggested wickedly, with a sexy smile.

"Well, damn, girl. Why your mouth like that?" He inched up behind her, still sitting on the bed, her ass all in his face.

"You don't like it?" Simone asked.

"No, I don't. I love it. Now, let me get some." Melvin leaned into her and started licking on Simone. Simone felt the wetness and the slow strokes of Melvin's tongue on her and returned to paradise. She had nothing on her mind but what was being done to her body. She felt so relaxed that she got weak in the knees. She dropped down and sat Indian style on the floor.

"Why you stop me? You can't take it, Wonder Woman?" He pushed Simone on her back and grabbed her legs and put them behind her knees with his long, strong arms. He began to eat her pussy like he was sucking on a melting ice cream cone. With every stroke, her body got closer to climax. She tried to resist as long as she could. She did not want to cum so soon, but it had been a long time since she had had sex this good. She wanted to savor the moment, but she could take it no longer.

"Go 'head, muthafucka, lick this pussy and make it explode!" As she said it, her body began to jerk, and she gyrated in his mouth. He was far from done.

Melvin picked Simone up and gently laid her on the bed. He stood up, put on a condom, and admired Simone's body. She still had on her two–piece, but her legs were open, revealing what the crotchless panties allowed.

"Girl, I want to take you away. I want to take you to an island and fuck you on a private beach of all white sand." Simone blushed and pictured it perfectly.

"Let's do it," she replied without thinking. She told herself that it would be better to kill him on a vacation anyway, that a lot of people die from natural causes when they travel. She didn't realize that she was only lying to herself.

"Candy, listen, I'm a real nigga. When I say something, I do it."

"So do it then. You said it already."

"I got you. Let me finish taking care of this first." Melvin slowly crawled in between Simone's legs and entered her. He put her legs underneath his chest so he could go deep, and he stroked her long and slowly until her body released again, this time slow and calm.

Melvin began to build his momentum. Now that he had taken care of her, he was ready to get his off. He pumped her forcefully, long and hard. She stared in his face as he looked down in hers.

"I want you, girl. I want you right now." Melvin began to moan and jerk. He growled, "Aw, shit! I'm cummin' all in this shit right now!

"Candy, you got that shit. You one of them got-it girls. You got it, baby." Melvin rolled over and lay on his back next to Simone. He kissed her on her lips and she put her arm on his chest and they fell asleep.

About two hours later Simone woke up. She looked over at Melvin and looked down at her pocketbook. He was in a deep sleep, and he was lying flat on his back. She looked in his face and tried to read his thoughts, his hopes, his dreams. She wanted to know if he would be someone who would mean anything to her life if she spared his. She didn't know him, but she wanted to learn about him.

Simone stared at Melvin for a long while, trying to muster the energy and motivation to take the syringe out of her bag and stab him in the heart with it. She wanted a reason to follow through, because he had already given her reason not to.

Melvin's eyes opened and he saw Simone staring at him. "What's up, pretty Candy? You checkin' me out I see. You want me to go back to sleep so you can keep getting your stare on?"

Simone sucked her teeth. "Nigga, I was just about to wake you up. I wasn't staring at you." She was relieved that he awoke before she forced herself to kill him. She promised herself she would do it if they went away on vacation or not; she just wanted to spend some more time with him first.

"Candy, did I tell you how good you feel?" Melvin started rubbing his hand along her cheek. She nodded yes and smiled. "So, I want to know who I'm feeling good with. I want to know the real you. I don't even think Candy is your name. When I say it it's not like it triggers a natural response in you. It's like you don't even know who I am calling when I say it."

Simone's face lost the grin and she tensed up. She reminded herself what she was really there for. "What is it that you want?" she asked and thought to herself, *Because I can end it for you right here and now.*

"Oh God, why chicks always gotta ask that question? I want to rock with you. I want us to rock out. I don't want this to turn into some bullshit where we realize that it was just a fuck thing and say fuck it. But right now I gotta get to you. Take this fuckin' wig off." Melvin playfully snatched Simone's black wig off to reveal her blonde hair. Simone got mad and grabbed it out of his hands and ran to the bathroom.

She looked at herself in the mirror and felt that a layer had been removed from her outside, a weight lifted. She felt that Melvin had uncovered something that she wanted to get to herself—her insides, her feelings. She went to put the wig back on but didn't want to. She wanted him to see her. She wanted him to know her name too but knew that he couldn't.

She fixed her blonde hair and adjusted her outfit. She was not ready to be naked in front of him, but she wanted him to see what she really looked like. She walked back out into the room. Melvin turned from looking at the television to Simone. His mouth almost dropped.

"You are beautiful. Can I get to know you? Can I uncover your desires and wash away your tears? I want to knock that wall down and cover you with my protection. Come here," Melvin demanded firmly in a sexy voice.

Simone went over to Melvin and sat next to him on the edge of the bed. He ran his fingers through her hair. Just then, Simone's cell phone rang. She excused herself and went into the bathroom.

"Hey, I got thirty thousand for you, but I need you now. Meet me at Madison Square Garden in exactly one hour," the voice on the other end said.

Simone said okay and hung up. She came back in the room and said, "I gotta go, Melvin." She didn't even want to leave him.

"Okay, but I got the room until the morning. Why don't you come back when you finish what you have to do?" Although she wanted to, she refused.

"I have a lot of running around to do with my sister tomorrow. When are we going away, *Mr. I don't front?* I need a vacation. Now. What about this weekend?" Simone didn't care that she sounded pushy and was rushing him; she needed a vacation. She knew that Melvin's days were numbered, and she wanted to have as many good memories as she could with him before it was all over for him.

"Where you wanna go, Princess? That's what I'm gonna call you until you tell me your name. Candy sounds like a hooker, and a princess is what you are." Melvin was falling hard for Simone.

"I want to go to Saint-Tropez since all the rappers be talkin' 'bout that shit. Let's go there for, like, three days." Simone put her hands on her hips.

"You got it," Melvin said and pulled her down to him and kissed her cheek.

Simone put her clothes back on over her lingerie and walked to the door. Melvin called her back over to him. She bent down and he whispered in her ear. "Make me love you, Princess."

Janay

Janay woke up and looked around her hotel room. After receiving her money from Western Union the day before, she went and purchased a few pieces of lingerie for Rich. She was going to make sure that he would be her new puppet on a string. Her phone rang from a blocked number, and she picked it up.

"Hello." Janay grabbed the television remote and turned the TV on.

"Is this Janay?" an unfamiliar voice asked.

"Who wants to know?" she asked rudely.

"This is Mr. Burrows. I have some of your money. Where can I meet you?" the voice asked. Janay did not remember what Mr. Burrows' voice had sounded like, but she assumed that it was him since he said it was.

"Did you get my number from Mr. Jamison?" She sat up excited, hearing *cha-ching* in her mind and seeing dollar signs in her eyes.

"Yes, I did," he answered.

"Okay, so you decided to cooperate? That was a great choice," Janay said confidently.

"I'd like to know where to meet you face to face."

Janay got an instant eerie feeling but ignored it. "Well, I'm out of town. I'm not in Atlanta right now, so it'd probably be best if you just wired it to me." Janay smiled in the mirror that was opposite the bed and quietly clapped her hands.

"Well, I am in New York on business, so I was hoping that we could meet. Mr. Jamison told me that he wired you money to New York. I am willing to work with you, but there are some things I would like to discuss with you."

She didn't trust the voice. "What is it that we have to discuss? You know what the situation is. You got yourself in a situation that I want to help you get out of. I'm sure you have a family that you want to protect and not expose to one foolish night that you had from drinking too much. Not to mention drugging." Janay was not going to back down; she was going to play hardball.

"Well, if you want the money, you will meet me. I will be at the Boat Basin on Seventy-ninth Street at eight o'clock tonight. I will be in a black Lincoln Town Car. Make sure you are alone." The person on the other end hung up.

Janay had eight hours to devise a plan on how to get the money without the trouble that she felt was lurking behind that phone call. She thought of who she could call to protect her. She had cousins in Paterson who were thorough and criminal. Her and Brielle's Aunt Janice was a crackhead and a drunk, with three bad sons. Janay called her Aunt Janice's number, and she answered sounding fucked up.

"Who the fuck is this?" Janice's groggy and scratchy voice answered.

"Aunt Janice, it's Janay. Where's the boys at?" She wasn't interested in talking to her aunt. She knew how she was doing—still smoking crack since the last time she saw her after Dante's funeral.

"Who? Oh, Janay. Oh, Butchie and Shoo Shoo locked up. I don't know where Monk is at. Where you at? You got some money?"

"What's his cell number?" Janay was either going to ignore her aunt's beggin' ass or curse her out, and she didn't have time to be bothered with her. "Come on, Aunt Janice, it's important. What's Monk's cell?"

"Damn, Janay, you always got a fuckin attitude, yo country ass. It's 862-329-4387." Janay hung up after entering the number into her phone. She dialed her cousin's number and a girl answered.

"Hello, can I speak to Monk?" Janay was feeling anxious and nervous from the call, but she knew that she couldn't let them intimidate her or she would lose. This was a fight that she had to win; she needed the money.

"Who is this?" the girl asked probingly.

"It's his cousin Janay and it's important. Can I speak to him?" Janay had no intention of being polite.

"Hold on... You got a cousin named Janay?" Janay heard the girl ask her cousin. She heard Monk tell the girl yes.

"What up, cousin? What's going on with you?" Monk said when he put the phone to his ear.

"I need a favor. Can you come to New York?"

"For what? Is there money in it for me, 'cause I know you about to have me involved in some bullshit. And I got a baby on the way. I can't be beatin' up cats for you and shit, and then you go right back and be with them, like you did to me when we was teenagers," Monk said jokingly but meaning what he said for real. Everyone in the family knew that Janay was grimy.

"Shut up, Monkey, this is serious. You wanna talk about being a teenager, I'ma put your nickname on blast. Now, I need you to come with me to pick some money up. I got you. Just make sure you have yo piece wit you," Janay said in a low but serious tone.

"Listen, Janay, you gonna have to tell me what the deal is." Monk was not in the mood for trouble.

"I just did. I'm going to pick up some money. I don't want to go by myself because I'm a woman, and it's this shady white dude. But he's a suit-and-tie guy; you don't have to worry about him. I just want him to know I'm serious about this paper he owes me. So what's up, you wit it?" Janay asked persistently.

"How much money you giving me?" Monk was not impressed with Janay's slick talking and knew his cousin was grimy.

"If he gives me the five thousand, then I'll give you a thousand, damn." She shook her head at her cousin's greed.

"Damn what? I just told you I'm about to have a baby. I need that paper."

"Okay, okay, damn. That's why I don't deal with my family—everyone is for self. Meet me at the George Washington Bridge at seven. I'm going to order a car service to pick me up and then pick you up. Just call me when you get to the bridge, and I'll tell you what I'm in." They agreed and hung up with no further discussion or conversation of how any of the family members were doing.

Janay took a shower and put some jeans and a short-sleeve T-shirt on with her sneakers. She was not trying to look cute. She had business to tend to. She went to the restaurant in her hotel, had lunch, went back to her room, watched a movie, took a nap, and had the car pick her up at six o'clock. A Hispanic man in an old, brown OJ picked her up. She had him drive to the George Washington Bridge and wait for her cousin to show. She felt comfortable knowing that he would be there with her. Janay's phone rang at 6:45 p.m., and it was her cousin.

"Yeah, Monk, where you at?" she asked nervously.

"I just stepped off the bus. I'm coming down the escalator. Where you at?" As he walked out on the street, he noticed his cousin waving him over from a car across the street. Monk crossed over and gave Janay a hug and kiss and joined her in the car. "What's up, cousin?" he asked, smiling. "You lookin' good."

"Yeah, well, it's a good thing you didn't see me a few days ago. I was stressin', losin' my damn mind. But shit is starting to look up. I'm getting this paper from these dumb-ass crackers. You lookin' good yourself. Well, you always was the cutest out of the three of you."

Monk flashed his charming smile. He was short, stocky, handsome, and muscular. He had deep dimples in the middle of his mocha-brown cheeks, eyes that were chinky like a Chinese man's, and thick eyebrows that showcased them. He was gorgeous.

"So, what you stressin' about?" The two were genuinely happy to see each other. They had spent many childhood summers together, both in New Jersey and in Georgia. They had many good memories.

"Brielle and her fuckin' crazy-ass man. She got me caught up in some shit. I have a murder trial starting in four days. I gotta get this money up just in case she decides to do some bullshit with the lawyer." Janay looked at Monk, hoping for sympathy.

"Yeah, I heard. You know I always thought she killed Cousin Tony," Monk confided in Janay.

"Shit, she did. She finally admitted it to me when I was up here for Dante's funeral. The bitch wasn't happy enough to get off on her husband's murder; she had to have his bitch killed too."

"So you did that shit, Janay?" She turned her head away, which gave him the answer. "Damn, girl, so how y'all bitches get caught?"

"I gave that bitch up before she gave me up," Janay said malevolently.

"Yeah, but my mother told me that you told before you even got a lawyer and sat down with Bree. That's wack, Janay, man. You should have held out; you ain't have to tell that fuckin' fast. You should have bailed out, brought it to her, and seen how she was gonna act. You the one that folded, Nay Nay." Janay got mad that Monk was taking Brielle's side.

"Damn, nigga, they had my blood at the scene. Brielle would have left me for dead in there."

"Nah, you buggin'." Monk looked at Janay and shook his head.

"What?! Fuck it. That bitch gotta pay if I gotta pay."

"Yeah, but neither one of y'all would have had to pay if you would have stuck together. Anyway, so what is this money shit right here about?" Monk looked for flaws in Janay's story to figure out if she was being straight up with him.

"I filmed these two corporate white boys who are married with children doing drugs and fucking each other and shit." Janay smiled at the shocked look on Monk's face.

"What?! Yo, you a crazy bitch. So, you blackmailing these niggas?"

Janay smiled and nodded her head yes while Monk shook his at her again.

"So, who's the chick you having a baby by? A new one?" Janay asked sarcastically. Monk looked at her strangely.

"Yo, Janay, what's wrong with you? Why do I have to be having a baby by a new chick? Why can't I still be with my first two kids' mother? No, I'm still with Tanisha. We are rais- ing our kids together. What, you don't think that's possible because we are from the hood?" Monk shook his head at Janay's ignorance.

"First of all, that's good that you are with the same girl, raising your kids, but it didn't sound like her, and she didn't say hello to me when I called, so I thought it was someone else. When is the baby due?"

"It wasn't her. It was her nosy-ass sister who was using my phone at the time and took it upon herself to answer it... It's a girl, my first daughter. Her name is Nia and she will be here in three weeks. I can't wait. And I'm gonna marry Tanisha next summer. Is that okay with you?" Monk looked at the picture of his pregnant girlfriend on his phone.

"Of course. You should have married her ass already, but we all know black men don't like to marry their baby mothers and make honest women out of them. Now, when we get there, just go to the car that the guy is waiting in and tell him I'm in this car and just to give you the money," Janay instructed bossily.

They pulled off of the West Side Highway and into the Boat Basin on 79th Street. There were only two cars in the parking lot. One was the black Town Car, and the other was a yellow cab. Their car pulled up alongside the black car and Monk got out. He knocked on the back window of the backseat door. Janay picked Monk's phone up off of the car seat and began to go through his text messages to see if he was cheating on his girl, to just be nosey.

The door was unlocked and Monk leaned in and got in the car. The car's windows were all tinted. Janay could not see inside the car to identify Mr. Burrows, but she really didn't care if it was him as long as he sent someone with the money.

A few minutes passed and Janay again tried to look inside of the black car. Just as she was about to get out of her car and knock on the window, the black car's back driver's side door opened, and Monk's body fell out of it and onto the ground. Janay screamed ,"Oh my God!" and jumped out of the car to see what was wrong with her cousin. The car screeched in reverse, turned around, and sped out of the parking lot too fast for her to get the license plate number. Janay screamed in anguish as she inspected her lifeless cousin. Blood was gushing out of Monk's head, and his clothes were soaked in blood. His eyes were shut and his mouth had no breath coming out of it. Janay yelled to the driver to call 911.

"Monkey! Monkey! What happened?!" Janay tried to wake Monk to no avail. He was dead. Janay hugged him and held him tightly in her arms while she sobbed helplessly. The driver stood over her and Monk as he told the 911 operator their location in Spanish. She tried to ask him if he got the license plate, and he shook his head no, without any other means of expressing himself to her. Janay looked down at her cousin and saw no pain, just the face of another young man dead in the street, a father who would no longer be there to raise his children. Her cell phone rang from a private number.

"Hello? What did you do that to my cousin for?" Janay ranted hysterically.

"I told you to bring no one. You are lucky because that could have been you. I suggest you destroy the tape and move on with your life. Be glad you were spared."

The phone hung up while Janay screamed, "Who is this?!" She dropped the phone and continued to wail in sorrow over her cousin's death at her hands.

Janay heard the sirens of the ambulance and police and turned around and saw them approaching in a blur through her water-drenched eyes. The EMS workers quickly jumped out and ran to Monk's body to try to see if there was anything they could do to revive him. Unfortunately, they pronounced him dead on the scene.

As the emergency technicians worked on Monk, the detectives who responded to the shooting call tried to question Janay.

"Miss, can you tell us your name?"

"Janay Roberts." She was trying to think of the story that she was going to give, but she couldn't think straight. All she could think about was her dead cousin.

"Miss, what is your relationship to the deceased?" One officer spoke to her while the other jotted down her answers.

"He is my cousin," she answered, still crying and wiping her tears. The Spanish driver went into the car and brought her back some tissues. They were awaiting an officer to come and question the driver in Spanish.

"Can you tell us what happened?" the officer asked cordially.

"My cousin came with me to pick up some money from somebody who owed me, and the guy shot him when he got in the car."

"Okay, so you know who shot your cousin? That's good. Can you tell us what happened from beginning to end?"

"We drove up. He got in their car. They shot him and threw his body out."

"So, Miss Roberts, did you see who shot him?" The officer looked Janay in the eye.

"No, I didn't see him shoot him because the windows were tinted, but I saw my cousin's body fall out of the car, with blood gushing out of his head. He saw it too." Janay pointed at the driver of her car. She was becoming agitated. "Officer, my cousin was just killed in front of my eyes. I can't do this right now." Janay did not want to give any more details because she did not want to tell the whole story.

"Yes, I understand that, ma'am, but we are hoping to catch the person who shot and killed your cousin." Janay let out a gasp at the sound of the officer's words and started sobbing extra hard. She buried her head in the officer's chest, hoping to buy herself some time.

"I have to call my aunt. I have to tell his fiancée. Oh my God, he has a baby on the way. Oh my God, I feel like I'm going to faint." Janay put her hand up to her head and her other arm on the detective to help herself remain standing. The officer signaled for the second ambulance that had arrived to help. Two emergency techs ran over and began to administer vital-sign tests on Janay. Holding both of her arms, they walked her over to the ambulance.

"I feel sick. Please make sure I am not going to have a heart attack! My cousin! Monkey! Monkey! Why'd they have to kill you?!" Janay was yelling at Monk's body, which was still on the ground, with a cover over it. The body was awaiting the coroner's arrival. "Monkey! Wake up, please!"

"Calm down, miss, please have a seat inside of the ambulance so that we can check you out." Janay dramatically climbed into the back of the ambulance with their help and continued to wail and rave. They performed some preliminary tests on Janay, while she attempted to raise her blood pressure with her hysteria. She was uncooperative as they tried to survey her current health and stability.

"I need to go to the hospital! I am having chest pains!" Janay put on an Oscar-worthy performance.

The ambulance workers immediately strapped her to the gurney and rushed her to Columbia-Presbyterian in Manhattan. As she was being rushed there, she tried to get her story straight in her mind, because she knew the cops would be visiting her at the hospital.

Simone

imone took her gloves off and pulled her shades off of her eyes. She leaned up to speak to the driver.

"Damn, Peter, that guy was cute. I'm sorry that I had to blast him like that." The Italian man who was driving the black Town Car looked in the rearview mirror at Simone and smiled.

"You know, Simone, I have met a few chicks with balls in my days, but I have to say, you are one of the ruthless ones. You showed that guy no mercy. You shot him before his buns got all the way down in his seat."

"Mr. Sicily, I follow orders. Johnny said someone was trying to put his cousin in a jam. He said shoot the girl and whoever comes with her. I shot him and waited for her to approach the car. She never did and we couldn't be sitting ducks with a dead body in the car. If he needs me to find the girl and take her down, I will." Simone was nervous but came across confident.

"I know you will, Simone. She sounded frantic when I made the call. Hopefully, she will get the message and back off and spare her own life. She sounded like a firecracker when I spoke to her this morning, so you never know. If she keeps up the game, she will end up the loser. But you are right; following orders is the way to go. You going back home?"

"Yes, you can drop me back home. I should have gotten a look at her but it's okay. We may have to cross paths again real soon."

"Oh, I wanted to see if you were up for some gambling at Yonkers Raceway." Peter Sicily was itching to scratch his gambling habit and thought that Simone's attractiveness would transfer to luck for him.

"Peter, you really need to try to stop the gambling. Haven't you lost enough because of it?"

"I know, Simone, but your beauty will bring me luck, I'm sure. I've lost so much that I will never get back. Can I at least have the enjoyment of my favorite pastime? When my business partner died, everything went downhill for me. My jewelry stores are suffering. My wife left me. The only thing that I enjoy is gambling. It makes me think that I can possibly win everything back."

"I guess it's hard out here for everyone, huh?" Simone said, not the least bit concerned for Peter Sicily's plight. She knew his story. He was a washed-up boss who lost his position in the Family because of his gambling habit, poor business practices, and constant feuds he has had within the organization. His nephew Joey was one of Simone's clients, whom she had done about five "jobs" for to date, and Peter had been her driver each time. She felt comfortable with Peter, although she trusted no one.

"Hey, life is short. You gotta take the ups and downs. I have nothing else to lose," Peter said wistfully.

Mr. Sicily asked Simone where she wanted to be dropped off. She texted Melvin that she was hungry and on her way back to the hotel. He texted her back that he couldn't wait to see her lovely face. She told Peter to drop her off at the Hilton in Times Square, which he did. She figured being with Melvin was way better than going home alone, like she normally did.

Simone felt no remorse over the day's murder. She had just been given thirty thousand dollars cash, all in hundreds, and it was making her pocketbook feel like a suitcase. As far as she was concerned, it was well worth it.

Simone went up to Melvin's room, and he was lying on the bed butt naked. She was open on him and loving every minute of him.

"Come get on this thing here." Melvin held his penis in his hands until Simone took her pants off. She went to straddle him and he stopped her. "No, take that off. All of it. I want to see all of you."

Simone did as she was told and dropped her two-piece on the ground. She lay on her stomach the way Melvin told her while he entered her from the back. He talked to her in her ear the whole time he pumped on her. He told her how much he could do for her and how good she looked and felt and how he meant every word that he was saying to her. Simone believed his every word.

About an hour later, when they finished having sex, they both agreed to go out to eat at Blue Fin, an upscale Sushi Bar. As they were walking across from their hotel to the restaurant, they did not see Joey Patron, Peter's nephew, sitting in a chauffeur-driven Town Car outside of their hotel.

Joey saw Simone and Melvin holding hands and walking across the street. He had been told by Peter where Simone had requested to get dropped off, because something had told him her story about Melvin standing her up just wasn't right.

He dialed Simone's cell phone after they were inside the restaurant to see if she would answer. She looked at Joey's number in the phone and did not. He gave her the benefit of the doubt and decided not to set up a hit on both of them where they were staying because he figured maybe she had gotten in touch with Melvin and was going to carry out the job that night.

Simone and Melvin had a good time eating and talking. He told her about the company that he worked for and how successful he had been as a sales manager. He didn't pry too much into her life, but just let her begin to feel comfortable in his.

They spent the night together and awoke early for Melvin to go to work and Simone to go home and get ready for Brielle to come and pick her up.

Brielle:

Brielle woke up Monday morning and remembered that she had a meeting with her therapist. She threw on a peach-colored Anne Klein pleated Capri pantsuit. Her hair needed doing, so she just put it into a bun.

When she entered the office, the white female doctor, Dr. Crawford, was waiting for her. Brielle followed her back into the private room and sat.

"Brielle, I know the trial is starting this week, so how are you feeling? Are you having nightmares or getting voices in your head?" She opened her pad and waited to write. Brielle crossed her arms and legs.

"Well, I haven't really had any horrible nightmares since I got out of jail, but I have been getting the voices," she answered without emotion.

"And you are against taking medication? I think you mentioned, correct?" the doctor asked.

"Yes, Doctor, I am. I don't need a chemical to control my mind. I just need a new lifestyle to rescue me from my old one. I may have done crazy things, but I am a product of what others have imposed on me. I didn't ask anyone to abuse me. I am ready to impose on myself the healing."

"Well, how do you propose to do so? Do you have a plan, and has it been put into motion?"

"No, I can't say that I have a plan. I do have some motivation, though. I am beginning to believe that God is the controller of my destiny, and if he is as good as people say and believe he is, then I am in good hands." The doctor looked at Brielle blankly, quickly wrote something, and cleared her throat.

"Well, that is good that you are starting to believe in a higher power, but you need practical means to mental health. You need viable methods to stay sane." The doctor shifted in her seat.

"No, I actually don't. I just need to continue to fight for my emotional and mental health. I can no longer let someone take their inner pain out on me. I am no longer going to be a victim of my past or anyone else's scapegoat. I refuse to."

"So, again, Brielle, what are you going to do?"

"I'm going to live and be free. I have a major fight ahead of me. I can't go feeling sorry for myself. I have to win this fight and then win the next one. Whenever life brings me trials, I have to fight to win, and I need my mind to be strong. I am willing and able," Brielle said confidently and with a huge smile on her face. She reassured herself as she spoke and thought about that woman who told her that yesterday didn't matter.

"Sometimes we feel that things are getting better and we don't focus on treatment and then the problems get worse."

"Dr. Crawford, I pay you one hundred fifty dollars an hour for you to ask me questions and for me to tell you what's on my mind. I have figured out that I was hated by the woman who created me, and that is very painful to experience. But my mom died a long time ago. She never knew me and never will. She will not destroy me any longer. I know that I chose men that had as many issues as I've had, so that we can both be messed up in the head. I have allowed other family members to abuse me, but from now on I live for me. I know my pitfalls; I just have to avoid them. I think counseling is great. It helped me see that I'm not doing all that bad, considering the circumstances I've been in. I'm doing much better. And I will continue to work on myself every day and leave the bullshit alone."

"Well, Brielle, do you wish to continue counseling with me? Or are you ready to try to go at it alone?" The doctor did not seem happy to Brielle. It was almost as though she wanted Brielle to be sick. *But then again, she gets paid for me to be loco.* Brielle laughed and stood up, her hour only half gone.

"You know, I am definitely ready to go at it alone. I thank you for all of your help, but I don't think that, with God, I am never alone."

Dr. Crawford stood up and shook Brielle's hand and said, "I'm here if you need to come back." Brielle smiled and closed the door to the office behind her. Brielle walked out of therapy with the belief that she would never ever be going back.

Brielle got in her Bentley Continental GT and called Simone.

"You ready, sis?"

"Yes, sis, I'm ready," Simone answered.

Brielle picked up Simone for a day of shopping, eating, and whatever they wanted to do.

Simone had on a pinstriped Tahari dress with a suit jacket and had her blonde hair done in spiral curls. The two were not only dressed to kill, but both had killed before, and neither knew just how treacherous the other one truly was.

Janay

Janay was rushed into the emergency room of the hospital, still complaining that her chest was hurting as they ran an EKG on her. She told the doctor on call that she was very upset that her cousin was just murdered and could not take any more excitement. She asked that the doctor not allow the police to question her until the next day. He agreed to do that.

She received a series of tests that took hours, and by the time she was given a room for observation, it was about midnight. She knew that her aunt had probably been notified of her cousin's death, and she was not sure how much truth she was going to give to her family either. She did not want to bear the responsibility of blame for Monk's murder and decided not to even call anyone and tell them where she was. It was Tuesday and her trial was starting on Thursday. She would try to remain in the hospital until Thursday morning, when she intended to sign herself out.

Janay woke up Wednesday morning to the knock on her door and entrance of two plainclothes officers.

"Good morning, Miss Roberts. Again, I am Detective Calhoun, and this is Detective Gruber. We would like to continue asking you some questions about the events leading up to the murder of your cousin, Montell Keys. How are you feeling this morning?"

"I am feeling horrible. Did my doctor okay this visit?" Janay sat up in her bed and pushed the nurse call button.

"Yes, he said that you seem to have been excited and anxious and for good reason; yet, however, not in any serious health danger. So, can you tell us again why you and your cousin were parked at the Boat Basin?"

"I was there to collect a debt." Janay was angry that they were allowed to enter her room without a doctor or nurse asking her permission first. She was wondering why it was taking the nurse so long to respond to her request for assistance.

"Okay, so what happened?"

"My cousin got in the car, and about three minutes later, his body was shoved out of the car and onto the ground and then the car sped off."

"So, do you know who was in the car?" They both looked at Janay intently.

"The guy who owed me the money," Janay replied flatly.

"And who is *the guy?*" the officer asked, sounding sarcastic.

"His name is Harry Burrows." Janay decided that she had no other choice but to be honest, because if it was revealed that she was lying, she might be suspected of having something to do with Monkey's death.

"And what is your relationship to this person?"

"He is a friend of a business acquaintance."

"And why did he owe you money?" The two men looked very interested in hearing the answer to that question as well. They were both standing at the foot of her bed, staring at her.

"He owed me money because he said that he would help me out with a court case that I had if I hooked him up with a friend of mine. We went out, I introduced the two, and he said that he would give me five thousand for setting up the blind date." Janay knew that Mr. Jamison would not admit to the reason he owed Janay the money, so she didn't feel the need to reveal the truth about that.

"Do you have his contact information?" one of the officers asked.

"No, I don't." Janay turned on the television set and tried to tune the officers out.

"Miss Roberts, we are merely trying to do our job and catch the person who killed your cousin. You said you saw Mr. Harry Burrows shoot and kill your cousin, Montell Keys; is that correct?"

Janay noticed that one of the officers was holding a tape recorder. "Yes. Mr. Harry Burrows killed my cousin. That is all that I have to say. I will not say anything else without a lawyer. Now, please, leave my hospital room."

The officers knew that they had to adhere to Miss Roberts' request because she was not a suspect or in custody, and they were in no way ready to charge her with any crime.

"Okay, Miss Roberts. We will be in touch." The two officers left her hospital room.

Janay spent the rest of the day watching TV, with her cell phone turned off. She did not know whether her family was calling her or if they knew that she was the last one to see Monk alive. She spoke to her lawyer, and they agreed to meet at a diner by the courthouse an hour before court would start to go over a few things. She was released from the hospital that evening, and she went back to her hotel room.

When Janay finally turned on her cell phone, she only had one message from Rich.

"Hey, Janay, I will be moving into my new place at the end of the week; however, I will be sharing it with your cousin-in-law for a few months. Call me when you get this message."

Janay was curious as to why Shawn was going to stay with Rich if he had planned on renting the place to him. She wondered if there may have been trouble in paradise with Shawn and Brielle. She quickly imagined herself in Shawn's bed and in his arms. She laughed at the vision and thought, *I would love that.*

Janay prepared her suit that she would be wearing to court the next day and got ready for bed.

Janay woke up early the next morning and was at the diner, waiting for Mr. Cifelli. He walked in about two minutes after she did and found her based on the description given to him over the phone. He walked up to her, introduced himself, shook her hand, and sat down.

"How are you feeling today, Miss Roberts?"

"I am just ready to get this over with. Will we be sitting with Brielle and Mr. Rabissi?" she asked.

"Yes, we will be at the same defense table; however, usually, the court will split the two cases. We are making a motion for the two of you to be tried together."

"Is that a good thing to do?" Janay asked calmly, in order not to sound worried.

"Yes, because we will show how Ms. Prescott was attending a funeral and how you have no motive. We are trying to get both of you off, scot-free."

"What about my confession?" Janay asked, fidgeting in her seat and beginning to sound nervous.

"Well, oftentimes people confess under duress. Sometimes confessions are coerced. We already made a motion to rescind your confession, but the judge did not make a decision on that yet. We still will move forward with the trial, however. I would suggest that you remain confident in your mind, because it carries over to your demeanor, just as nervousness shows. So, just think positive. Are you ready? We will meet them over at the courthouse now."

Janay and Mr. Cifelli walked silently together to the courthouse. When they got in the courtroom, Brielle was seated next to Mr. Rabissi, but Shawn was not present. Janay gathered that something must be going on between the two, especially after the message she received from Rich. She was going to pretend that everything between she and Brielle was fine in the eyes of the attorneys, and Brielle planned to do the same thing.

Brielle stood up and turned around when she saw Janay and Mr. Cifelli approaching. The two cousins gave a loose hug and gave fake love and kisses on the cheek that barely touched skin.

"Hey, Brielle, where's Shawn?" Janay used the moment as an opportunity to pry.

"Oh, he had to go out of town on family business." Brielle knew that it was going to be hard for her to play the role, but she had to do it. "How are you? I haven't spoken to you in a few days."

"Oh, I'm good. I'm staying at the W Hotel in Midtown. I will probably start staying with Rich at Shawn's place once he moves in," Janay lied.

Brielle cringed at the thought of Janay staying at Shawn's brownstone. She wondered why Shawn would still be renting the place out since they were broken up. She wondered if he already had a new girl and a new home away from home. She kept a straight face.

"Oh, that's good. So, things must be going well with you and Rich." Brielle flashed a fake smile, which was returned to her by Janay.

Just then, the bailiff ordered the courtroom to rise and receive the judge. They stood along with everyone else, and then Brielle and Janay sat down.

Brielle looked around the courtroom, hoping to see Shawn appear in one of the many spots that she had been looking for him all morning. The door to the courtroom opened when all were directed to be seated and in walked Simone.

Simone was dressed like she was attending a funeral. She had on an all-black sleeveless linen dress with a wide-brim hat and large Chanel shades. Her dress had large pearl-colored buttons going down the back of it, matching her pearl-colored Michael Kors bag, and her expensive hosiery had a seam down the back that accentuated her three-inch black alligator slingback shoes. She looked like Jackie O.

Brielle smiled when she saw Simone. Janay turned around and looked Simone up and down and turned back around without acknowledging her. Simone took a seat in the first row, behind Brielle and Janay's table.

Brielle

Judge Champlain read the case, and the prosecution began to present their case to the judge and jury. Brielle looked over the jury and was curious as to why the jury was predominantly white. She leaned over and questioned Paolo. "Why aren't there more black people on the jury?" she asked, concerned.

"The prosecution dismissed just about everyone we tried to select. It's okay, though; some of them have participated in the Civil Rights movement. One is married to an African-American man...don't worry." He patted Brielle on the back.

The state district attorney made his opening statements. "Ladies and gentlemen, my name is Aaron Lewis. I have been a prosecutor for twenty years, and I must say that this is one murder that has caused me many sleepless nights. I just cannot fathom how two women can be so conniving, so vindictive, and so crass that they can orchestrate the murder of a woman who is eight months pregnant. These two young ladies—who are family, I might add—did just that. They plotted, planned, and carried out the murder of the late Monique Troy. They not only killed her, but her unborn child. I believe that they should be charged with the murder of the fetus as well; however, Monique Troy sat in her cousin's kitchen eating with her family when Janay Roberts stormed in through a back door and shot her in cold blood. The woman you are looking at, with the crimson hair, not only has hair like fire, but a heart that must be as evil as hell is. Janay Roberts carried out the murder at the suggestion and bribery of her dear cousin Brielle Prescott, who, I might add, killed her own husband shortly before this."

Mr. Rabissi quickly stood and yelled, "Your Honor, I object. My client accidentally killed her husband in self-defense, and that information should be scratched from the transcripts right now."

"Mr. Rabissi, your objection is overruled. Now, please be seated." Brielle immediately got nervous. She looked behind her at Simone, who gave her a thumbs-up to tell her that things would be okay. She noticed Monique's family staring at her with disdain. Her high school friend and the one who Monique was staying with had so much hate in her eyes. Brielle could not stand to look Shanta in the eyes, so she turned back around. Brielle could not believe that loving Dante had led to this.

The prosecutor continued as Brielle and Janay remained in the hot seat. "Thank you, Your Honor. That is very essential to this case. Brielle Prescott killed her husband because he was cheating on her with Monique Troy."

"I object, Your Honor. My client was never charged with murder; that is a false accusation."

"Sustained. Mr. Lewis, please keep your statements based on fact."

Mr. Lewis paced back and forth like a tiger ready to kill his prey. "I apologize, Your Honor. Monique Troy was pregnant by Dante Prescott, Brielle's husband. Monique Troy was killed by Janay Roberts, and Brielle Prescott paid her to do it. That concludes my opening statements."

There were gasps and reactions from Monique's family, and the courtroom was filled with sobbing and whispers.

Paolo stood up and took his position between the judge and jury and in front of the court. He nodded to Mr. Lewis and began. "Brielle Prescott was a battered woman. She was emotionally, mentally, and physically abused by her cheating husband. She lost three—not one, but three—children due to the stress of Dante Prescott. The night that she miscarried for the third time, her husband's mistress had pictures of the two of them together sent to Brielle's home. Brielle was upset and confronted her husband about it, and he tried to kill her. He tried to choke her to death. Luckily, my client was able to reach onto her kitchen counter, grab a knife, and save her life by taking his. This woman is a victim. She is not a murderer. Brielle Prescott wanted to move on with her life. She wanted to put the past behind her; however, Monique Troy began to taunt her, flaunt her pregnancy in Mrs. Prescott's face, and blackmail her. My client did not pursue Miss Troy. She tried to stay away from her. Miss Troy came to my client's home to ask for money. If my client was such a murderer, she could have killed Miss Troy then. My client was able to move on and find someone else who was willing to treat her kindly and marry her. She had no intention of ruining her own future by committing murder and going to prison. She may have had a serious and understandable loathing for the deceased Miss Troy, but on the day of Miss Troy's murder, my client was at her fiancée's mother's funeral. Brielle Prescott had nothing to do with the murder of Monique Troy."

Paolo sat down and Elliot stood up. "Ladies and gentleman, my client is Janay Roberts. Miss Roberts is being wrongly accused of murder. There is no evidence to prove that Janay killed Monique. There is no gun, there are no witnesses, and she certainly had no motive. Although the two defendants are cousins, Miss Roberts would not put her freedom on the line to murder someone that she did not know, whom she had no conflict with. My client is an innocent bystander. She was in Brooklyn with a boyfriend at the time of the murder. My client is innocent."

Mr. Cifelli sat down and patted Janay on the leg. Janay was hoping that that was enough to get her off, but she knew that the trial had just begun, and she was ready and willing to turn her back on Brielle again if necessary.

The prosecutor stood up and began to present the evidence. "These men, who are being paid very well, I'm sure—"

"Objection, Your Honor," Mr. Cifelli stood up and called. "How much we are being paid has nothing to do with this case." He readjusted his tie and sat back down.

"Objection sustained. Again, Mr. Lewis, stick to the relevant details of the case."

Mr. Lewis cleared his throat and said, "Yes, Your Honor. These two attorneys are claiming the innocence of their clients, claiming no motive. Well, there most certainly is motive on both of these ladies' parts. Brielle Prescott had Monique killed because she did not want to have to give her any money. Brielle Prescott had Monique killed because she didn't want to have to face seeing Monique around town with her dead husband's child. Monique was killed because Brielle Prescott felt slighted. Janay Roberts killed Monique Troy for the money. I am ready to bring the first witness to the stand."

Shanta was called and she got up and walked past Brielle and rolled her eyes at her. Brielle was instantly angered and rolled her eyes back. Shanta was given a Bible to take the oath on, and then she sat down in the witness chair.

"Miss, please state your full name," Mr. Lewis directed at Monique's cousin.

"My name is Shanta Latice Davis." Shanta looked at Brielle and Brielle looked right back at her.

"And what is your relationship to the deceased?" Mr. Lewis tapped his foot on the floor, awaiting Shanta's response.

"She was my cousin." A tear rolled down Shanta's cheek.

"Miss Davis, I know this is hard for you, because you were there when she died. Can you describe the night that your cousin was killed?"

Shanta used a tissue to wipe her eyes and began to speak. "We had a nice day that day. We went to buy the baby's furniture for her room." Shanta wiped her eyes again and continued. "We went to the grocery store. Monique's favorite food was lobster, and she had a craving. We had some lobsters steamed at ShopRite and went home to enjoy them." She stopped talking and was choked up. She put her finger up to request a minute.

Brielle discreetly looked around the courtroom to analyze the reaction. Monique's family was all crying. The jury looked sympathetic. Brielle looked at Janay with disdain and thought, *Bitch, you just had to run your fucking mouth, didn't you? You better hope we get off.* Janay returned a loathful stare at her cousin Brielle.

Shanta continued. "So, just as we were finished eating and about to scrape the plates—well, actually, my daughter was up scraping her plate and I was taking the garbage out back—I saw someone run past me and into the house. I ran behind the person, and they pointed the gun at Monique and shot, like, three times. Monique's chair fell backwards and she fell back onto the floor. My girls started screaming and the person ran out. I started running after them, and then when they got out of my yard, I ran back to try to help Monique." Shanta buried her head in her hands and began to sob. The prosecutor looked from Brielle to Janay and shook his head at them while tapping his feet and giving Shanta a few seconds to compose herself.

"Miss Davis, we are almost done. I know this is extremely hard. So, you said that your daughters were there; correct?"

"Objection, Your Honor. The witness already stated that her children were present."

"Overruled, Mr. Cifelli. Please be seated."

"Yes, my daughters were there." Shanta looked at Janay with contempt. "They saw their pregnant cousin killed."

"How many people did you see, and can you identify them in this courtroom right now?"

"One person ran in and was alone. I can't because the person was in all black, with one of those hats that only has openings for your eyes and mouth. I couldn't see the person's face at all."

"Thank you, Miss Davis. I have no further questions."

Brielle and Janay's defense declined from cross-examining Shanta because they knew that would be seen as malicious and mean by the jury. They probably would request to question her at a later date.

Shanta wept as she walked past the defense table. She gathered some phlegm in her mouth and spit on Janay as she passed. The spit landed on the side of Janay's face. Janay jumped up to assault Shanta, and Mr. Cifelli grabbed her arm.

The court officers were about to run over when Janay and Mr. Cifelli sat down. Janay wiped the spit off of her face and had to hold it until a tissue was requested and brought to her.

Brielle wanted to laugh and say, "Yeah, I feel the same way. I should have spit in her fucking face for telling," and then her mother's voice said, *No, bitch, you should have killed her!*

Brielle instantly begin to cry out. She grabbed her head and started banging it to make her mother's voice stop. "Why are you still bothering me?! Leave me alone! You are still ruining my life!" She got up and started screaming, "Stop! Stop! I hate you!"

The judge began to bang his gavel on his podium and demanded that Mr. Rabissi control Brielle. Simone ran around the divider and grabbed Brielle and shook her. Brielle's eyes were glazed over. Simone whispered for her to get herself together. Paolo Rabissi and the rest of the onlookers had horrified looks on their faces.

"This court is in intermission! Counsel, approach the bench."

Mr. Rabissi went to the judge, who asked him how much time he needed. He turned around to see Brielle sobbing in Simone's arms. Her head was buried in Simone's chest. He turned around and asked for an adjournment until the next day.

"This court will resume tomorrow morning at 9 a.m." The judge tapped his gavel and watched intently as Brielle was put back in her seat. Simone's calls to her did not seem to get through. Monique's family began to talk and complain among themselves that Brielle should not be given any sympathy or the chance to end the court session. The bailiff announced that everyone had to leave the room. Another one walked over and told the legal team that Brielle could stay until the room cleared out. Mr. Rabissi thanked the judge, who removed himself to his chambers.

The prosecutor took his time talking to Monique's family, who seemed to be asking why court was being adjourned. After they left Janay cut in to Brielle.

"Bitch, are you crazy?" Janay sneered at Brielle in a low voice so that they would not get kicked out but not low enough for the prosecutor not to hear. He looked over at the two women and noticed the tension between them.

He walked over and asked Mr. Cifelli to talk with him. They went out into the hallway to conference, while Mr. Rabissi tried to understand what was going on.

"You just made us look guilty as hell. What the fuck is wrong with you?" Brielle began to come back from her daze and Janay continued. "You start crying after the witness gets off the stand? Are you trying to fry me?"

"Listen, Janay, I don't want to hear shit that you have to say right now. We would not be here if you didn't open your fucking mouth."

She regained her composure and addressed Paolo. "Paolo, I am very sorry. I have been having some issues dealing with some things that happened in my past, and I just became very overwhelmed. Is she right? Did I mess up our case?"

He looked at her, very concerned, and thought before he answered. Simone was listening for the answer just as intently as Brielle and Janay were. She was worried about Brielle. "Well, it was a disturbing outburst, and it came at a not-so-good time. Shanta Davis is the only witness that the prosecution has. I mean, they have character witnesses for Monique that we will object to hearing, because we are not attacking Miss Troy's character. We must show sympathy to her. But you have a right to be upset. Any innocent person would be upset to be on trial for murder, so it may not have that much of an impact. However, it cannot, in any manner, happen again. Are you okay to proceed, or do we need to try to have the trial postponed until a few weeks pass? Is there anything that we need to share with the judge that may help him give us a few weeks?"

"I don't want to wait weeks for this to be over. Why Brielle has to always act like a psycho is a question that I would love to have answered," Janay said disgustedly.

"And why you didn't have loyalty to her instead of telling is a question that I would love to have—"Simone began to say when Janay cut her off.

"Listen, little Brielle, you don't even know the half about your half-ass sister anyway, so keep your mouth shut." Janay looked to Mr. Rabissi to ask him a question when Simone responded to her comment.

"And you don't know me, so I suggest you keep your comments to yourself," Simone said and stood up to challenge Janay.

"Ladies, I really don't think this is the place for this and I see that you two really are not on each other's team and that is going to show. It's basically like this: Either the two of you are going to get off or the two of you are going to go to prison. I don't see it happening any other way. You two need each other."

Mr. Cifelli came walking back into the courtroom and asked Mr. Rabissi to come over and talk to him. Mr. Rabissi asked the ladies to excuse him. Janay sat down and put her head in her hands.

"Listen, sis, you gotta tell me what's wrong. What can I do to help?" Simone whispered in Brielle's ear.

Brielle looked at Janay and back at Simone and decided against telling her to kill Janay, although that is what she really wanted to do. "I just need to return to counseling. I have a lot on my mind."

"Is everything okay with Shawn?" Simone asked.

Brielle looked again at Janay's head, which was still down, and shook her head no while saying yes to Simone so that Janay would not hear her say no.

"Good, we will talk when we leave here." Simone sat back down behind the defense table. Brielle and Janay waited to hear from Mr. Cifelli what Mr. Lewis had requested to talk to him for. The three ladies were quiet and kept to their own thoughts while waiting.

After about fifteen minutes the two lawyers came over. Mr. Cifelli spoke first. "Ladies, this is a very serious case, and you cannot show discord between you. The district attorney just asked me to take a plea where Janay confesses and turns state evidence towards Brielle for a five-year sentence. That would mean that Brielle would have no leg to stand on and probably face a life sentence, since New Jersey abolished the death penalty in 2007."

Brielle looked at Janay, who smiled back at her. "Well, if you think I am paying your legal fees so that you can turn on me, you are crazier than you claim I am. Mr. Cifelli is a part of *our* team, not yours. If I don't pay him, he will not represent you." Janay decided against speaking her thoughts. She would ask Mr. Cifelli in private if she could pay him herself and separate their cases. She would gladly do five years to see Brielle rot in prison.

"Relax, Brielle, I am on *your* team," Janay said sarcastically, while Simone sat behind them, looking at Janay in disgust. "So, what did you tell him, Mr. Cifelli?" Janay asked, putting him on the spot.

"Well, naturally, I told him that I would talk to you about it. However, I can only represent you if it is not in conflict to our first client, Brielle. If you are interested in taking the plea bargain, you will have to find other counsel."

Janay did not think that that would be too bad of an idea. She just didn't have much money, and she knew that any lawyer taking on this sensationalized case was gonna want big bucks.

"Okay, so where do we stand for tomorrow?" Simone asked from behind them.

Everyone turned around. Mr. Rabissi looked at Brielle for permission to answer Simone's question and Brielle nodded yes. "Well, we will express to the judge and jury that you have been under a tremendous amount of stress and that you just felt very overwhelmed and that *we* apologize. The only two witnesses are Shanta and Janay. So, the next step is to get the confession thrown out. We will ask about that motion tomorrow. Our whole case and strategy really depends on whether he will let the confession be recanted and removed from the record. So, let's hope that we get a win tomorrow. Ladies, go home and get some rest."

The ladies gathered their purses and walked outside. Janay and Brielle said nothing to each other. Janay hailed a cab and left.

The two girls walked to the parking lot to their cars. Simone agreed to follow Brielle to her house. Brielle was impressed to see Simone's new burgundy tricked out BMW X6.

"Girl, what did you say you do again?" Brielle asked and laughed.

"I'm in between jobs right now, so I do what I gotta do to survive."

"Well, from the looks of my Bentley and your X6, we are surviving pretty close to living, girl. We are poppin'!"

"Oh God, Brielle! Nobody says that anymore." Simone laughed.

"Who cares what they say? I do me! Let's go!" Brielle got in her car, and Simone got in hers.

Simone pulled in front of Brielle's house and parked, while Brielle pulled in her driveway. Simone got out and, as Brielle was putting the key in the door, asked, "Are you okay? You scared me in the courtroom."

Brielle turned around and winked. "I'll be fine. I guess I'm buggin' out because I miss Shawn. My mind is starting to play tricks on me. I wish he was there today, but I don't blame him for not being there. I was a bitch to him the other night." Brielle flashed a fake smile and tried to laugh it off, but Simone didn't buy it.

"Well, what the hell happened? Why wasn't he there today?"

"I broke it off. I can't stand a lying-ass man." Simone was secretly glad that she may have a chance to have Brielle to herself, without Shawn being the center of Brielle's attention.

"Yeah, well, he should have still came to show support," Simone said in an attempt to give Brielle more reason to let Shawn go.

"That's a man for you. They all drop the ball," Brielle replied. Simone followed Brielle into the kitchen and looked around, feeling at home.

"Yup, they sure do. But don't worry, we have each other," Simone said, and Brielle had another message from her mom. *You better watch this girl. She is sneaky, like her whorish mother. She is not to be trusted.*

Brielle brushed her mother's voice out of her head without letting Simone notice her frustration. She realized that she had only been starting to hear her mother's voice again since she and Shawn had broken up.

"Yup, that we do." Brielle was eager for a chance to start a new beginning with her sister and without Shawn.

"Don't worry, sis. Everything will be all right; we just need to focus on the trial first. Do you think Janay is going to crack under the pressure and try to take the deal?"

Brielle sat down on the stool by the island, and Simone sat across from her. Brielle had a worried look on her face. "Simone, I'm gonna be honest. I wouldn't put it past her. She is a cutthroat. She is only for self. The only thing that will stop her from finding another lawyer is money. If she doesn't have the money, then she will have to stay on our team. But if she does, then it's just a matter of time."

Simone began thinking of a way to make sure that didn't happen. She was not going to let Janay ruin Brielle's life. She would start to put her plan together before it was too late. "You know what? Fuck Janay. She better not cross you, if she knows what's good for her. I didn't like that bitch the moment I laid eyes on her, and now I have a legitimate reason not to like her."

Brielle read into the subtle threat that Simone had made against Janay and addressed it. "Look, Simone, I can't take everything in my own hands anymore. It only leads to more trouble. I don't even want to think about it. Let's just see what happens in court tomorrow. For now let's pop this champagne. I was saving this one for the end of trial, but after today I might not be too good."

Simone shook her head. "I don't want to hear that negative talk and shit. It ain't going down, trust me."

The doorbell rang and Brielle opened the door to a deliveryman. He was holding three dozen yellow roses.

"I'm looking for Brielle Prescott," the driver said.

"That's me," Brielle answered curiously.

"These are for you. Enjoy."

Brielle signed for the flowers and eagerly read the card. The flowers were from Shawn and the card read, "I am not the same without you. If you take me back, I will forever be true. You are for me and I am for you. Love you for life, Shawn."

Brielle smiled when she read the card. Simone stood over her shoulder and read the card too.

"Girl, don't pay that no mind. He's another man who knows he fucked up. He should have thought about that." Simone walked back into the living room and sat back down.

Brielle put the flowers on the island in the kitchen and admired them for a few minutes and then contemplated calling Shawn. She decided to wait to call him after Simone left. Brielle felt like she was hanging with the twin sister she always wanted but never had. Simone was younger and more strong-willed and unforgiving than Brielle was. She felt like Simone was older than she was, and she looked forward to having someone who was loyal to her. Brielle was not going to let anything come between her and Simone.

Janay

anay got out of the cab at the W Hotel, where she was still staying, and received a phone call as she entered the lobby. She went to take a seat instead of going straight to her room.

"Hello," she answered.

"Miss Roberts, this is Detective Calhoun. Your cousin Montell did not have any identification on him. We know that you identified the body, but we need to notify his next of kin. He also had no cell phone. Who should we contact?" Janay thought as quickly as she could. She did not want her family knowing that she was connected to Monkey's murder.

"He has no family. He lives with me and my mom in Atlanta." There were a few minutes of silence on the other end of the phone.

"Well, in reading my notes, I see that you mentioned at the murder scene that you had to call your aunt and his fiancée. May I have their numbers?" Janay kept her reaction calm.

"No, I'm sorry, sir. I meant *my* mother, his aunt. His mother died years ago. His fiancée I don't know. He told me that day that he had some girl pregnant and that he planned on marrying her, but I don't know who she is. It was the first time he mentioned it to me."

"So, does your mom know? May I have her number?"

"Yes, of course I told her. We were all he had. It's so sad."

"Well, will you be having a funeral service here, or will he be buried in Atlanta?" Janay wondered why he was so curious about this. She figured he didn't believe her story and was trying to make her crack under pressure.

Janay recited her home number as her mother's number, knowing that the detective would get the machine.

"My mom is really taking this hard, so she may not be up to talking. We are going to cremate his remains. That is what he said he wanted us to do if anything ever happened to him. When will his body be released to me?" she asked as innocently as she could.

"Well, we are still investigating, so I can't tell you that yet. Do you have any more information that might help us with the case?"

She shook her head, thinking it's typical of the police to want everyone to do their job for them. At that moment she realized that she should have held out instead of giving up Brielle. She shrugged her shoulders to return to not caring about Brielle. Brielle had a new puppet; she didn't care about Janay, so Janay wasn't going to care about Brielle.

"I was going to ask you the same question. You haven't found anything out?"

"Well, nothing concrete. There was a call with a license plate, but the plate on the car seems to have been a dummy, from a nonregistered car that was reported stolen years ago. They must have been professionals. But don't give up hope; tips come in that help all the time. Give us a call back in a few days, and I should have an answer on the release of your cousin's body."

Janay said okay and hung up. She wanted to call Mr. Jamison but she was scared. She didn't know if he was in on Mr. Burrows' plan to kill her. She took Monk's cell phone out of her pocketbook and plugged it in with the charger that she had bought for it before going back to her hotel. There were numerous text messages. She couldn't listen to the voice messages because Monkey had a password. The phone rang. She answered it.

"Hello?"

"Who the fuck is this? Where is Monk?" a very upset girl screamed on the other end of the phone.

"Bitch, who are you? I'm his girlfriend. He is busy," Janay said calmly.

"His what?! I'm having his baby. Let me speak to Monk. And how long have you been seeing him? We have three kids!" the girl screeched angrily.

"So what, bitch? He don't want you no more! Stop calling this phone!" Janay hung up. She felt bad for the girl, but she couldn't tell her the truth. She figured that would be better for her pregnant ass to hear than that her man was dead. The girl called back so many times that Janay turned the phone off.

"Damn, this is fucked up." Janay spoke out loud, feeling angry instead of sorry.

"Monk was only trying to help me. Why did he have to die?" She punched her fists as if she was about to fight someone.

Janay needed a distraction from her anguish. She thought about Rich and called him.

"Hello, stranger. What have you been up to?" Janay was not in the mood for joyful talk, but she needed something to do.

"Oh, I've just been taking care of some business. I would love to see you, though. Where are you?"

"I'm at Shawn's brownstone. You want to come through?" Janay's eyes lit up.

"Sure. I'll take a cab. Be there shortly." Janay was going to find out what was going on with Brielle and Shawn and hopefully get at Shawn. *He probably realized how crazy Brielle was and left her insane ass alone, leaving room for me to step in,* she thought.

Janay took a shower and put on some extra-tight jeans, stiletto sandals, and a seductive blouse. She was ready and her game face was on.

She went outside and hailed a cab to Harlem. *Please let Shawn be there.*

The cab pulled up to the brownstone. She paid, walked up the steps, and rang the doorbell. Shawn came to the door and opened it. Rich must have told Shawn that Janay was coming because he did not look surprised to see her.

"Hey, cousin-in-law," she said and leaned in to kiss Shawn. He stepped back and let her in, ignoring the attempt she had made to kiss him. He knew Janay was grimy and wasn't going to play her game. He did not care for her and didn't care if she noticed it or not.

"Rich walked to the store; he'll be right back," Shawn said with regret. He did not want to be caught anywhere alone with Janay, let alone his house. Brielle would really kill him if she found that out, and he knew that Janay had a vendetta against Brielle.

"Oh, no problem. So, I didn't see you in court today. Is everything okay with you and Brielle?" Janay asked innocently.

"Yes, everything is fine. I had something that I couldn't get out of," Shawn lied with a cool demeanor.

"Oh, so then you will be there tomorrow then?" Janay sat on the couch, hoping that Shawn would notice her breasts bulging out of her sleeveless shirt.

"Uh, most likely. I have a business to run so that I can pay you guys' legal fees, you know. You both are in good hands with Rabissi and Cifelli, so there's no need for me to worry. I just gotta get that paper up to make sure they do the job right." He gave a fake chuckle and turned to go upstairs to his room.

"So, where's Brielle?" Janay pried further.

"She's with Simone," he said, throwing the dig back.

"What do you think about *that* Simone? I don't trust her." Janay tried hard to entice Shawn into conversation.

"I'm glad that Brielle has someone that she could be close to. It's sad that the two of you have such animosity with each other now." Shawn wanted Janay to know that his loyalty was to Brielle no matter what.

"You don't know Brielle like I do. She's been messed up in the head her whole life."

"Listen, Janay, I don't have anything personally against you, but I love Brielle. I want to marry her. We all have issues. We have all been a product of our environments, tragedies, and upbringings. No one is in a position to judge anyone else. I have to go lay down; excuse me."

Shawn went upstairs and Janay was slighted by his rejection of her interaction with him. Her desire to win against Brielle was getting the best of her. She sat and pondered her next move. Rich still hadn't come back after a half hour, so she decided to look around.

Janay walked upstairs and noticed Shawn's bedroom door closed. She quietly turned the knob to his bedroom and saw him sleeping. She tiptoed in his room, took off her clothes, and used her camera phone to take pictures of her naked body in front of Shawn. She positioned herself in front of the bed, with him lying down in the background, and took various poses. She was rushing because she didn't want Shawn to wake up nor did she want Rich to come in and catch her. When she found the perfect shot, she hurriedly grabbed her clothes and snuck into the bathroom to get dressed.

She made her way back down the stairs and back onto the couch just as Rich was coming in.

"Hey, how long have you been here? Why didn't you call me to tell me you were here already?" He lifted her up and gave her a hug and kiss.

"Oh, I just got here. Shawn let me in and said you would be right back, so I didn't want to bother you. How's it going with the two of you?"

"Oh, Shawn is truly a generous dude. He could have made me wait to move in until he was ready to move out, but he understood my urgency to have a place to lay my head that wasn't a burden to my friends and family."

"So, you never told me why he didn't move yet." Janay rubbed on Rich's penis through his pants. He instantly got hard.

"Oh, he didn't really say. I've been trying to stay out of his way. I don't want to impose on him. But I'd like to impose on you. You wanna see my room?" Rich took Janay's hand and led her to the back of the brownstone behind the kitchen. There was a bedroom off to the left, across from another bathroom. Janay was mad that Rich's room wasn't across from Shawn's so that she could mistakenly walk in Shawn's room with no clothes on and act like she had made a mistake coming from the bathroom after having sex with Rich. She figured she'd give him a chance to see what he was missing.

"Oh, so at least you have your own part of the house." Janay sat on Rich's bed and looked around it.

"Oh yeah. Two grown men need their own space. I wouldn't want Shawn running into you naked, coming from the bathroom." Rich laughed and Janay laughed at the fact that she was just hoping the same thing *would* happen that he was hoping wouldn't.

"So, let's christen the room. This will be the first time we are doing it in *my* bed." Rich began to rub Janay's breasts and lift her shirt up.

"Okay, we can do that. But after that can you go get me something to eat?" Janay was not ready to give up the opportunity to be in the house alone with Shawn. She tried to convince herself that Shawn was just playing hard to get and that all he needed to do was see her body without covering, and he would want to take a shot.

"Sure. I can go around the corner. There is a great Spanish restaurant. Well, we can go together," Rich said, clueless.

"Maybe. But I may want to lay in the bed butt naked and wait for you to come back so I can *feed* you some more after you *feed* me."

Rich smiled at the thought. He pulled off the cargo shorts that he had on, and his penis was exposed through his boxers. Janay pulled him toward her by the back of his knees. She put his penis inside of her mouth and began to caress it with her tongue. It began to grow in her mouth, and she played tricks with it. She looked up at Rich, who was looking down at her. She stared in his eyes and thought, *I wish you were Shawn.* She slurped on him and made him a slave to her wet strokes. He began to gyrate and attempt to put all of himself down her throat.

She went in for the kill and moved her head up and down as fast as the speed of light. Rich began to moan and she knew that her job was almost complete and she knew that her customer-satisfaction rating would be very high. He let out a long moan, and she felt his salty discharge in her mouth. She held it in her mouth and went to the bathroom to spit his cum in the toilet.

"I would have swallowed if it was Shawn." She laughed.

Janay returned to Rich's room, where he was stretched out on his back, with his private tool still exposed.

"Damn, girl, you know what you are doing." He patted the bed for her to sit next to him. "I'm really curious to know why you don't have a man with a tight head game like that."

"Because no man is worthy of my undivided attention. Would you like to apply for the job?" she asked seductively while rubbing on his chest.

"Nah, I just came out of a marriage; commitment is not in my vocabulary right now, but like I told you before, I'm very honest. I won't play games with you. You will always know where I stand."

"So then, what am I here for?" Janay asked as if she wanted a relationship with him, knowing that she could care less.

"Janay, we are both adults, and we know that rushing into things can bring disastrous results. Well, at least by the time we are adults, if we have had relationships at a young age, that is one thing we all should have learned. I just met you. I'm getting to know you. I won't make any promises that I can't keep."

Janay laughed at him on the inside and thought, *Please, you are not the one.* "Well then, could you at least keep your promise and go get me something to eat?" Janay wanted one more shot at Shawn, because she didn't know whether he would be there again when she came there.

"Even though you just sucked the life out of me, you did it so good, I can't say no. What would you like?"

"Bring me the Spanish food that you were telling me about."

"Why don't you take the walk with me?" Rich asked as he dressed.

"I don't feel like it. I just put in some major mouth work. I need to rest it so I can eat." They both laughed. "Go 'head now; that drink made me hungry."

"You nasty, girl, you nasty…" Rich sang, like the old Biggie song.

"Yup, and damn proud of it. Now go!" Janay got up and followed Rich to the door to have an easy getaway up the stairs once Rich left.

Janay got to Shawn's door and listened for sound. She didn't hear anything. She slowly pushed the door open. Shawn was dead to the world. She gently pulled the covers off of him

and figured her only chance to change his mind would be se-
ducing him. She noticed his penis hanging out of his boxers
and got on her knees. She crawled up and put her mouth on
him.

Shawn jumped up and could not believe his eyes. He sat up
and stuffed himself back inside.

"Janay, what the fuck do you think you are doing? Do you
know Brielle will kill you if she found out?" He grabbed a pair
of basketball shorts and put them on.

"Yeah, but why would she have to find out? We are grown
adults, Shawn. Come on, I just want the chance to know you. I
won't tell her and you don't have to." Shawn grabbed Janay's
arm and led her to the hallway. He shoved her out of his room.

"Janay, I love Brielle. I thought I made that clear downstairs. You think I don't know that you just want to use me to
get back at her? I'm not going to be your pawn. And where the
hell is Rich?" Shawn got ready to close his door, and Janay put
her hand on it to stop him.

"Come on, Shawn, please? Just let me get a taste. I think
about you a lot. I know that if you would have met me first, we
could have been a nice couple." Shawn shook his head and was
shocked at Janay's audacity.

"Rich went to the store to get me something to eat. He ain't
my man, so what does it matter?"

"Janay, go back downstairs or you will leave out of my
fucking house, bitch! I feel sorry for you. You don't even realize how twisted you are mentally, and you talk about Brielle?
You need help." Shawn slammed his door in Janay's face and
locked it.

She yelled to him from the other side of the door, "Oh, it's
like that? What if you let me suck you, and if it's good, you
give me a shot?" Janay could not stand being brushed off, and
it made her feel even worse that she was being rejected because
of Brielle.

"Janay, get the fuck from around my room before I tell
Rich! I'm not responsible for that man, and if he can't tell that

you are a skank ho, then that's his problem, but you will not come in between me and Brielle!"

Janay shrugged her shoulders and walked back downstairs. She went into Rich's room without remorse, and got in Rich's bed. She would have to settle for him for now, but she sure was going to hold those pictures of herself in Shawn's room for the perfectly opportunity. She knew they would come in handy one way or another.

Shawn

Shawn paced the floor of his room. He wanted to call Brielle and tell her what had just transpired with Janay, but he didn't want her to switch it around and try to place blame on him. He knew that she had probably received the flowers by then and was hoping that she would call to say thank you.

He decided to pick up the phone and call her to see what kind of mood she was in, but her voice mail picked up. "Brielle, I need to see you. We really need to talk. Things cannot end this way." He hung up and left the house. He wanted to be nowhere near Janay. He felt that because he rejected her, her wrath would only grow stronger, as she had a point to prove. He knew that it wasn't the last he would hear about Brielle.

He called Paolo to find out how the day in court had gone. "Hey, Shawn, we missed you today in court. Is everything okay?"

"Sure, I just couldn't make it. Why, what happened?"

"Well, Brielle had sort of a breakdown." Shawn immediately got nervous. He knew that would not be a good look for Brielle.

"What kind of breakdown?" Shawn felt a lump in his throat. He missed Brielle so bad and knew that whatever happened probably wouldn't have if he had been there.

"Uh, after the witness, the cousin, got off the stand, Brielle started screaming as if she were screaming at someone. She was saying, "Leave me alone." It was really weird and it couldn't have been at the worst time. I don't mean to impose or pry, Shawn, but I've known you a very long time. Is everything okay with Brielle?"

Shawn thought about how to answer the question without going into too much detail. "Brielle has had a lot of trauma in her life. She has some unresolved issues with her deceased mother, and when she is under pressure, she reverts back to bad memories of the abuse she received from her mother as a young girl. I've got to make sure she goes back to counseling." Shawn really didn't want to tell Paolo that they had broken up.

"Well, I think you should be there tomorrow. She was probably even more nervous because you weren't there. She didn't seem as confident as she has the couple of times that I have seen the two of you. I gotta tell you, man, it was really eerie."

Shawn shook his head at the thought of Brielle having a fit in the courtroom without him to calm and comfort her. Again, his mind confirmed for him the fact that he was not going to move on. He had to have her back so that he could love, protect, and care for her. That was his desire, not his obligation.

"I know. I'll make sure I'm there. See you in the morning. Thank you for telling me. Oh, before you hang up, do you think it will negatively affect the outcome of the case? Did the outburst make her look guilty?" Shawn awaited Paolo's reply as Paolo tried to put the answer as nicely as possible.

"Well, the jury didn't seem to be too concerned for Brielle's anguish after having heard Shanta's tearful recap of the night's events. And then the prosecution offered Janay five years to turn state's evidence against Brielle."

"What! What did the jealous bitch say?" Shawn realized what he had said and excused himself. "Pardon me, Paolo, I'm just aggravated. I don't mean to be hostile against you; you have nothing to do with this."

"No, it's okay. I tell you, the tension between those two is too thick to cut with a chainsaw. I mean, those two really hate each other. And Brielle's little sister seems to be ready to take Janay somewhere and beat her brains out. I tell you, those three women scare me worse than the mob." They both laughed.

"Yeah, you know what they say, 'Hell hath no fury like a woman scorned,' and those three sure have had their fair share of contempt and mistreatment. They are emotionally bruised kittens. I don't know that much about her sister, but she sure seems to fit right in." They both laughed again.

"Well, Brielle is lucky that you still love her either way. You know most men wouldn't want to take that on as a project. I don't mean Brielle is bad, but you know what I mean." Paolo rethought his comment and explained.

"No, listen, me and Brielle have a lot in common, and, believe me, if I thought she was a lost cause, I most certainly wouldn't be bothered. Janay seems to be the unsalvageable one. That one is really a piece of work." Shawn's phone showed another call coming in.

He got off the phone with Paolo and answered Peter Sicily's call. He was not in the mood for him right now. "Mr. Sicily, what can I do for you?" Shawn asked dryly.

"I thought you were going to reach out to me. I told you I need some more money." Shawn's blood started boiling. He needed to get this matter out of the way so that he could focus on Brielle. He was tired of being blackmailed. He was going to have to get rid of Peter for good.

"Oh, I'm so sorry, Peter. I was trying to get the money up. Can you meet me tonight?" Shawn tried not to sound too angry, but calm.

"Oh, tonight? Uh, sure thing. Where do you want to meet?" Peter Sicily had a bad feeling about Shawn's unusual compliance without complaining.

"I'll get back to you. How much do you need?" Shawn began to put his plan in mind.

"I could use about twenty grand. I just came from Yonkers Raceway, and I blew my daughter's wedding money. I have to pay for the reception hall tomorrow."

"So, you just think I keep thousands of dollars to the side to fix your fuckups? You don't think I have a family and responsibilities?"

"I don't think you will be able to take care of that from behind prison walls." Peter Sicily was being arrogant and cocky as far as Shawn was concerned, and Shawn was going to bring him back down from that cloud.

"No problem, Peter. I'll call you in an hour to tell you where to meet me." Shawn hung up and dialed his cousin Rock's number.

"What's the deal, cuzzo?" Rock asked.

"Yo, I gotta get rid of Sicily, man."

"Might as well, nigga, instead of keep paying. Say the word. When?"

"Tonight." Shawn knew that he didn't need any trouble, but he was also fed up with Mr. Sicily. Enough was enough.

"Well, we need to make this airtight, man. I ain't trying to go back behind no bars. Come over here so we can put this together, man. Bryan is here already. How long you gonna be?"

"I'm coming now." Shawn hung up his house phone, threw his sneakers on, and got in his Benz. He didn't feel good; he felt pressure. He needed to relieve the pressure.

Shawn drove downtown to Rock's condo in Midtown. Rock's girl worked in the entertainment industry and had a lot of paper and a plush condominium. He was buzzed into the posh building and took the elevator to the fifteenth floor. Rock was standing in the doorway when Shawn got off the elevator, and he saw the stress in Shawn's face.

"Listen, we got too much to lose. We gotta do this right," Shawn said. He walked past Rock, giving him a pound, and inside to give Bryan a pound. He sat down and took a deep breath.

"Don't worry, man, it'll be okay," Rock replied.

Shawn didn't feel as optimistic.

"Don't pout nigga, let's do this!" Bryan said. "You know we got ya back, cuz."

"Yeah, but anything can happen. Anything can go wrong. I really don't want to take this risk, but I feel like I have no other choice." Rock passed Shawn an open can of beer. Shawn refused it. "We can't be drinking right now. We gotta put a plan together. Do y'all have any ideas? I'm supposed to meet this nigga tonight and give him twenty Gs. This is the last time this nigga almost gets a dime from me. He wants me to be his fuckin' black slave for life. It's a wrap."

"Now you talkin', nigga. Rock already got a plan." Bryan motioned for Shawn to listen to Rock.

Rock stood up, animated, and demonstrated his plan. "I say we let you meet him, give him the money, and then we follow him home and blast him on the way inside. That way no one who may see you get in the car with him can finger you. You will have an airtight alibi. Make sure you take your girl out to dinner somewhere, or as soon as he pulls off from you, go somewhere public where you know there will be cameras on you so you can prove you were at that place at the time of this nigga's death. Me and Bryan ain't got no ties to this nigga, so all we need to make sure is that no one sees us. Soon as he gets out of his car, we will blast him and peel off quietly. You dig?"

Bryan and Shawn sat there thinking about Rock's suggestion. "So, we need a car that ain't as big and white as your damn truck, Bryan. Even if we rent a car, the rental company knows who rented the car if someone calls in the license plate." Shawn was more worried than he had ever been in his life. He could not go to prison and leave Brielle out in the world to fend for herself.

"Listen, we gon' pay a crackhead to steal someone's license plate. We will put it on the car we drive and take it off and throw it out when we are done." Rock had it all figured out. Shawn smiled. "See, I'm telling you, it ain't that hard," Rock assured him confidently.

"Okay, so I'll go rent the car since I'll be driving my car to meet him. Who's gonna get the license plates?" Shawn was beginning to gain some energy and motivation.

"I will," Bryan said. "Since Rock devised the whole plan, I'll handle that."

"Okay, so where should I tell him to meet me?" Shawn asked.

"Well, tell him you want to meet him somewhere with a lot of traffic, so that he won't be suspicious. If you tell him to meet you in a secluded location, he may have something waiting for you. He may think something is up." Shawn was thankful that his cousins were willing to put their lives on the line for him, and he would do the same for them. "Does he live in Jersey?" Bryan asked.

"As far as I know, he still lives in Franklin Lakes, a rich-ass town in Jersey."

"Well, tell him Jersey. Shit, we'll follow him wherever he ends up." Bryan paced the floor, angry that this man has been able to get this off for so long.

"Okay, let me go and rent the car. Be ready about nine; it needs to be dark outside." Shawn got up and got to the door. "And no drinking. Get your minds right right now. This is serious business," he instructed.

"You got it, boss," Rock said.

"Come on, Rock, you have to drive my car until we get off the rental lot." Bryan got up and followed Shawn and Rock outside.

Shawn rented the car in New York but was going to have Mr. Sicily meet him somewhere in Jersey. Then he would drop by and pay Brielle an unannounced visit to see if she was up to no good.

The day seemed to speed by. Shawn rented the car and told Rock to wait for his call. He knew that Rock had the firearms covered too.

Before he called Mr. Sicily, he prayed. "Lord, I don't believe that I cannot call on you when I am doing wrong. I can call on you whenever I need you. I need you now. I need your protection, grace, and mercy. I don't need to go to prison. I need my woman back."

Shawn called Mr. Sicily and told him that they should meet in the parking lot of Wal-Mart on Route 46 in Lodi, New Jersey, at 10 p.m. It was a heavily trafficked parking lot and strip mall. Mr. Sicily very calmly agreed.

Shawn said, "That way neither one of us can pull any funny stuff."

"That sounds good to me," Peter Sicily said, and they ended the call.

Shawn left his house at eight-thirty, with Rock and Bryan in the rental car behind him.

Simone

Simone and Brielle talked and listened to music for about two hours. Then Simone's phone rang. She looked at her ringing cell phone and noticed Peter Sicily calling. She went into the bathroom by the kitchen, away from Brielle, to take the call.

"Hey, Peter, what's up? You got a job for me?" Simone whispered.

"I sure do, darlin', and I need you right now. How fast can you meet me at the Wal-Mart parking lot in Lodi?"

"In New Jersey? What's the address?" Simone wrote the address down. "Okay, I'll put the address in my GPS. How far is it from Fort Lee? I'm already out in New Jersey."

"Oh, you're real close. So, just meet me in the parking lot at nine-thirty. When you see my car, wait for me to pull out, and then pull out and follow me. We will drive somewhere and talk. And make it nine instead."

"Okay. So I'll see you then. If I have any problems, I'll call you back. How much money are we talking, Peter? Jersey is scary. The cops are always around. It's very risky."

"Twenty thousand."

"Okay, I'll be there." Simone hung up just as Brielle was knocking on the bathroom door.

"Is everything all right, sis?" Brielle asked, concerned.

"Oh yeah. I gotta go. I got a little date." Brielle smiled and nudged Simone's arm, and Simone nudged her back with her elbow.

"That's good, lil' sis. Have a good time," Brielle said and then seemed to frown and look like she had a serious thought. Simone picked up that something wasn't right.

"Oh, I just have a lot on my mind," Brielle answered.

"What are you gonna do about Shawn? Do you want him back?"

"I haven't been thinking about it. I've tried to push him out of my mind every time he pops into it, but I need to really think about it. Shawn was good to me, and I can't deny that. No man will care to make sure you go to counseling and get better.

Most will just walk away when they see things are heavy. Shawn didn't do that."

"Well, think about it then," Simone said, seeming agitated.

"What's wrong, Simone?"

"I just feel like he will do it again. They always do it again." Simone put her shoes on and grabbed her pocketbook off the island as Brielle followed her to the door. Brielle took a sip of her wine.

"Shawn is different. Or he was different." Brielle paused. "I know that I need him. I hadn't had any thoughts of my mother for a while. I had started feeling safe and sane, dammit. A couple of days without him, and her voice is popping back into my head again. Shawn is good for me."

"All right. If you feel like you need him, then call him," Simone said sarcastically. "I'll be here for you no matter what. If he fucks up again, I'll be here."

Brielle didn't like how Simone was being negative. "Simone, this is something that I must do for myself. I must decide on my own. I thank you for being here and caring, though; I do. You just met Shawn, so I can understand how you would view him, but he is a good man."

"If you say so, sis. I gotta go. I'll call you tomorrow," Simone said with an attitude. She opened the door and turned around. She and Brielle opened their arms and gave each other a hug. They kissed each other on the cheek and then looked in each other's eyes.

"Brielle, I'm glad that I met you and that we are sisters. I never would have thought that I would get another sister. I miss Mariah so much, but it's like you are making up for it in some way. You are more than a friend; you are my real sister. I will be here for you until the day I die. I'm not losing another sister." Brielle smiled at Simone's reiteration.

"Well, Simone, you are the sister that I always wanted but never had. What a miracle it is to be a grown woman and get a sister just when I need one the most. You are not an evil cousin"—they both smirked and thought of Janay—"but a real sister and I will be here for you until the day I die. I'm not losing my only sister."

"I think they call it a blessing, but what do we know about God? We are lost and scorned ladies," Simone said and walked to her BMW.

"Maybe we need to find out together!" Brielle yelled as Simone got in her car. She waved, started her truck, and pulled off.

Brielle went back in the living room and sat back on the couch. She thought about Shawn. She pictured in her mind the day that they first met and how good he looked when she opened the door and saw him standing there. She picked up her phone and dialed his number. The call went straight to voice mail.

Simone drove her X6 and thought about Brielle. She didn't understand why Brielle needed Shawn now that she was in the picture. Men were nothing to keep as far as Simone was concerned. They brought nothing but pain and misery to women. Simone hated men but she was still attracted to them. She never was attracted to the same sex. She thought about how attracted she was to Melvin. She knew that it wasn't going anywhere, so she pushed the thought of him out of her mind.

Simone looked at the clock in her dashboard, and it read nine o'clock. She set her navigation system with the address for Wal-Mart. It would only take her eight minutes to get to her destination. She put on Jeezy's "Trap or Die 2" to prepare herself mentally for street war. She had to reach the place in her mind where fear didn't exist and survival was the only option.

Simone pulled into the parking lot of Wal-Mart and circled around until she saw Peter's Lincoln. She pulled up next to him, and he nodded, acknowledging her. She stayed in her car as he had instructed but let him pull out of his spot and followed him out of the lot.

Mr. Sicily drove to a nearby Friendly's parking lot and pulled in. Simone followed and parked next to him. She got out and got into his car. He leaned over and kissed her cheek.

"Okay, girl, I hope you're ready. This is what we are going to do. There is a guy that I've been blackmailing for a while now. He's pretty fed up. I can hear it in his voice that he's ready to cancel out me and his bill with me, so I've gotta do it first. I cannot risk my life for his money any longer. He is bringing me twenty thousand. I am giving you the whole thing. I am going to let him get in the car, and you are going to shoot him. Since we are in New Jersey and not a secluded location, I will call the police and tell them that he tried to rob me. That strip mall has not yet installed cameras into their parking lot. I know this because I know the owner of one of the stores in there. They will be getting cameras in the lot in three weeks, so I will just tell the police that we had a business involvement a few years ago and that he called me and asked me to meet him somewhere so he could talk to me. I will say I told him that I had to pick up some money and then I could meet him. I will say he got in the car, pulled the gun out on me, and tried to rob me, so I shot him."

"So, what do you need me for then? If you are going to claim self-defense, why don't you just do it?" Simone asked.

"I have to get the money. I don't need to struggle with him and he gets the best of me, shoots me, and takes his money back. He will be caught off guard if he is looking at me, and you just pop him as soon as he sits down." Simone played the scene out in her head.

"Yeah, but he will see me in the backseat when he gets in the car." Simone was getting agitated.

"Then walk up to my driver's-side window like you're asking for directions, reach in, and shoot him."

"What if someone sees me? Then your story will be blown apart." Simone didn't like Peter's plan; he hadn't thought things out enough, and the place may be too heavily trafficked.

"It'll be dark outside. I am going to pull almost behind the buildings, like, on the side where people only park when the parking lot is full and they have to park there. It's off to the side of the lot." Simone still wasn't impressed.

Peter continued. "Okay, so what if you act like you're my whore for the night? I'll introduce you and your beauty will most certainly distract him. He will be off his guard, and then you can blast him from the front seat when he gets in the back."

"Listen, Peter, I am not trying to be involved in this when the police are called. I don't do interrogations; I don't make that a part of my plan. If you are going to claim that he tried to rob you, then he will need to be shot in the back, like, when he's trying to get away. But then, how can you be sure he will die? You can't shoot him in his head; that'll seem like it's personal."

"You can shoot anyone anywhere if you are trying to save your own life—"

Simone cut Peter off. "You didn't let me finish. So, he will need two shots to the back, and I will sit in the car to the right of you. When I see him open your car door, I will shoot him in the back. You will grab the money, and I will jump out of my car, pass you the gun, and act like I'm trying to call the police to help you. I will then get back in my car and drive off, while everyone will begin to start gathering around. If someone takes my license plate, I will tell the police all that I saw was the guy fall out of your car and I asked you if you needed me to call the police and you will say you told me that you know him, you will call the police, and that you don't need my help. And I hope nobody does turn my license number in, because if they do, I will want another ten grand. Do we have an agreement?" Peter Sicily knew that Simone meant business.

"Okay, you got it, hon," Mr. Sicily said reluctantly.

"And don't forget to shoot the gun off so that you will have the gun powder on your hands. And was this hit okayed? Did you get the word that you can get rid of this guy?" Simone did not want to be doing something against the mob, only for it.

"I don't need the okay. He doesn't work for the Family anymore, but they will not protect him because he's a nigger, and he is making off with a business that should have been kept *in* the Family. He was left a sanitation company by a boss."

"You sure where you are going to park is secluded?"

Peter nodded his head yes. "Remember, you will wait until he has his back to you, and just shoot two times," Peter said.

"I told *you* the plan, Peter. What kind of car is he driving, or what does he look like? Do you have a picture of him?" Simone asked sternly. She did not like the fact that Peter didn't have a picture of the girl who she was supposed to shoot the last time and ended up shooting the guy who had come with her.

"I don't have a picture. I told you this is not an ordered hit. I know he drives a burgundy Mercedes-Benz with New York plates. He is a tall, brown-skinned black guy with braids." For a second Simone thought it might be Shawn but put the thought out of her head. She didn't know enough about Shawn to know that he was exactly who Peter Sicily was referring to.

"Okay, let's go. I want to get this over with. You know, Peter, I know it's none of my business, but just because you are not a boss anymore doesn't mean you have to act like a driver. Get yourself together." Peter passed her the gun that she was supposed to use. It was his legally registered gun.

Simone got out of Peter's car and back into her own. She followed him back to the Wal-Mart parking lot, thinking about how washed up Peter was. He had gambled and messed up so much that he wasn't even in the ranks of the mob anymore. He had become a gopher who did anything for small change. She decided that she was going to start distancing herself from Mr. Sicily, because he was not influential enough for her. He was a major fuckup in her eyes, and she no longer had much respect for him, even though his money came in handy. She was going to get Joey to put her on with other mobsters to get better-paying jobs. The first problem was deciding what she was going to do about Melvin's situation.

They pulled their cars into the lot, and Peter parked in the far corner of the parking lot to find as much privacy as he possibly could. He knew that the parking lot did not have cameras in it, but he wanted to be off to the side to eliminate the number of possible eyewitnesses. Simone pulled her X6 to the right of Peter Sicily's car and held the gun in her lap. She lowered her seat as much as she could and waited. Her windows were tinted and she had some dark black shades on and put a scarf around her head but let her blonde hair hang down.

About fifteen minutes later Simone noticed a burgundy Benz pull to the side of the lot that they were on. Instantly, she knew by the outline of his body that it was Shawn. She had a few seconds to contemplate whether to follow through. She knew that if he died, she would have Brielle to herself, but if he lived, he might be able to identify her, and then she would lose Brielle forever.

Shawn pulled his car on the other side of Peter's and got out with a small bag in his hand. Simone leaned down in her chair and rolled down her window as he approached Peter's passenger's-side door. As Shawn pulled on the door to open it, his instincts had him look into the car next to Peter's, and he was shocked to see Simone's very familiar face.

Before he could say a word, Simone panicked and shot him in his stomach. Shawn ducked and tried to make it back to his car, with the bag still in his hand. Mr. Sicily jumped out of his car to try to grab the bag just as Simone shot at Shawn again. Shawn was kneeling down in the front of Peter's car with his gun drawn, staring in Simone's face. He was shocked that she was trying to shoot him.

Simone threw the gun out of her car and backed it up. She noticed two black guys in her mirror running toward their direction. She quickly put her car in reverse, backed out, and then put the car in drive and screeched out of the parking lot.

Simone drove as quickly as she could, without speeding and catching the attention of the police, to the George Washington Bridge. She paid her toll and traveled down the Henry Hudson Parkway in anguish. She could not believe that she had shot Shawn, Brielle's love.

She began to scream at herself, "You did it this time! You fucked up. That nigga ain't gonna die! Brielle will hate you for the rest of her life!"

Simone began to cry, "Mariah, I don't know what to do! What should I do now? My life is over! How can I fix this?" She sped downtown, feeling like killing herself. She had finally done that fateful job. The one that many hit men face—the job that ends it all and either winds you up dead or in prison for life.

She made it to the parking garage where she parks her car and ran inside her loft. She paced back and forth while downing every bottle of alcohol that she had in her place one label at a time. She paced, drank, and talked.

Simone took a swig from a bottle of Remy and asked herself, "What is my next move?" Her survival instincts began to kick in as she asked herself very important and relevant questions. "What if he dies? He got shot in his stomach. A stomach wound is very dangerous. If he dies, the guys that were running over weren't close enough to see my plate. They were coming from the middle of the parking lot. No one else seemed to be out of their cars or in the parking lot but them. Okay, so they don't know me or who I am. Good. Peter is not going to tell on me, because I can tell on him. He will probably stick with the story that he shot him because he tried to rob him. Okay. If he doesn't die, then he will know that I did this. But will he tell the police or do me himself? I don't know what type of nigga he is, but he from the city. He seems thorough, like he may have done time too. He may not be a snitch. Okay. Will he tell Brielle? No, not until after he does me in. Then he may just never tell her what happened. He surely won't want to tell her he had something to do with my death. So, that will be our little secret, me and Shawn's. So, I gotta get him before he gets me. That's if he's still alive. Okay. If the police come checking for me, I will tell them that I was just parked there, and I drove off when the gun started going off. I don't know anything, didn't see anything. Okay. What about Peter? Will he want to kill me if this nigga doesn't die? That's a hard one. I've been loyal. I've handled every job. Sometimes things don't go as planned. As long as I don't tell the police on him and he sticks to his story, I'm good with him. He knows I won't tell if he don't. Shit, this may not be so bad after all. I just gotta make sure Brielle never finds this shit out!"

Simone, still nervous even after convincing herself that everything was going to be all right, drank herself drunk until she passed out. She kept going over and over the scenario that she had worked out in her head, each time boosting her confidence that everything would turn out fine.

Shawn

Shawn felt his breathing getting heavy. He saw Peter Sicily come over to him and snatch the bag. He was sitting on the ground, and everything seemed to be moving in slow motion.

Peter backed up his car and sped off. Shawn's cousins were running toward him. He mustered up just enough energy to yell at them, "Get the fuck back in the car! Go handle that motherfucker and get my bag of money back!"

They ran back to the truck and took off out of the parking lot in the direction that they saw Peter's car go in.

Shawn knew that Peter would be more concerned about police cars than to realize his cousins following him. He felt himself going in and out of consciousness, and by that time there were three people over him, one calling the police from his cell phone.

"Don't worry, guy, they're on their way," is the last thing Shawn remembered the guy who called say to him before he passed out.

The ambulance and police came about three minutes later and put Shawn into the ambulance, while the police asked the three people and other latecomers what they had seen.

Actually, because of the location of the incident and the time that it had occurred, no one had seen anything. There were about twenty people gathered around, and only the three who were initially there had only noticed Shawn lying on the ground, not anything that happened beforehand.

Shawn was rushed to the trauma center at Hackensack University Medical Center and was induced into a coma because of the amount of blood that he had lost. He was in the intensive care unit.

Shawn was in three hours of surgery, and by the time he was out, his brothers and sister were at the hospital by his side. He was still induced. They decided not to call Brielle, because they didn't know the circumstances of Shawn's and her breakup.

They stood vigil by Shawn and prayed over and for him. His pastor, who had eulogized his mother, came to pray with him and his family as well.

Peter Sicily was nervous and jittery as he drove down Route 46 in anticipation of being pulled over by the police. He knew that because Shawn was alive when he left, the chances of him living were possible. He was not dead at the scene, and Peter had, at the last second, pulled off without going with his first plan. Things hadn't gone as planned, and he had to leave so that Shawn and his stories didn't conflict if questioned by the police. Peter knew that Shawn, being questioned by himself, would come up with a story that would make the incident appear random and not personal.

As far as where Peter thought Shawn would take the incident was something that he would consider at a later time. Peter kept checking his rearview mirror for the lights and sirens of an approaching pursuing officer.

He did not see any sign of them. He began to calm down some and drive easier. He cruised to the main street near his home and drove two more blocks to turn left onto his street. He was playing his classical music and thinking about life. He was glad that he had managed to take the bag of money from Shawn. That was a plus. He knew that if Shawn lived, there would be no more blackmailing, and they would have to verbally call a truce. Shawn was a man of his word and so was Peter. Peter's word was all he really had left. He would tell Shawn that their feud was over.

Rock and Bryan were following a good distance behind Peter's car. Rock was driving and they had immediately called Shawn's brother to tell him what had happened.

Rock said, "Listen, you gonna shoot him when he get out of the car?"

"Nah, I'm gonna run up on him before he makes it all the way out. If I shoot him from the car, I might not get him good enough. I gotta get out, blast him, and get back in. This ain't

Compton, nigga; we ain't doin a drive-by." They both started laughing, then Bryan said, "This gotta be perfect and precise. One false move could have a town of Jersey police on us." Rock agreed with Bryan.

"Now, he pulled over, pull over!" Rock did as Bryan commanded, and Bryan jumped out, ran up to Peter's driver's-side window, and pumped four bullets into the window. He reached in the broken window and leaned over Peter and snatched the bag of money and ran back into the car. Rock immediately pulled off and drove at a fast rate to get some distance between them and the crime scene before slowing down.

"Did you get him?" Rock asked, curious and wide-eyed.

"Did I get him? Nigga, he's got!" They both started laughing and Rock proceeded to drive to the hospital where they had to check on their cousin.

They went to the hospital and waited in the waiting room with other family members. They both were glad that they at least put a stop to the man who may have killed their cousin. The doctors said it would be days before they could give a prognosis on Shawn's physical state and his chance of survival.

Brielle

Brielle left Shawn a message that said, "Baby, I love the flowers and I love you. Call me back if you want to, and I hope you do, because I really love you."

She finished the second bottle of wine and, after eating, felt sick. She was nauseous and she broke out in a heavy sweat. She made it to the bathroom just in time to throw up in the toilet.

Brielle figured it was her nerves acting up because of the trial and the situation with Shawn. She dreaded having to go back to court, fearing another disaster might happen that would move her closer to a guilty verdict. She had forced herself to be strong when Shawn was by her side, but without him near and with her, she was starting to crumble. Simone being around her helped too. She needed some comfort and support. She needed Shawn.

Brielle wanted to call Shawn back. She thought about it and told herself, *Shit, I was just his fiancée a week ago. Why can't I call his ass right back?* Brielle picked up the phone and dialed Shawn's cell phone number again.

When it went straight to voice mail, she left another message. "Shawn, I need you to be with me in court tomorrow. It was a disaster today. I need you with me. I want us to work this out."

Brielle hung up the phone and had to rush to the bathroom to throw up again. She did not make it to the toilet and vomited all over the hallway floor. She started sobbing as she wet some towels and wiped it up.

"Who can I depend on? Why do I never have anyone to really love me? Why?"

Just as she said that, she heard a commercial coming from the television in her bedroom. It seemed to be much louder than the other programming that was on. She heard a man's voice… "Who can you turn to when you feel like no one is there? You can turn to Jesus. He is your best friend. He is your healer, your confidante, and your protector. What friend can be better than that?"

Brielle went to her bedroom door to look at the commercial. The voice she heard was that of Bishop TD Jakes, and he was promoting his Potter's House Worship weekend in Texas. Brielle was very interested in learning more. She decided to ask Simone in court the next day if she wanted to go.

Brielle was very tired and went to bed by eleven. She tossed and turned the whole night, knowing that if Shawn was there, she would have been sleeping like a baby. When she looked at the clock and saw that it read 3 a.m. and Shawn never called her back, she called his house phone.

"Well, damn. I called you twice and left messages and here it is three in the morning and your ass is not even home. What the fuck did you send me flowers for if you are already seeing someone else? I am not a toy, Shawn. I guess you changed your mind that fast. I guess it's really over."

She hung up and took two sleeping pills so that she could at least get five hours of sleep before having to get up and get ready for court. Before she knew it the alarm clock was ringing and reading 8 a.m.

Brielle jumped up and took a shower. Once out of the shower, the nausea returned, and she threw up two more times before leaving for court. She tried to dress classy and professional to build her spirits and make her look like anything but a contract killer. She had on a pinstriped silver skirt suit made by Betsey Johnson that was very Audrey Hepburnish. It was inspired by the sixties. Her patent leather gray pumps by Dolce & Gabbana were three inches high and very expensive-looking. She pulled her hair back in a bun to look as conservative as possible.

When Brielle got to court, she looked around for Shawn and Simone but saw neither of them. She was not happy to see Janay and barely gave her an audible hello, which Janay returned just as unenthusiastically.

Brielle was unusually nervous and jittery. Paolo noticed the flush look in her face and asked her what was wrong. "Brielle, is everything okay?" he whispered in her ear.

"Paolo, I'm feeling really dizzy and nauseous. I think I am just a bit overwhelmed." She drank a sip from the glass of orange juice that was on their defense table.

"Well, you know after what happened yesterday, they may think we are trying to pull something if we ask for another adjournment. Do you think that you can hold up for today and then maybe we can ask him at the end of the day to wait to resume until Monday?"

"I will try to do the best I can." Brielle wanted to crawl under a rock. She felt just that miserable, and the absence of her sister and her man made her feel worse.

"Did you speak to Shawn, Paolo?" Brielle asked, feeling herself getting upset.

"Yes. He said that he would be coming today, but I see no sign of him." Paolo loosened his tie a bit in anticipation of the type of day that he was going to have.

Brielle smiled and instantly felt ten times better after hearing that Shawn would be coming to court.

She tried to psych herself up to feeling better so that she would look better for Shawn. She knew that she looked just as messed up as she felt, but she was going to fight the feeling for the sake of feeling better when Shawn got there.

The judge approached the bench from his chamber, and everyone in the courtroom rose to their feet at the direction of the bailiff.

Brielle looked over at Janay, who, at the same time, looked back at her and gave her a smirk. Brielle was not in the mood for Janay's tricks and was two seconds from slapping her.

She knew that she could only stare back and give her a look of death. Brielle was sick of Janay and wanted to find a way to beat the case without her. She came to the conclusion that Shawn should not be providing her with an attorney.

Brielle was in a daze during the proceedings. She was daydreaming about Shawn, looking back and forth at the door, waiting for him or Simone to come through it, and trying to keep herself from getting sick right there on the table. Paolo sent his assistant to get her some crackers, and they were coming in handy with her nervous stomach.

The prosecution opened and the district attorney continued where he left off the day before, dishing dirt on Brielle.

"Good morning, ladies and gentlemen. We are here again to continue to prove the guilt of Mrs. Brielle Prescott and Janay Roberts—"

Paolo stood. "Objection, Your Honor. The prosecutor said he is here to continue to prove the guilt of Miss Prescott and Miss Roberts. These two ladies are presumed innocent until this case is closed and the jury reaches a verdict, Your Honor."

"Objection sustained. Mr. Lewis, please watch your wordplay."

Mr. Lewis nodded in acceptance of the judge's order and continued. "Ladies and gentlemen, this is a pretty open-and-shut case. You have a jilted wife, a pregnant mistress, a cousin in trouble and in need of money and willing to commit murder to get it."

"Objection, Your Honor." Janay's lawyer spoke. "My client has not been found guilty of any charges as of yet."

"Objection sustained. Mr. Lewis, do you have any witnesses to call to the stand today?"

"Yes, actually, I would like to call Detective Monroe to the stand. He is the detective who was at the scene of the crime and who took Mrs. Roberts' confession."

"Okay, well, we are not going to hear questions based on the confession as of yet, because I have not decided on whether the confession will be admitted into evidence or not. So, please, Mr. Lewis, refrain from any of those questions at this time."

"Yes, Your Honor."

The detective took the oath and answered questions regarding the scene of the crime. The questions were not detrimental to Brielle or Janay because neither one of them was there, but then the prosecutor asked the last few questions.

"So, Detective Monroe, was there any evidence at the scene that points to either one of the defendants?" Mr. Lewis looked Janay dead in the eye and then back at the detective.

Detective Monroe nodded his head yes and said, "Yes, DNA of blood collected at the scene matched that of Janay Roberts." Some spectators simultaneously gasped as he said that.

"Okay, so we know that Janay Roberts has been at that house. Is that a fact?"

"Yes, that is a fact, Mr. Lewis," the detective said, also looking directly at Janay, who had a scowl on her face as she looked at both of the gentlemen in front of her.

"Thank you, Detective. No further questions, Your Honor," Mr. Lewis said and returned to his seat.

Mr. Cifelli stood up and approached the bench to cross-examine the detective.

"Detective Monroe, can you tell the court where the blood of Miss Roberts was found?"

"It was found on the back porch, where the perpetrator entered and left the house from."

"Okay, so was there any blood found of Miss Roberts inside the house?" Mr. Cifelli looked at the jury.

"No, there was no blood found inside the home."

Just then, Simone walked in, wearing a conservative, taffeta baby blue skirt set that was trimmed with ribbon and baby blue Jimmy Choo pumps that looked like blue marble swirls. She was decked out as usual. Simone walked right up behind Brielle, who smiled and felt relieved to see her but was reminded that Shawn still hadn't come. Simone leaned over the railing and kissed Brielle on her head and took an empty seat about three rows back.

"So, is it safe to say that we don't know if Miss Roberts entered the home?" The detective hesitated, seeming to replay the question in his mind before answering.

"We did not find DNA evidence of her being in the home."

"Okay, does her DNA evidence outside of the home prove that she is the person who shot Miss Troy?"

"Objection, Your Honor. Her DNA being outside shows that she was at the scene."

"Overruled, Counselor. Please let the detective answer the question." The judge turned his attention back to the detective.

"No, her DNA evidence outside of the home does not prove that she is the person who shot Miss Troy." The detective seemed agitated to have to have answered the question with that truthful answer.

"Thank you, Detective Monroe. No further questions." The officer returned to his seat from the bench, and Mr. Cifelli returned to his seat.

The prosecution asked for the DNA expert to come to the stand and discuss the freshness of the bloodstains on the back porch. The medical examiner sat down after taking his oath. He expressed that the blood could have been no older than two hours. Mr. Cifelli re-asked the same question in terms of that information not proving the guilt of Janay. He also got the expert to agree that someone who was with her could have been the shooter. The prosecution objected, reminding the court that when Shanta testified, she said that only one person ran in and ran away. The objection was sustained.

The court proceeding was ending for the day. Brielle was happy that Simone had made it, because she surely did not intend on seeking comfort from Janay or going anywhere with her.

After the judge dismissed the jury with their rules of not talking to anyone about the case, Simone and Brielle joined hands and walked outside. Janay did not even bother to say good-bye as she went her own way.

By the time Simone and Brielle began to walk down the court steps, Brielle knew something was wrong. She felt woozy and faint and blacked out on the concrete steps.

The ambulance was called and Brielle was rushed to Hackensack University Medical Center, where Shawn was unconscious and surrounded by family.

Simone

Simone was allowed to ride in the ambulance with Brielle, who was out cold. The emergency-response workers were checking Brielle's vital signs.

Simone had decided to go to court because she figured that if Brielle knew anything about her being the one who shot Shawn, she would have called. She intended not to say anything since she did not know what the situation with Shawn was or if Brielle even knew. She knew when she got to court that Brielle didn't know, because she would have been distraught from worrying about him.

Brielle was taken to the emergency room and into a space to continue to be worked on. Simone went outside when she saw Joey calling. She was uncomfortable about lying to him but she had to.

"Hey, listen. What's going on? I spoke to you on Monday; it's Wednesday. Did you set that next date up?"

"Yeah, I'm gonna see him next Friday. He will be out of town on a business trip until then."

"Listen, do I need to let someone else handle this? There's a lot going on. Peter got killed last night. Did you see him? Did he have something going on?" Simone knew that she could not tell Joey that she was with Peter, but she tried to cover herself in case Joey got a hold of his cell phone.

"Damn, I'm sorry to hear that. That's fucked up. Are you okay?" Simone had to sound like she cared, although she didn't. "He called me last night to go gambling with him. Maybe he pissed someone off and made them lose a lot of money or something." She did not want to be involved.

"Well, somebody followed him home and shot him. Maybe you are right and maybe there's more to it than that. I need to meet with you. When are you gonna be available?"

Simone got a bad feeling. "Well, my sister just got rushed to the hospital. I'm all the way Upstate New York. What's the matter?"

"I don't want this black piece of shit turning evidence on me. How do you know he's out of town?" Joey knew that something was up because he saw her with Melvin. He began to suspect that she was becoming a turncoat.

"Joey, what makes you so sure that he is going to tell on you? Did you talk to him?"

"Simone, of all the things we've done together, this is the first time I'm feeling like something fishy is going on. Do you need to tell me something?" Simone wanted desperately to tell Joey that she was catching feelings for Melvin and that she believed that they could work something out to make sure he didn't roll over on Joey, but she knew he wouldn't be cooperative. He just wanted Melvin dead.

"Listen, Joey, of all the work we've done, you don't trust me yet? I've spoken to him plenty over the phone. He just doesn't seem like the snitching type. And wouldn't it make sense to let him know that you know the police are trying to get him to talk about you? Give the man the benefit of the doubt. Of all that we've done together, this is the first time I'm feeling like this might be the wrong move."

"Simone, my life and my freedom are on the line. Handle that motherfucker!" Joey hung up.

Simone called Melvin. "Hey, beautiful. I was just thinking about you. Can I see you tonight? And I want to see where you live." Simone wanted Melvin in her bed. She never brought men home, but this time things felt different. She wanted him to share her private serenity that she only had at home. Simone was not on edge when she was in the safety of her own home. She knew that it would not be a good idea to show him where she lived, just in case he didn't die when it was time to kill him. Then he would send the police right to her. *I don't want to kill him*, she thought to herself, finally admitting her feelings to herself.

"Okay, well, my sister fainted after court. When I leave from here, I will call you."

"Is this some real shit or that bullshit you women be doing, stalling a nigga out and frontin' and shit? Am I gonna see you for real or not?"

She loved his demanding personality. "Yes, I am going to see you. Why can't I see where you live then?"

"You can, after I see where you live. I asked first. Ha-ha, how you like them apples? Or should I say, 'How you like these nuts?' Call me. I want you tonight." Melvin hung up and left Simone blushing on the other end and hot in her pants.

Simone went back into the emergency room and to Brielle's holding area. Brielle was coming out of her daze but was still groggy.

"What did the doctor say?" Simone asked, concerned.

"They are running some tests. They should have some results shortly. Do you have somewhere that you have to go, because I'm fine?" Brielle tried to sit up but was too weak.

"No, I'm here with you for a while. At least until visiting is over." Simone rubbed Brielle's leg. She was really concerned about her sister and curious as to what the deal was with Shawn.

"Good, 'cause I lied. I'm not good. I called Shawn three times, and he has yet to call me back. Paolo said that he told him that he would be in court today, and he didn't even show up. That's odd. I mean, I could see if he didn't send me the flowers, but it just doesn't make sense."

"He's probably starting to enjoy his freedom," Simone said harshly.

"Simone, he said he wanted to be with me on the card."

"He's trying to buy some time. He just wants to keep you on a string." Brielle didn't like her negativity and decided not to mention Shawn to her anymore.

They sat and watched TV for a couple of hours until the doctor came back. He opened the curtain that divided her from the others in the emergency room and came in smiling.

"Miss Prescott, I hope the news that I am about to give you is happy for you."

Brielle looked at the doctor, confused. "I hope so too, Doc," Brielle joked.

"Well, Miss Prescott, there is nothing unhealthy about you. You are just expecting." Brielle thought that she heard wrong.

"Expecting? A baby? What?" She busted out crying and the doctor became the confused one.

"Uh, Miss Prescott, there are options. This does not have to be a bad thing even if you don't want this child."

"Doctor, if you only knew how bad I want this child. I want nothing more in the world. I just didn't expect it, and my child's father and I recently separated from each other."

"Well, no better reason to reconcile. But I can only give you a health diagnosis, not advice. I wish you the best. I will release you and you need to see your OB-GYN as soon as possible. I wish you all the best." The doctor told her that the nurse would be bringing her the discharge papers to sign, and then she would be free to go.

When the doctor left the room, Brielle began to sob uncontrollably.

"What's the matter, Brielle? If Shawn doesn't want the baby, you can raise the baby on your own. Plenty of women have done it, and you know I'll be there to help."

"It's not that. I just don't know if I can handle it mentally. I have lost three children. I cannot bear to lose another child."

"Well, don't let anything that a man does affect you. Just worry about the baby." Brielle was offended that Simone was insinuating that her losing her children was under Brielle's control, as if she could have prevented it.

The nurse came in and let Brielle sign the papers. Brielle and Simone were walking down the corridor to the exit to catch a cab back to the courthouse to get Simone's car when Brielle heard someone call her name.

"Brielle, you passed the room. He is right here." Simone instantly felt shook. She knew that whoever the woman was who was calling Simone had something to do with Shawn.

Brielle turned around and saw Shawn's sister. She rushed to the door. "Shawn is here? What is he doing here? What happened?"

Simone stopped in the hallway and did not approach the room. She didn't want Shawn to take one look at her and start screaming to Brielle that Simone was the one who had shot him. Simone was frozen. Brielle went in the room. Simone slowly continued to walk toward the door.

"Oh my God, Shawn was shot last night, Brielle." Brielle had to catch herself from fainting again. She pushed past the people who were blocking her view to see Shawn lying in the hospital, bed with his eyes closed. He had an oxygen tube in his mouth. He was not breathing on his own. He had different machines that he was hooked up to.

Brielle was overwhelmed but she kept herself from getting too upset, thinking of what Simone had said. She went over to Shawn and rubbed his face. She buried her head in his chest, while most of his family moved out into the hallway to give her some privacy.

"What happened to you, baby? I need you." Shawn's sister came up by Brielle.

"Someone shot him in a parking lot last night and robbed him." Shawn's sister started crying for the hundredth time.

"So, what did the doctor say?" Brielle would have loved to cheer up the moment by announcing her baby news, but she was unsure of how safe the pregnancy was. She wanted to see her obstetrician before telling anyone.

"These days are very critical. They have him in a coma to give his body a rest and a chance to build up strength. They will be able to give us a better prognosis in a few days. I'm so sorry we didn't call you, but we knew that you guys had separated, and we didn't know what the circumstances were. So, who told you?"

"Um, I just came here to visit someone, and I was going to the main corridor to go home."

"Well, God works in mysterious ways for you to end up on this very hallway, in this very hospital, with no idea that you were walking past your ex-fiancé."

Brielle didn't like how that sounded. "We just broke up and I am hoping that we can come together and work things out for the baby." Brielle was just as shocked as Shawn's sister was to hear herself say what she had said.

"What?!" she exclaimed in a loud whisper.

"Oh my God. Listen, I just found out. I am not trying to make this about me. Please don't say anything right now. I want to be the one to tell him." His sister nodded her head in agreement.

"Well, you need to go and get some rest. We have been taking turns staying and in shifts. You can come back tomorrow, and we will let you and Shawn be alone."

"Thank you so much, sis. I appreciate it so much. I have had a crazy day. I will be back tomorrow. I have to go to court, but after court I will come straight here."

"Okay, and don't worry. You have to focus on the baby. God will watch and keep Shawn, because he knows that the baby that he blessed you with needs his father." Brielle's tears streamed down her face, and she knew that she had to go.

"Thank you. I must go. See you tomorrow."

Brielle went outside and Simone was sitting away from the door a bit. Brielle walked over to her.

"Is he gonna be okay?" Simone asked. She was extremely nervous.

"He's in an induced coma. It's very critical. God, please don't let Shawn die."

Simone grabbed Brielle's shoulders and gently shook her. "I told you about being strong. It's not about you or Shawn right now. It's about my niece in your stomach. It's gonna be a girl. You have got to put all your might into keeping this baby. Do you hear me?"

Brielle listened intently to Simone. She was glad that Simone had made that point. Brielle decided that nothing was more important than having this baby and, because of that, beating Monique's murder trial.

"I'm very serious, Brielle. A baby brings hope. Our lives need a boost of good energy. This girl will be special; she won't be harmed like we were. We will make sure of it, me and you. Okay?" Simone looked into Brielle's eyes.

"But what if Shawn...you know what? Fuck that, my baby is going to make it regardless."

"That's right. Now, let's get you home."

Simone put her arm in Brielle's, and they went outside and took a taxi to the street where Simone's car was parked. They got in the car, and Simone dropped Brielle off. She made Brielle promise that she would go straight to bed.

Simone pulled off and called Melvin. She had to keep off of her mind the fact that she had shot Shawn. She ignored the fact because it was too heavy to realize. She knew that one day soon, she would be dealing with that fact in some way, but she just did not know how.

Melvin lived in Harlem, so Simone picked him up on the way downtown. When he got in the car, he grabbed her chin and pulled her face to him.

"Hi, baby. Look at you, lookin' all pretty in that beautiful blonde hair. You my Barbie doll?" Melvin kissed Simone all over her face as she answered him.

"Of course I am your Barbie doll. Which Barbie do you want me to be tonight?" Simone looked over at Melvin and winked. He shot her a smile, his dimples showing, and they made her melt.

"I want you to be Dominatrix Barbie. You got your black five-inch-heel boots?"

"I sure do, baby, but I don't have no whip."

"Oh, we gon' do without the whip. I ain't on that whippin' shit. That's some perverted, sick shit right there." They both started laughing.

"Yeah, I was about to have a whole new outlook on you, and, believe me, it wasn't a good one. I don't want no man who likes to be treated like a bitch."

"Don't worry, I'm all man, Simone." Simone had finally told Melvin her name when she went back to see him at the hotel. "I just want you to order me to do whatever you want me to do to please you. You got a problem with that?" Melvin put his hand between Simone's legs while she drove. He rubbed her legs through her clothes.

"Oh yeah? I can think of a few things that I would love to order you to do."

"Name them. I ain't neva scurred." They laughed again.

"Well, whip your dick out right now, and let me see you jerk off while I'm driving. That will turn me on."

"Oh, I get it. You can't wait to see Charlie. Here he go. Say hi to Charlie." Melvin rubbed on himself while Simone drove and took glances at his hand workout.

They got to her loft, and Simone went in the back and came out with a black-lace crotchless one-piece. She had her patent leather fuck-me pumps on with it. Melvin whipped out a bottle of Patron and Simone told him that he had to do what she commanded and if he didn't do it right, he would have to take a shot of Patron.

Simone made Melvin give her a body massage, foot massage, make her something to eat, and clean her kitchen in the nude. They both took random shots of the Patron, which made the game get freakier and more fun. By the time the bottle was done, they were both naked and passed out on the area rug in the middle of the floor.

Simone and Melvin jumped up the next morning and got a kick out of how they both fell asleep before any real action happened. Melvin said that he was glad, because he wanted more than sex when it came to her.

"Melvin, please."

"I'm telling you the truth," he confessed.

"So, let's go online and book our trip then. That's how you test a man. If he's only about the pussy, he ain't gonna pay money to take you out the country just to get it."

"You know, Simone, I can understand how I would be hard to believe, but I'll prove it to you. When I get back we will have tickets to Saint-Tropez. I'll do it at work; I gotta get dressed and go."

"Yeah, I gotta go to Brielle's trial. Will I see you later?" Simone was shocked that she had asked Melvin that. She wasn't one to care about a man enough to want to be with him all the time, not until now.

They left her loft together, and Simone dropped Melvin off at his job in Midtown. They kissed and agreed to see each other later on.

Simone went to the courthouse to support Brielle another day. She was relieved to know that Shawn would not be there to blow her cover. She had some time to figure out what she was going to do if Shawn didn't die and alleviate that problem.

Janay

anay woke up in her hotel room alone. She hadn't heard from Rich since the day she saw him. She had called him several times, but he never took or returned her calls. She figured that Shawn must have told him what she had done. Janay was in no mood for men. As far as she was concerned, it was because of a no-good man that she was in this predicament. She had no time for men; she had a murder trial to beat.

Janay had been contemplating whether or not to take the DA up on his offer. She decided that it would be the best thing for her, especially if the judge does not keep her confession from being admitted into evidence. If he admits the evidence, she is as good as fried. She sees no way that they will be able to beat the case that way. She will just have to take the plea bargain and let Brielle rot in prison by her damn self.

Janay put on a very plain blue pantsuit; it was not designer. She noticed how Brielle and Simone had been dressing in expensive clothes, and she felt that the jury would have less sympathy if they think these black women have money. Everyone feels sorry for the poor, so she was going to go to court looking like she was needy and innocent.

When Janay saw Brielle walk in, she noticed that she looked much better than she had the day before. She also realized that Shawn had not been there yet. She was happy at the thought that Brielle may have lost Shawn. *Maybe he realized just how crazy that bitch is*, she thought to herself and then giggled.

Brielle gave Janay a head nod and sat. Janay turned the other way without even a nonverbal hello.

Aunt Janelle was in the courtroom. She had been too sick to travel before then, having just been diagnosed with multiple sclerosis. Janay and Brielle's grandmother was also there because Aunt Janelle was staying with her. The judge came into the courtroom, all rose, and then they began.

The district attorney, to Brielle's surprise, called Dante's sister to the stand. Brielle knew that she would end up looking like a horrible villain by the time she got off, as if Shanta hadn't done enough damage to her character.

Dante's sister hated Brielle and she did everything to paint her as a sadistic fatal attraction who killed her brother in cold blood. Paolo really showed how greatly skilled he was when he cross-examined her. He made her look like a jealous sister-in-law who really knew nothing about her brother and his abuse to Brielle. He also made it apparent that she was stretching the truth to get revenge on Brielle for defending herself from Dante. The day was off to a good start for the defense, and the prosecution's first battle was lost.

The judge seemed to be a fair judge who really did not play sides. He objected and sustained to the objections of both legal teams the way he saw fit, without trying to win any popularity contests.

The prosecutor attempted to then attack Janay. He brought to the stand her former boss. He tried to degrade her character.

In the middle of the interrogation, two detectives approached the bench to speak to the judge. The judge excused and removed himself and went to his chambers with the detectives and both legal teams.

Everyone was stunned and curious to know what was going on; everyone except Janay. She recognized the two detectives from the scene of Monk's murder and knew that they were there for her.

Janay contemplated running from the courtroom and becoming a fugitive, but she knew that she would not make it to the street with all of the officers that were all over the courthouse. She sat to see what disaster was about to come her way.

The officers came out and approached Janay. The judge spoke to the courtroom. "Ladies and gentlemen, I must adjourn this proceeding again. This trial is definitely bringing a lot more than to be expected; however, there is another investigation that is going on and must be addressed at this time. We will resume on Monday, not tomorrow. Have a nice weekend, everyone." He banged his gavel, got up, and walked into his chambers. He did not stay for the drama that was about to unfold in his courtroom. He knew the officers would do their jobs.

"Janay Roberts, please stand. You are under arrest for conspiracy to murder, blackmail, and hindering a police investigation."

Janay started screaming. "What the fuck are you talking about? Get the fuck out of here. That was my cousin!"

The court officers restrained her, while Aunt Janelle ran to her side. They cuffed Janay as Aunt Janelle asked what was going on.

Janay was removed from the courthouse and put in a car to be taken to the county jail. Aunt Janelle was asked to come down to the station to talk further, but they did fill her in on the preliminaries of what was going on while their grandmother, Brielle, and Janay stood right there.

"Your daughter was at the scene when your nephew, Montell Keys, was murdered." They all gasped and Simone had a funny feeling that she was yet mixed up in another incident involving someone close to Brielle. She listened further to make sure. Her mind was yelling, *Unbelievable!*

"Monkey's dead?" their grandmother yelled. Aunt Janelle was in shock.

"Montell Keys was shot about two weeks ago in New York. We questioned your daughter, who was with him when he got shot. She was elusive about a lot of information and pretended to be his only surviving relative. I gave your daughter the opportunity to be truthful, but then a young lady called, asking if a young man had been found and gave his name. She also said that she had called his cell phone, and a woman answered, saying that he was busy. So, we tracked the cell phone, and it led us to Janay."

"Oh my God, what has happened to my daughter?" Aunt Janelle said, sobbing. "This is all from greed. She just became so greedy for money, and it took over her whole life."

"I can't believe that Montell died and Janay didn't tell us." Brielle looked at Simone, who had a weird look on her face.

"Oh, Aunt Janelle, this is my sister, Simone, that I told you about. My father had at least two good things that he had something to do with in his lifetime." Aunt Janelle shook her head.

"Brielle, let he who has no sin cast the first stone. We are all screwed up in the brain in some way, shape, or form. I swear. It just can't get any worse than this, or I should say, 'Please, Lord, don't let it'? I'm sorry. Hi, Simone, I'm just runnin' my mouth. But anyway, I think the Lord may have given me MS so that I don't kill myself with Janay's bullshit. He is making me sit down instead of being able to try to fix her life. She made it; I can't fix it. And I gotta live mine."

"Let's go to the station," Brielle's grandmother said to Aunt Janelle. Brielle was never close to her grandmother because she felt that her grandmother must have been the reason why Brielle's mother was so abusive. Janay always thought her grandmother must have beaten her mother when she was a child. Plus, Janay was always her grandmother's favorite, which was another reason Brielle didn't like her. She figured only an evil woman could love Janay. Janay's own mother couldn't stand her, and Aunt Janelle was an angel in Brielle's eyes. She knew that Aunt Janelle wished that she had a different type of daughter. She sure didn't raise Janay to be so grimy; Janay was just born bad.

"Aunt Janelle, I have to go home. I need to get some rest." She figured she'd tell her the baby news later.

"Okay, well, I have the rental car, it's okay. I'm gonna take Grandma to see about Janay. I'm gonna come by your house probably Saturday if you're not doing anything."

"Okay."

They said their good-byes and nice-to-meet-you to Simone and went their separate ways.

Janay was read her rights while in the police car and told about herself. The detective was turned around, speaking to her.

"Miss Roberts, I asked you who in his family could be notified. What is it that you are trying to cover up?"

"I have the right to remain silent, remember?" Janay knew better than to talk to the detectives. She had a lawyer and she was going to call him as soon as she got situated at the jail. She couldn't believe that her life had amounted to all this trouble.

When Janay got her call she called Mr. Cifelli and he answered. "Mr. Cifelli, why were they able to do that to me?"

"Well, they approached the judge as if you were a flight risk. I think they did it to influence the jury. The judge—because, off the record, you are affiliated with three deaths—decided to let them interrupt court proceedings. The district attorney likes it because now they will again try to get you to cop a plea."

"So, you didn't object to them taking me on the spot?" Janay asked angrily.

"I had no say-so in the matter. The judge heard them and made his decision."

"So, now what?" Janay asked? She figured that they had made their scene and expected to be able to be released at that point. She was very wrong.

"Well, until they post bail, you will have to stay there. They will bring you to court from there."

Janay panicked. "I have to stay here?! But these are bullshit charges!"

"Well, you tried to hide a murder, hide the contact information of family members who had a right to know, and you are already in a murder trial. That is not a small thing."

"But that was my cousin," Janay said desperately.

"Janay, the criminal justice system is crooked. They will use all the ammunition they have and pull it out when ready. This is a technicality but the prosecution is at favor now because they found something more on you. This does not literally affect our case, but it actually affects the jury's mind."

"But that's prejudice; that's against the law. Can't you do something about it?" Janay began to cry.

"We are going to move slowly, as not to stir trouble. We want the judge to throw the conviction out, so we can't go bitching about everything and get on his bad side. Judge Champlain is a fair judge.I think because that was your cousin, the way that you chose to treat his death is really going to make you look bad. You tried to deny your family the right they have to know, bury, and memorialize your relative. But listen, the bottom line is you will either bail out or be brought to court from there. They will probably lessen those charges, but they are hoping that you will tell more. They think you know who killed your cousin or why, and they want you to tell. They used this way to let you know how serious they are."

"Okay, thank you, Mr. Cifelli. I'm sure my mom and grandma are on their way to pick me up, so I guess I'll see you in court on Monday."

Aunt Janelle and Grandma bailed Janay out, took her to the hotel to get her belongings and check out, and brought Janay to stay with them in Paterson. Neither her grandmother nor her mother had a word to say to her. They were disgusted with Janay.

Janay was scared to face the family to tell them what happened with Monkey. She never felt so ashamed of herself in her entire life. This was the first time she really felt any remorse for her actions.

Brielle

Brielle and Simone walked out of the courtroom and to the parking lot.

"I cannot believe that Janay had something to do with my cousin's death." Brielle shook her head and walked with her head down.

"Girl, that bitch is something else. I don't think I met a bitch as grimy as her. Damn, that's fucked up."

Brielle looked over at Simone and realized that she really had just met her. Although they were blood and shared the same genes, if Janay could grow up with Brielle and turn out to be like that, how would she know what Simone was capable of or had done in her life?

"It's just crazy how we expect the people we love not to hurt us, but it's the very people who are close to you who will hurt you the most."

Simone knew exactly what Brielle was talking about. "Brielle, sometimes we don't intentionally hurt others. It's like we are in a tug-of-war with our needs and the needs of others. If something that we need or even want to do conflicts with someone that we care for, which side do we choose? We may even not realize the damage that our actions are going to make until the damage is already done. It's not always a plot or plan, but sometimes just a circumstance or coincidence."

"Yeah, you are right. We try to please others as we are pleasing ourselves, and sometimes the two things are on opposite ends of the spectrum. That's why I guess it's important to forgive."

Brielle had an idea. She decided to go to her mother's grave site. She didn't want Simone to go; she wanted to go alone. There were some things that she had to let go of to be able to start her new life.

"What are you about to do, Simone?" Brielle asked as they reached Brielle's car.

"I have to take care of something. Call me later. You okay?" Simone went over and hugged Brielle.

"Yes, I'm fine. I love you, sister." Brielle kissed Simone's cheek and Simone told Brielle that she loved her too.

Brielle drove to the cemetery after buying a dozen yellow roses and tulips—those were her mother's favorite flowers. She didn't know if it was intuition or coincidence that had her wearing all yellow as well: a yellow crisscross linen cardigan and silk cropped pants by Brunello Cucinelli, with matching yellow leather Valentino pumps that had a hand-tied leather bow at the back tip.

When she got to the grave, she put the portable chair that she was carrying down and sat.

"Ma, I came here to tell you that I forgive you. I have to move on, and I cannot have you putting negative thoughts in my mind. I had a horrible upbringing and I blamed you. But it doesn't matter now. I am alive and I have life inside of me. I have hope. I have a chance to do it better than you did. I should have felt sorry for you but I didn't. Maybe it was selfish of me to expect so much from you when you didn't have it to give, but I will not let you take it away from me. I am going to heal. I am going to be healthy, mentally. I am going to be the best damn mother on Earth. All I ask is that you leave me alone. Don't haunt me. I understand that you had it hard too. Just let me forgive you and let me go."

Brielle walked back to her car and got in. She sat there for a second to see if she would shed any tears. She didn't. She thought about visiting Dante's grave but she didn't. Dante was not an issue for her anymore; Shawn was. She replaced the love that she had for Dante with the love she gave to Shawn. She had to see Shawn next and tell him about their baby.

Brielle drove to the hospital, and Sylvia, Shawn's sister, smiled when she saw her.

"I've been talking in his ear, and he is showing some signs that he hears me. He is flinching and stuff. I said your name and his lips moved. They have stopped the medicine to keep him under, so it's about him coming out now, waking up out of it. They said maybe two days or so. His vitals are good, though. How are you feeling?"

Brielle said that she was fine. She knew that, being in New York, his sister didn't know what was going on with Brielle and her case. Shawn had promised not to tell his family about it unless he had to. If Brielle got off, then Shawn would never have to tell.

Sylvia left so that Brielle could be alone with Shawn. Brielle stood back and just looked at Shawn. She stared at him. She imagined what it would be like without him. She felt that Shawn was the only man left for her. She couldn't see herself with anyone else; it didn't matter how long or short they had been together. Shawn had saved her life, and now she was going to save his.

Brielle started rubbing Shawn's feet gently. She rubbed both of his feet and then his calves and legs. As she caressed and massaged him, she talked to him as if he was conscious.

"You know, Shawn, that I was lost until I met you? I don't know where I would be right now if it weren't for you. There is no way that you can leave me." She reached for Shawn's hand and held it. She massaged both of his hands and then sat down on one side of the bed and kept squeezing his hand. She squeezed it and then just held it while she watched television.

She sat there for about an hour. As she was about to change the channel, she felt Shawn squeeze her hand. She looked over and he was looking at her. She immediately jumped up and put her face close to his to see if he knew who he was looking at. She whispered in his ear, as not to startle or frighten him.

"Shawn, I knew you weren't going to die. I knew it in the bottom of my soul that it wasn't over for us. Do you know how much I love you?" She looked in his eyes, and she saw tears fill up in them. He squeezed her hand again.

"Shawn, I have something very special for you. I have to wait until the right time, but I want you to know that you must get better for me to give it to you. And you are going to love it, I know."

Shawn tried to crack a smile, but his lips were all chapped and dry, with the plastic tube sticking out of his mouth. He coughed and scared Brielle. She immediately pushed the button to alert the nurses' station that he needed assistance.

Two nurses came in. They walked over and saw Shawn's eyes open and called for the doctor.

"Very good, Mr. Ellison; you are up. Don't try to talk or move; just relax."

Brielle stood off to the side and put her hand on her stomach. The man who was lying in that bed was the love of her life and he had given her new life inside of her body and she was going to give that baby to him. She was not going to lose it.

"Okay, miss, we have to do some tests on him. Can you please wait in the waiting room?"

Brielle went to the waiting room. She was so excited about Shawn coming to. She called Simone to tell her the good news, but Simone's voice mail picked up. "Simone, Shawn came out of the coma. He looked at me and squeezed my hand. He cried when I told him I loved him! I am so happy."

She sat in the waiting room until the nurse came to get her. She said that Shawn had gone back to sleep and they suggested that he be left to rest since his being aware may cause him to be in pain and wear on or put stress on his body.

"Nurse, does he ever have a guard? Since he's been shot and the police don't know who did it."

"Well, this intensive care unit is very secure. You have to be buzzed into this area, so, normally, unless a patient pays for private security, we just follow the safety procedures of the hospital itself."

"Do you have any companies' numbers that I can call to hire a bodyguard?"

"Yes, when you leave the room, stop by the nurses' station to get it. I'll write some numbers down for you."

Brielle thanked her and went in the room to say good-bye. She laid her head on Shawn's chest to hear his heartbeat. She wished that he could wrap his arms around her and hold her tightly. He was the air that she breathed.

Brielle got in the car and was on her way home when her phone rang. It was Aunt Janelle's cell phone number.

"Are you okay, Aunt Janelle?"

"No, Brielle, I'm not. My family has fallen apart, and my daughter seems to be a major orchestrator of that fact."

"But you know you have to take care of yourself. You have to keep your strength up to fight your own fight right now."

"I need you to come to Grandma's house, Brielle. We are all here and Janay is about to tell everyone what happened to Monk. I think you should be here too."

"Aunt Janelle, I don't think that is a good idea."

"Well, I do. Please come on."

"Okay, I'm on my way."

Brielle drove in the direction of Paterson, New Jersey, but not without beginning to rethink about the bad memories of her childhood. She never really went back to Paterson to visit her family because that part of her life she never wanted to deal with. The only way she felt that she could escape her horrible past was to never return to the people and places of her youth, and to her that meant cutting off her family, which is what she did. She did not feel connected to them anyway.

Brielle pulled up to her grandmother's house. She lived in a run-down two-family house that was overcrowded with relatives. They all treated Brielle like an outsider just as much as she acted like one. She walked into the house and living room, which had about twenty people all lined along the walls, sitting, and standing.

Janay was sitting in the middle of the room. She was disgusted to see Brielle.

"Okay, Janay, we want to know what is going on. What happened to my son?" their aunt—Monk's mother—asked.

"I asked him to come somewhere with me to pick up some money from someone that owed me. When we got there he got out of the car." She started to cry. "He got into the car and somebody shot him. They just shot him and took off."

"Yeah, bitch, then you tried to make me think my man was fuckin' you! I'm pregnant and you tried to make me think my man just up and left me. I knew that wasn't true. Monk loved me. He should have never went to help you!" No one stopped Monk's girl because she had every right to hate Janay.

"I just didn't know how to tell my family that it was my fault. I would have never called him if I thought he would die."

"Well, you thought something might happen if you asked him to go with you," Grandma said. No one was giving Janay any slack.

"I'm sorry. I'm so sorry. At least I'm not that crazy bitch standing right there, who purposely killed her husband and his mistress and is trying to make me fry for it."

"Fuck you, Janay. Stop always trying to pass the buck! You a grimy-ass bitch, and what goes around comes around," Brielle said from the doorway.

Janay got up to approach Brielle, and Aunt Janelle stopped her.

"Bitch, if I wasn't pregnant, I would kick your fuckin' ass."

"What, bitch? You lying!"

"You wish! I am going to change my life, Janay. You will never change." Brielle walked out of her grandmother's house feeling like that would be the last time she would ever go there or see those people. She wasn't mad, but she knew that it was time to get even with Janay and be done with it.

Brielle got in her car and called Paolo. "Hey, Paolo, I was so in deep thought today and with all the crazy stuff that happened, I meant to tell you that Shawn had gotten shot."

"I know. I just didn't want to tell you and upset you. Is he doing okay?"

"Yes, he is coming back to consciousness. I was calling because I want to know if I can offer to turn state's evidence against Janay. "Can we offer to the prosecution to let us testify against her for immunity? Or for them to drop the charges against me?"

"Wow. Well, are you sure about this? Or can I ask what makes you want to do that?"

"My cousin is only going to get what she gave. She chose to tell on me instead of just getting out and talking to a lawyer first at least. I think at that moment, she wanted to see me go down so bad that she didn't even realize that she was taking herself down too. She must have really thought that all she had to do was tell on me, and she would get off. So, I'm just returning the favor. It's either her or me, and it *must* be me. This is my last chance at a new life. I have been given a life inside of me. I'll be damned if I remain loyal to someone who has no loyalty to me."

"Uh, okay. So, of course, that will mean that you are no longer going to pay for her legal fees. Mr. Cifelli will not be her attorney, and your case, if you still have one, will be separate from hers. With the looks of things, that will be much better for you either way. She is not looking good, and it was going to tarnish your image, no matter how small, in the jury's eyes."

"Well, now it's going to be every bitch for herself. Pardon my language."

"No problem, Brielle. We have tomorrow to work on that before court resumes on Monday. You have a good evening."

"You too, Paolo."

Simone

imone left Brielle and had an idea. She knew that she must work quickly to accomplish her goal.

She dialed Joey's number. "Hey, Joey, you still need to meet up with me?"

"Uh, yeah, uh, I gotta see you. Can you meet later?"

"No, I need to meet now. You busy?"

"No. Where do you want to meet?"

"Listen, I'm at the Holiday Inn on Fifty-sixth Street. I'm in Room 516. We can talk there?"

"I wanted to meet you outside somewhere." Simone didn't like how that sounded, as if he wanted to do something to her but wouldn't want to be seen inside somewhere with her.

"What's the problem, Joey? You can't come to my hotel room? I'm damn sure not going to leave your dead body in my hotel room, if that's what you're worried about." Simone made that sarcastic statement to take Joey off of his guard. She knew that he would have to come to her room by himself, but outside anyone could be with him, and she wouldn't know it. She didn't actually know that Joey already had a hit out on her, but she felt that way, and she would get him to cancel the hit against her. A dead man couldn't pay a hit, so only a family member would carry out a murder if it was personal.

She got the needle ready to inject into Joey. She had used her fake ID to reserve the room, and she didn't care about leaving his dead ass in there that way.

Simone knew that she would have to take the stairs all the way down to the lobby and quickly make her way out to her car. As long as she got away from the murder, she knew she would be good. Hotels have everyone's DNA anyway; those housekeepers don't always clean that well, so it would be hard to prove when she was there if any traces of her being there were found.

Simone knew that Joey was the last job that she had to do. She planned on moving on after this was done. She was interested in being with Melvin and maybe having a baby or even getting married. *One day; don't push it*, she told herself.

When Joey knocked on the door and Simone opened it, she let him in and checked to see if anyone was out in the hallway. There was no one. Simone knew that Joey didn't trust her, and she didn't trust him.

"Do I need to pat you down?" she asked him.

"No, I need you to go with me someplace, though. I have a job for you." Joey was again trying to get Simone outside.

"Listen, Joey, what is the deal here?"

"What the fuck are you talking about? You tell me what the deal is. I saw you with Melvin."

Simone reached under the bed, grabbed the needle, and lunged at Joey. He stood up to block her and knocked the needle out of her hand. He grabbed her by the throat and started choking her. Simone could not break loose from Joey's grip. She spit in his eye, and his natural reaction was to reach for his eye. Before he could grab her again, she rolled over on the floor, picked the syringe up, and kicked him in his chest. Joey fell back onto the floor, on his back. She jumped on him, straddled him like they were having sex, and stabbed him directly in the heart. He tried to pull it out as she pushed the syringe to release all of the potassium chloride into his blood.

Joey managed to push her off of him and stand up. He was grabbing his chest, and he said, "I knew you was gonna try me, you cunt!"

Simone ran to the closet and grabbed the iron and smashed him in the back of his head with the pointed part of it. He fell onto his stomach, with his head turned to one side.

Simone looked in his eyes, which had a blank stare, and knew he was a goner. Joey was dead and so was her life as a killer. She grabbed her pocketbook and walked out of the room, with her shades on and her hair tucked under a baseball cap. She had changed her clothes from the suit to jeans and sneakers while in the room.

Simone made it to her car and started driving. Alicia Keys' song "Unthinkable" came on and she started singing: "If you ask me, I'm ready…I'm ready. If you ask me, I'm ready."

Then she began to talk to herself out loud. "I never would have thought I would want to end this life. The money was good but, girl, you must be in love. You want to give it all up and be with Melvin." She started laughing. "I don't believe it myself. Maybe he will change my last name from Alexander to Richards. Simone Richards. Hmmm..." She smiled.

Simone pulled up to a light and looked over to her right, to the car that had pulled to the side of her from behind. The guy seemed to need directions. He rolled down his window and waved for her to roll down hers. As she rolled down her passenger's-side window, Joey's brother Daniel pulled out his gun, and, before shooting straight into her car, he said, "This is for not following orders!" Daniel emptied his weapon and sped off.

Simone received ten bullets to the face. Joey's brother had been in the car waiting to follow her, as per Joey's command after he got her to come outside. Daniel had no idea that his brother was dead. He was following the directions to follow and shoot Simone when she left the hotel. Simone died instantly.

Brielle

Brielle spent the weekend at the hospital, by Shawn's side. He still was not speaking, but he was alert and sitting up. She decided not to tell him about the baby until she could hear his response. She knew that his eyes would show joy, but he wouldn't be able to say anything.

On Sunday, after not hearing from Simone since Thursday, she went to Simone's loft to see detectives in her apartment. She was told that Simone was shot on Thursday evening.

Brielle told the officers that she was Simone's sister, and they let her in based on pictures that Simone had up of her and Brielle. Brielle looked around Simone's place, realizing that Simone was really a stranger. They had not known each other long enough to really learn each other's true personalities.

Brielle came across a box marked "Heaven" and opened it up. She read the letter that was on the very top.

Dear Mariah,

You will not believe this. Not only did I do a hit and it ended up being Brielle's fiancé, but I think the guy that I killed a few weeks ago was her cousin.

I went to do a job with Peter, and then he started telling me bits and pieces about the girl that was blackmailing his cousin with some dirty pictures and that the girl was here for a murder trial. I think that is Janay that he was talking about, which means the guy was Brielle's cousin too.

Then Peter calls me yesterday and tells me he has a job. I go and am shocked to see Brielle's fiancé—well, they broke up, but he was the job. When he saw me I panicked and shot him in the stomach. I don't know if he died or not yet.

Can my life get any worse?
Love, Simone

Brielle was frozen while reading the letter. She was numb. As she read the letter, she heard Simone's voice reciting it. Her eyes widened in horror. She dropped the letter and ran out of Simone's loft.

Brielle made it home and got ready for court the next day. She tried not to think of Simone and how such a good beginning turned into such a sudden and tragic end. She was upset that she couldn't keep her sister, the only one she ever had, but she was happy to at least have a life growing inside of her.

Brielle believed that Simone's death was a part of the cycle of one family member dying to make way for a new one coming.

Brielle didn't love Simone long enough to hate her nor was she glad that she had died. Brielle was glad that she got the chance to feel what having a real sister was like, and, regardless, Simone was her real sister.

Brielle was curious as to how Shawn would feel when he found out or if he already knew that Simone had shot him. She would surely be asking him when the time came.

Monday morning came and Brielle was sharp. She had on a teal tweed and cotton tapered dress with buttons on the sides, like a tuxedo dress, and she had crème-colored shoes to match. She was ready to win the battle and the war.

When Brielle entered the courtroom, Paolo met her and told her that everything was a go, that the prosecutor knew what they were going to do and was in support of it. They had gone from wanting Brielle to wanting Janay since getting both without the testimony of the other was not very likely to happen.

"Judge Champlain, there is a new offer that the prosecution has given us that we have decided to take. My colleague will no longer be representing Miss Roberts. Miss Prescott has agreed to testify against Miss Roberts in return for immunity."

"I knew it, you backstabbing bitch!"

Judge Champlain yelled for order in the court and told Janay to be quiet. "Miss Roberts, were you aware of this?"

"No."

"Do you have the money to get a lawyer, or will you need a public defender?"

"I don't know."

"Okay, well, we have adjourned this trial two times already. I must give you the chance for counsel; however, court will resume in two days. I apologize, ladies and gentlemen."

On Wednesday Janay was appointed a public defender after no one in her family gave her the money that she asked for for her defense.

The prosecutor called Brielle to the stand as the first witness. She took her oath while smiling at Janay.

"Miss Prescott, can you tell me why you think that your cousin tried to frame you for Monique Troy's murder?"

"Well, for one, my cousin and I have always had a bad love-hate relationship. She was always going against me. I think that she killed Monique first and then was going to try to blackmail me, but she got arrested first and lied about me having something to do with it."

"Where were you on the night of the murder?"

"I was at my fiance's mother's funeral." Brielle looked confident and sure of herself.

"And you had no idea that Janay would kill Monique?"

"Not at all. Like I said, I'm sure she would have threatened me that she would make it seem like I did it to get money from me to pay for her defense in her Atlanta case." Janay sat there with tears rolling down her face. She knew that there was no way, with the evidence mounting against her and Brielle's lie that she was going to get off. The jury had *Guilty* already written on the foreheads. She was facing life in prison if convicted. She leaned over and whispered in her public defender's ear.

Janay's lawyer waved to the judge and stood. "Your Honor, in lieu of the new developments, my client would like to ask the prosecution if they have a plea deal that they can put on the table for her."

As Brielle left the witness stand, she walked past Janay, leaned down, and whispered in her ear, "That was for me and Monkey. Payback is a bitch, ain't it?"

The defense was told that the prosecution needed to see what kind of deal they could offer her. Court was adjourned until a week later.

The following week Janay pled guilty to the murder of Monique Troy and accepted a twenty-year sentence. Due to her sentence, Atlanta did not pursue the charges against her any further. They never dropped the charges, but didn't spend the money to fly her in for trial and court costs, knowing that she was going to be incarcerated for twenty years. The charges that she received due to Monk's death and the blackmailing of Mr. Jamison was reduced, and she was given five years to run concurrent with the twenty years.

Brielle spent the next two months by Shawn's side. He was released from the hospital, and he was elated when he found out that Brielle was pregnant. She told him the first night they stayed at her home.

"Do you remember when I told you in your hospital bed that I had something for you?" Brielle asked and Shawn lied and said yes.

"Well, I have a baby for you," Brielle said, cheesing from ear to ear.

"Queen, you are now a goddess. You are carrying the world inside of you and it's my world. You and my baby are my world."

Brielle knew that she had to wait for Shawn to talk before she told him about her being pregnant because he said the perfect thing about it.

"Shawn, do you know who shot you?" Brielle asked him.

"No, baby, why?"

"Because I know you do. You saw my sister shoot you."

"Baby, what are you talking about?" Shawn seemed sincere but Brielle didn't buy it, even though she realized that he may have memory loss from the traumatic event.

"Simone shot you, Shawn."

"I know, baby." They both laughed and he strained a little bit.

"You lucky 'cause I was about to punch you in your stomach. I almost forgot. Why'd you act like you didn't know?"

"Because it doesn't matter now. If she hadn't died, I would have to forgive her."

Brielle looked at him like he was lying.

"Brielle, not because I'm so great and, honestly, not because that's what Jesus would do. I would have to because she was your sister, and you were so happy to have her. More importantly because she gave me back what I gave to someone else only I didn't die. Who am I to not forgive her when I have taken a life before? Shit, at least she didn't kill me. I get another chance to do things right and better and better." Brielle smiled and leaned over and kissed Shawn.

"Shawn, you have such a way with words. You make everything make so much sense even when that shit doesn't make no sense at all. I don't know how I would have forgiven her." Brielle thought about the good things that Simone had said to her and the good talks that the two of them had and rephrased her statement. "I mean, if I hadn't read her little diary. She wrote letters to her sister who was killed. She put that she didn't know you were the person she was supposed to shoot, and when she saw you, she got nervous and shot you by accident. That's not even the half."

Shawn cut Brielle off before she could continue talking about Simone. "That might not be the half, but that's the whole of what I want to hear about it. We're just gonna let that go. You were able to meet your sister before she died. You don't know what she had done in her life before you met her. Her day was obviously coming, but you two were a blessing to each other for that short time. You will never forget her."

"You're right. And that's why I left her diary right there. I want to remember her the way I knew her. None of it matters now, nothing but my husband-to-be and our baby."

"You lucky I didn't pawn that damn ring, you throwing my ring like that."

"Shut up. Let it go." Brielle put her finger over Shawn's lips and then kissed him.

Shawn, Brielle, & Simone

Four Months later Shawn and Brielle traveled to Saint-Tropez to get married. They invited family members to come, but Brielle was happy that her family couldn't afford it and would not be there. Aunt Janelle was the only one from her family who was there. Shawn's brothers and sister and their spouses were there as well. Brielle was happy to be gaining a new family, because the one she had was no good for her. In her eyes they would only poison the rest of her life and her child's life if she kept them in it, which she decided against doing.

Brielle always wanted to go to France. Saint-Tropez was the closest thing to paradise that Brielle had ever seen. They stayed on Nikki Beach, an exquisite location and a favorite vacation destination of the world's most beautiful, celebrated, rich, and powerful people. She felt like royalty.

The day they got married was a beautiful day. Brielle looked fabulously beautiful. She had a crystal-embroidered gown by none other than Vera Wang. Her dress was strapless and iced out. The top of the dress was like a corset, and the bottom flared like an A-line dress with a long train, of course. Her baby bump made her shine like the queen she was. Her hair was pinned up, and her tiara glistened in the sun like it was full of diamonds. She felt like it was a fairy tale out of a book.

Shawn and Brielle got married on the cliffs in Cap Camarat. The French Riviera surrounded them on all sides. It looked like they got married on a mountain close to heaven.

They wrote their own vows to each other.

Shawn's vows read: "I love you in an unconditional way. I love you the way Jesus does, with no holds barred. When I looked in your eyes, they told me that you were suffering and that I was the only remedy for you. I took that challenge on because you were me. I knew that we had been matched up somewhere in the sky and that it was coming to pass. I have dealt with hell and heaven in dealing with you. But the reward that comes from walking through the fire with someone is that you get to experience when they become a phoenix. I forgive you for your mistakes; you have learned from them. You are a new creature, and I know that with you, I am safe. My heart is healed when I am with you because God has used you to bless me."

Brielle's vows read: "There is no pain in loving you. Pain had been my middle name, the thing that I loved to hate but loved to have. I knew no reciprocated love until I met you. Yes, I had loved others, but no one loved me back but you. I knew hate, anger, betrayal, and revenge when I met you. I now know respect, acceptance, forgiveness, and emotional health. I am healing because of you. I am healing because of God. I know God because of you. I will never ever, ever stop loving you.

Shawn and Brielle stayed an extra week on their honeymoon after their family members returned home. When they reached Brielle's house, which was now their home, Shawn took a shower while Brielle made something quick and easy for them to eat.

They were both jetlagged and exhausted from the excitement of their wedding bliss and had agreed to eat and go straight to bed.

Brielle put a frozen entrée in the oven and went through the mail. The doorbell rang and Brielle felt déjà vu as she signed for an envelope from UPS. It reminded her of the day she received the pictures of Dante and Monique.

Brielle slowly opened the package and took the pictures out. Her jaw dropped as she saw pictures of Janay, naked, inside Shawn's room. There was a sleeping Shawn and Janay standing in front of him. Brielle began to see images of Dante, Peyton, the rapist, and Darren. Her Cousin Tony's face flashed in front of her. Brielle's mind exploded with a kaleidoscope of all of the men she had killed.

She began to get cramps. She was four months pregnant and had not had any previous problems with this pregnancy. She slowly sat down, tightly holding her stomach with one hand and beginning to read the letter that was enclosed with the pictures with the other.

Dear Brielle,

You thought you won but you didn't. I would never let you beat me. I may be going to prison, but you are going to the crazy house this time for sure. I fucked Dante, I fucked Darren, and I fucked Shawn. None of your men could resist me. You were just a trophy to those muthafuckas, but they really wanted me. You may be all pretty on the outside, but they know you're all fucked up on the inside. I'm hoping that the baby I am carrying is Shawn's. Our children will be able to grow up hating each other like we did. My mother will make sure that you keep the cousins tight. You know her favorite saying: Family ties bind the heart. LOL. So, anyway, I just wanted you to know that we will always be connected. You can run but you can't hide, bitch!

Love and hate,

Janay

Brielle's stomach tightened. She sat on the kitchen stool, staring at the knives in the knife holder. She felt her blood boiling. She let out a scream. "Noooooooooooooooooooooo! I will not lose another baby! We will all have to die!"

Brielle blacked out. She jumped up and grabbed the longest kitchen knife and ran upstairs. She stormed through the bathroom door, holding the knife above her head, ready to end her horrible nightmare of a life.

The End

ABOUT THE AUTHOR

Ericka Williams is a *tour de force*, a phenomenal woman. She is a compassionate person who not only cares about herself and hers, but cares about humanity. All of her books are themed to show the unlimited access of human beings to redemption. She is a Christian, spreading the message that Jesus saves no matter who you are, what you've done, or what other people think of you. She uses societal ills, her own experiences, and real situations that we all face to show that there is a light at the end of every tunnel if you take God's hand and let him lead the way. She may not fit the mold of a "saint," but she sure is a believer, and she knows that we only have the obligation to spread the Word the way that we personally know how.

Ericka Williams is a mother of two, an elementary school language arts teacher, an actor, a director, and a producer of short films. She is currently in the cast of The Cartel Publications feature *Pitbulls in a Skirt*, being released in the summer of 2011. She continues to write books, act, and prepare to fulfill her dream of having her books turned into films.

Ericka Williams is a humanitarian, a mentor, a public speaker and above all, a Child of God. You may contact her at www.erickaw.com, erickawilliamsinfo@yahoo.com, or (212) 201-9329. You may "like" her at Ericka Monique Williams on Facebook, or follow her on Twitter @AuthorErickaw

IN STORES NOW

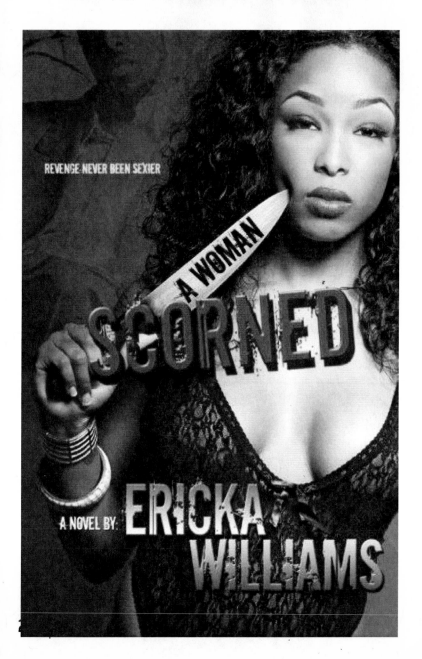

REVENGE NEVER BEEN SEXIER

A WOMAN
SCORNED

A NOVEL BY: ERICKA WILLIAMS

IN STORES NOW

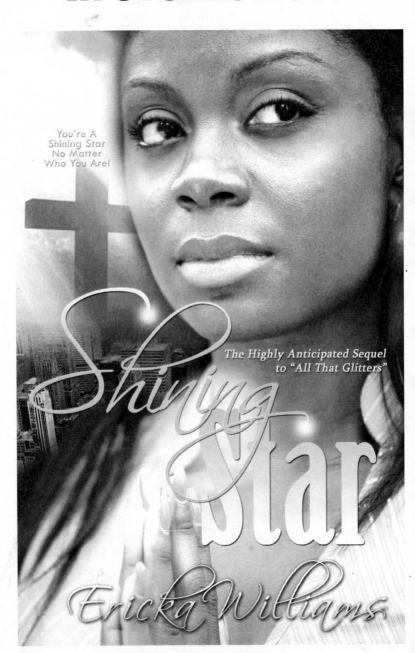

You're A
Shining Star
No Matter
Who You Are!

The Highly Anticipated Sequel
to "All That Glitters"

Shining Star

Ericka Williams

IN STORES NOW

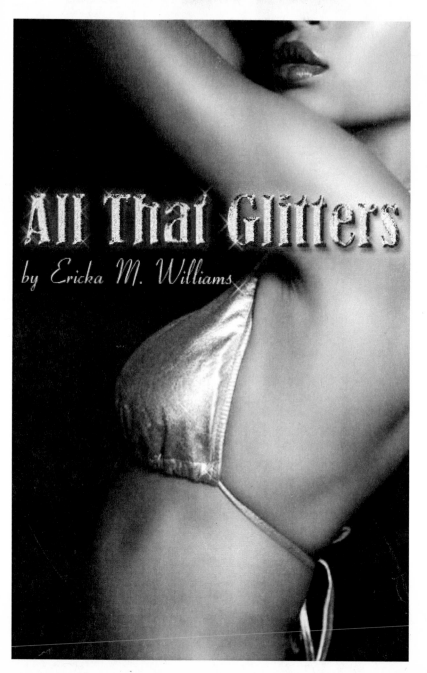

All That Glitters
by Ericka M. Williams

COMING SOON

They Rob from the Rich....
and Splurge in the Hood!

THE
ROBBIN'
HOODS

A Novel

THE BEST SELLING AUTHOR OF "A WOMAN SCORNED"

ERICKA WILLIAMS